By the Same Author

The Music Programme

THE
COVER
ARTIST

PAUL MICOU

Simon & Schuster
New York London Toronto Sydney Tokyo Singapore

Simon & Schuster
Simon & Schuster Building
Rockefeller Center
1230 Avenue of the Americas
New York, New York 10020

Copyright © 1990 by Paul Micou
All rights reserved
including the right of reproduction
in whole or in part in any form.
Originally published in Great Britain by
Bantam Press, a division of
Transworld Publishers, Ltd.
SIMON & SCHUSTER and colophon
are registered trademarks
of Simon & Schuster Inc.
Designed by Caroline Cunningham
Manufactured in the United States of America

3 5 7 9 10 8 6 4 2

Library of Congress Cataloging in Publication Data

Micou, Paul.
The cover artist / Paul Micou.
p.   cm.
"Orginally published in Great Britain by Bantam Press"—T.p.
verso.
I. Title.
PS3563.I354C6   1991
813'.54—dc20   90-22084
                                CIP
ISBN 0-671-72938-1

For Anna U

ONE

I

"*COME ON, ELIZABETH,*" *SAID OSCAR LEMOINE.* "*STOP DROOLING.*"

"What's the matter with your dog?" asked the American customs officer.

"Tranquilizers, sir, for the flight from France. She is terrified of air travel."

Oscar Lemoine dreaded authority. He addressed the official with such deference that he might have been facing a foreign tribunal on charges of espionage rather than returning innocently to the country of his birth.

"Lemoine," said the customs officer. "French?"

"Goodness, no. American, sir." Oscar snapped to attention.

"No, I meant the name. Lemoine. Just curious."

"Possibly French, sir. But not me. I am American." Oscar told the strict truth, despite his biological father's being half French.

"Are you sure your dog is okay?"

Elizabeth struggled splay-leggedly to remain standing on the slippery, gum-stained floor.

"She'll be fine, sir."

"Occupation?"

"She's just a dog, sir. An aging black labrador."

"I meant *your* occupation."

"Of course, sir. I am a cartoonist and caricaturist."

"Is that right?"

"I swear it."

"Today's your birthday."

"Yes, sir. Twenty-eight."

"Been away, what—" he leafed through Oscar's passport—"a year and a half?"

"Yes, sir, almost."

"You don't look like your picture."

Oscar thought it a bad sign that the customs officer wanted to make personal remarks. These men and women were supposed to be gruff and unyielding.

"No, sir. I've changed."

"You got yourself a nice tan."

"Thank you, sir. And plenty of exercise. I gained some weight."

Hearty eating, outdoor exercise and sunshine had transformed Oscar from a sluglike city creature into quite a sturdy and attractive specimen.

"Not what I need exercise for," sighed the customs officer, who was obese. "Open the bags, please."

Oscar's luggage included art supplies, part of a varied wardrobe purchased during his stay in France, and Elizabeth's few belongings. He had left most of his goods and chattels behind, for he could not yet be sure he had absorbed his fill of sun and abandon.

"This a cartoon?" asked the customs man, who held between his fingers one of Oscar's works in progress.

"A sketch, sir. For a caricature."

The problem was that the sketch seemed to be pornographic, at least in the eyes of a customs man.

"It's for a magazine, sir. Perhaps you've heard of it? There's a copy in there somewhere."

Oscar helped him find an issue of the *Lowdown*. He pointed at the cover. "That's mine," said Oscar proudly. "I do the nudes for their cover."

The official inspected the magazine cover with the frown of a doctor studying a chest X ray.

"Haven't seen it," said the customs man. "I know *her*, though." He referred to the subject of Oscar's nude caricature, a broadcasting celebrity. "I'll be damned."

There was a lull in international arrivals, so the customs officer took his time picking through Oscar's possessions.

"Any fruits or vegetables? Plants? Tobacco? Firearms?"

"No, none, nothing, not at all, never."

Oscar had long known that a career in international intrigue was closed to him. Interrogators would be driven insane with boredom by his detailed confessions.

"Welcome," said the customs man at last, helping Oscar to close his cases. "You be careful out there in New York City."

Pushing a baggage cart, with Elizabeth limping drunkenly behind him, Oscar stepped out of the terminal into the choking fumes of his homeland. During the flight, circling before landing, Oscar had gazed out over the thrumming engines and felt a certain awe and nostalgia for his mighty city. On the ground, breathing jet exhaust and the humid smell of melting tarmac, a thousand memories returned to him. He felt the traveler's uneasy sensation of never having left a place, as if New York had frozen in time while he went about his business on another continent, only to swirl into action upon his return.

He was happy—or at least interested—to be part of the formicating masses once again.

Oscar hoped he had returned to New York a new and more presentable man. His stay in the French coastal resort of Val d'Argent had begun as self-imposed exile, as an effort to step back, however briefly, from a progression of events in New York that had become too much for him to manage. After several years hoping that things would start to go well in New York, they had gone too well, too quickly, for the comfort of a naturally reserved and bashful young man. His occupation, that of cartoonist and caricaturist, had not changed since high school; a monumental stroke of good fortune had changed everything else, when a childhood friend commissioned one of Oscar's renderings for the cover of a new and horrible-sounding magazine. Oscar was given to understand that his friend, a maddeningly wealthy entrepreneurial thrill-seeker named Brian Fable, needed to lose a great deal of money in a hurry, and knew of no better way than to found yet another doomed magazine of trend and hype. Fable hurriedly enlisted the services of old friends, including Oscar, to slap together the flagship issue of his brainchild, which he called the *Lowdown*. Oscar simply handed over an example of his motif of the past three years—a gaudy, full-color nude caricature of a recently deceased Mafia don—and waited for word that the *Lowdown* had fulfilled its mandate and collapsed.

To everyone's surprise, and not least to Brian Fable's panicked accountants, the first issue of the *Lowdown* disappeared from magazine racks as if a ravenous subculture had waited years for its appearance. This unintended success was attributed by an annoyed Brian Fable to Oscar's cover caricature, which screamed out from the stalls that if people missed a chance to buy it they would be passing up a collector's item. Some found the first caricature offensive, others found it profound or amusing, but either way the lurid full-frontal nudity of an assassinated crime boss performing a pirouette on his own grave was unique enough to spark the interest the founder had hoped to avoid.

Having lived for a quarter of a century without anyone taking the slightest notice of him, Oscar suddenly found himself at the center of some considerable attention. He was introduced to the double-edged phenomenon of minor urban celebrity. People knew his name and profession before he was introduced to them; they asked him questions and actually listened to his responses. Oscar found this small-scale notoriety disconcerting, and in most ways unpleasant. Still, the positive side of having cut himself a slice of city cachet was not lost on Oscar, who might have complained to anyone who cared to hear his woes that before the success of his *Lowdown* covers women had seemed to look straight through him, had appeared annoyed or insulted or merely surprised when he chose to speak to them. This had not been due to any gross disfigurement or other failing in his actually rather pleasant looks—up to that point his strongest asset—but to a fact of life he had been too naive or romantic to recognize: women in his circles were attracted to glamour.

After making this important discovery, Oscar did not have long to wallow in the unfairness of it all—something he certainly would have done had Brian Fable not intervened by providing Oscar with a sufficient glamour quotient that women actually began to seek him out. Humble draftsman had mutated into talked-about caricaturist; "Oscar" was now known as "Lemoine." And yet Oscar managed to endure only a year of this attention before fleeing to Val d'Argent where he could work in peace, and where he hoped to cultivate the more extroverted personality that would be required to carry on in New York if he ever chose to return. This move was interpreted as arrogance, which greatly enhanced his image back home.

"Taxicab, sir?" said a grizzled old driver who wore a heavy

coat in the sweltering Indian-summer weather, interrupting Oscar's retrospective daydream.

Oscar was stunned by the taxi driver's politeness, but somewhat affronted at the same time: could it be that one of his hometown's tourist attractions, the venomous and uncouth cabdriver, had disappeared during the cartoonist's absence? Oscar need not have worried: the driver engaged in a colorful exchange of racist insults with an airport porter, leaving Oscar to load his own luggage into the boot, and to carry his disoriented dog to the backseat. When the driver was good and ready he took the controls and shot out of the airport exit in a cloud of smoke. They bounced onto the freeway and came almost immediately to a halt in a traffic jam of heroic density; the driver cursed as if his automotive will had never before been thwarted on the city's roads.

Elizabeth put her head on Oscar's thigh and closed her eyes. Oscar stroked her shiny black head and she responded with a lethargic wag of her tail. He rolled down his window, preferring car exhaust to the smell of his driver's soggy cigar. He reclined in his seat, crumpled and flustered by his long travels, and found to his surprise that after only a few minutes back home he had begun to reminisce about his life abroad.

II

THINGS HAD STARTED WELL IN VAL D'ARGENT. OSCAR LIVED IN A GUEST cottage on a dramatic hillside overlooking the Mediterranean, on property owned by a family friend of Brian Fable's. In Val d'Argent the expression "guest cottage" was invariably taken to mean a two-story red-tile-roofed three-bedroom mini-villa with swimming pool and private drive. Fable's family friends were happy to have a trusted tenant who planned to live on the premises year-round, and a reasonable rent was swiftly agreed.

For many months Oscar led a life of peaceful quasi-solitude, spent long days at his drafting table perfecting the art of the nude caricature, ventured only rarely into society. He posted his work to the *Lowdown* and received regular checks and bundles of hate mail in return. He gulped deep breaths of salty air and ample quantities of local wine. He walked his dog Elizabeth along the famous seaside cliffs. He sprouted muscles swimming in a pool lined by cypress trees. By the time Val d'Argent high society discovered him, Oscar had become the bronzed, fit, golden embodiment of the personality he had hoped to develop on this neutral ground. Women, young and old, began to throw themselves at him on the terraces of their husbands' villas, in the front seats of their fathers' sports cars, in the bedrooms of their boyfriends' hotel suites. Oscar very rarely acquiesced to these advances—just often enough to earn the respect of a scandal-hungry Val d'Argent society. He learned discretion and abandon in equal measures, and he learned to work with a hangover.

Oscar Lemoine had almost resigned himself to living this way, perhaps forever, when his recently conditioned emotional detachment was shattered by the apparition—for that is how she seemed to Oscar—of a woman named Veronique.

A sunset-cocktail party at someone's swimming pool found Oscar practicing his newfound suaveness on a woman who, like so many of the Europeans Oscar met in Val d'Argent, seemed annoyed that he claimed never to have heard of her. Part of being suave, Oscar had learned, was an ability to talk about the most trivial topics without for a moment losing a tone of voice more suited to a description of spiritual epiphany. It was in the middle of one such rave that his attention was diverted by a new arrival on the far side of the pool, whose effect on Oscar called to mind every cliché involving rooms darkening and eyes meeting, music playing and time standing still. What was not a cliché, and what Oscar actually felt, was that unconsciously he had known her forever; she had materialized like the glimpses of past lives insane people took seriously. Oscar knew that his instantaneous and powerful attraction to her was somehow mystical, and tried to reason with himself that she could not be substantially more beautiful than the two sensational young women who were the first to greet her.

And yet, of course, she was. Heads on all sides, male and female, turned to watch her entrance: men gaped; women flinched and readjusted their clothing. The level of conversation diminished appreciably. Ice cubes stopped clinking in their glasses. Oscar, who had never been ashamed of superficial physical attraction, felt something drop in the pit of his stomach when the breathtaking new arrival glided into full view: she extended a brown, delicate arm to shake the hand of the first man to greet her; her white-blond hair, cropped short at the back and sides in a style recently popularized by a local princess, tossed in a gust of wind; her amazing smile shone across the pool; she wore a loose dress and a white sweater around her shoulders; her slender body defined poise.

The woman Oscar had been talking to was self-absorbed enough not to notice the cartoonist's *coup de foudre.* To be polite he let her finish her next sentence before excusing himself and drifting nearer to the new arrival with Elizabeth at his side. He stopped halfway around the swimming pool, a point that happily coincided with a well-stocked bar, and inwardly criticized himself for acting so hastily. With his back to the new guest he asked the bartender for a glass of wine, and while this was poured he argued to himself that his social self-education had not progressed far enough to warrant approaching such a glorious woman. Besides, Oscar told himself, he must have exaggerated her appeal: surely it was simply a matter of contrast between her pretty smile and the stupefyingly boring conversation with the supposedly famous French woman that made the new arrival appear unique. He would take a sip of wine and a deep breath, and he would turn around to see that she had melted into the crowd, just another sun-kissed jet-setter like all the others. He sipped his wine, he breathed deeply, and turned toward the young woman.

A mighty orchestra swelled in his ears. He felt himself being drawn in her direction—one step, then another, his sandaled feet hoisted and dropped like a marionette's. Her eyes gleamed in the sunset; the evening breeze swept off the water and up the cliffs and billowed her skirt between her legs. Oscar raised his chin in rapture as he approached, and thought he could detect a warmth emanating from her side of the pool. She nodded kindly and smiled at what her companions were saying, and then, as if disturbed by the pulsing rays of Oscar's infatuation, looked up. The sight of her green eyes stopped Oscar dead, and made him look down as if ashamed. He saw that if he had taken one more step he would have plunged into the shallow end of the swimming pool. Other guests had noticed his trajectory, and again there was a perceptible lowering of the level of conversation.

Oscar pantomimed an investigation of the pool's marble edge, and even dipped a big toe into the water as if his intention all along had been to gauge its temperature. He whistled tunelessly, in the manner of lunatics, and sipped again at his wine. He kept his head down, and was thankful that his tan would conceal the inevitable burning blush. He reached down to pet his worried dog. He waited for the babble of conversation to return to its normal pitch, then turned away from the swimming pool without daring to look back at the young woman. He searched his immediate vicinity for a familiar face, but saw no one he knew well enough to interrupt. He put his wineglass down on the barman's table, folded his arms, surveyed the shoreline far below the terrace and pre-tended to be lost in appreciation of such extraordinary natural beauty. He counted slowly to fifty, believing this to be a sufficient interval that no one would remember his peculiar behavior. His plan was to turn in the opposite direction from the new arrival, to leave the premises as inconspicuously as possible, and, after instructing someone to take good care of Elizabeth, to throw himself from the cliffs to his death.

This was not to be. When he turned around, with Elizabeth at his heels, he came face-to-face with the sensational young woman and her entourage, which had gravitated with her toward the nearby bar. She stood before him with one hand through the arm of an elderly white-haired man who spoke German in a loud voice to the group at large. It was an uncomfortable moment for Oscar, who felt that his face had frozen into a teeth-baring, baboonlike grimace of shock and surprise. He was saved, as he had been on so many occasions, by his dog. Elizabeth padded ahead and looked up at the young woman with her ears back and a dog's best approximation of a courteous smile. Oscar had no choice but to follow her.

Fending off the nervous tic in the corner of his eye that was a recurring physical symptom of his shyness, Oscar shook hands with each member of the group, including the catalyst of his infatuation, Veronique. He was delighted to learn that she was at least partly French. As the ice was broken he reminded himself to lavish thanks on Elizabeth for having the social courage to make these introductions possible.

The elderly German was introduced to Oscar by Veronique first as "Herr Dohrmann," then as "Hansie," a silly-sounding nickname that did not jibe with his sinister appearance: his creased leathery face was slashed on one side by what appeared to be an ancient dueling scar; wisps of white hair hung over vicious eyebrows; one of his eyes was palest green, the other, near the beginning of his crescent-shaped scar, was soupy gray and probably blind.

Conversation was easy, thanks to Elizabeth.

"Give me two laps," said Oscar, and the labrador dutifully trotted down to the end of the swimming pool, dived in, swam two lengths, and climbed out again using the steps in the corner. She politely moved behind a potted palm to shake herself, then returned to the group and sat down next to Oscar. When wet, Elizabeth looked more like a baby seal than a dog.

"What a good girl," said Veronique, in English. Then she looked at the German and said, in French, "We've never had a dog who could swim that well."

Oscar decided that Herr Dohrmann was Veronique's father. That could account for her blondeness and her familiarity with the old man. That she spoke French to the German did not arouse Oscar's suspicions, so internationally inbred were the denizens of Val d'Argent. The fact that she called the man "Hansie" registered in Oscar's mind only because it reminded him of his first girlfriend in New York, who called all of her fathers by their first names.

When Herr Dohrmann and the other members of his group were moved along by one of the party's hosts, Oscar was amazed and terrified to find that Veronique chose to stay with him and Elizabeth. He went into a kind of trance as they exchanged recent biographies, and could not look into her eyes without trembling. He stared instead at her left collarbone. Everything Veronique said confirmed the idea that Herr Dohrmann was her father. Oscar could practically hear Elizabeth's telepathic voice: "This may be your last chance. Ask her to do something fun."

Oscar heard himself blurt out an invitation, the first thing that came into his head. To his great surprise, by the time Veronique and "Hansie" had purred away from the party an hour later in their low-slung black convertible, she had agreed to meet Oscar the following night for a snorkel in the world-famous Honclours Caves. It puzzled Oscar slightly when she leaned forward and whispered, "Don't tell anyone."

III

OSCAR SPENT MOST OF THE STOP-AND-GO CAB RIDE INTO MANHATTAN remembering this scene, and trying to reassure his black labrador that she was not going to die of a drug overdose.

"Now, Elizabeth," he said, "try to keep your tongue in your mouth."

Elizabeth stared up at her master with crossed eyes that

somehow managed to communicate an accusation of maltreatment, and struggled with uncoordinated paws to stay on the slippery seat of the jerking taxi. Her tongue lolled lifelessly from one side of her graying muzzle.

"You have to pull yourself together," said Oscar. "We have a party to go to."

The cabdriver stared suspiciously into his rearview mirror and chomped messily on his cigar. Someone was shouting angrily in a foreign language on the taxi's radio.

"Come on, girl. Buck up," said Oscar.

Slowly, Elizabeth began to respond. Her eyes focused, and her expression returned to its usual one of general disapproval. Soon she had managed to sit up on her haunches to take in the dreadful sights of her native city. Oscar held her up to the window, and together dog and master winced at each passing atrocity until, at last, the mighty skyline loomed and Manhattan was a postcard.

The new offices of the *Lowdown* were actually quite high up—on the forty-second floor of the Hoyt Tower. Oscar stashed his gear behind the guard's desk on the ground floor. He led Elizabeth into the elevator, straightened his hair and tie in the mirror, brushed at the shoulders of his blazer. He strode from the elevator through the receptionist's vacant office and into the party little more than twelve hours after having dived into his pool before breakfast in Val d'Argent.

Despite all the publicity to the contrary, alcohol was still the drug of choice in New York; sold openly and easily administered, the substance was everywhere in evidence. So it was, in its various popular forms, at the party thrown on the occasion of the *Lowdown*'s third anniversary. The magazine's survival in a field that had left so many entrepreneurial corpses littering the literary streets was cause enough for celebration, but such was the orientation of most of those assembled that no excuse was needed for their rapid descent into excess. Conversation had grown noisy and reckless. A layer of cigarette smoke clung to the acoustically tiled ceiling. The folks in advertising had burst into song, and many of them were doing and saying things they would have to drink heavily—again—to forget.

Because it was in great measure Oscar's controversial work that had sent the *Lowdown*'s circulation soaring to heights the founder would never have proposed even to his most gullible investors, the cartoonist arrived to be showered with confetti, toasted with all kinds of alcoholic drinks, and wildly praised in a series of slurred speeches by the small group of people he had done so much to enrich. The atmosphere was one of giddy goodwill, of an enduring camaraderie based on three years' sometimes hard-earned but mostly fortuitous success. Oscar was congratulated on his birthday, then criticized for being too tanned and handsome for someone who supposedly had a job to do. When the speeches were over and the assembled staffers had returned to the faster-paced drinking formal toasting can sometimes quell, Oscar Lemoine was cornered by his old friend Brian Fable.

"Ah," said the blond, gangling Fable, looming over his most prized employee, "the man they called Essential. Welcome home." His gratitude, like his cocktail, overflowed. His blond hair had thinned considerably, and he appeared to have chipped one of his front teeth.

Oscar shook Fable's hand, which as usual meant suffering a series of athletic thumps on the back, pokes in the ribs and touslings of hair, so that ticklish Oscar spilled most of his own drink fending off Fable's greeting. Despite having known Fable since preadolescence, Oscar's feelings about the man were decidedly mixed. Fable's untempered brashness had always verged on vulgarity, and was even less becoming in an adult.

"And if it isn't the bitch they called Unruly," Fable said, leaning over to pet Elizabeth. Elizabeth looked up at the tall man and yawned pinkly. "How can you still be alive?"

"She isn't unruly," said Oscar, who was at his most defensive when it came to his dog. "She has never been unruly in her life. Have you, Elizabeth? Good girl."

Fable shook his head. "People and their pets. Fascinating." He was about to say more, but someone had caught his eye in the crowd. He reached out a long arm, gained purchase on his victim, and pulled a woman to his side.

"Ow," said Gail Gardener, loyal denizen of the pasteup room and the only other person still working for the magazine who had been present at the creation of the *Lowdown*.

"Ah," said Fable, touching Gail in ways so unsuitable to the workplace that Oscar thought them likely to bring about litigation, "if it isn't the gal they called Desirable." He kissed her on top of her head and made guttural noises—just two of the many things it would be unlikely for someone to do without the ancient and well-documented effects of drink on human inhibitions.

Oscar found he could muster only the most bashful of smiles. He was grateful in such circumstances to have Elizabeth at his side, who soon monopolized Gail's attention.

"Oh, yes," said Gail, crouching down to pat her on the head. "Oh, yes, aren't you beautiful."

"Thank you," said the possessive Oscar.

"Can you shake my hand?" Gail asked Elizabeth. "Can you, girl?"

"Shake," said Oscar, with a nonchalance he hoped would convey to Gail that Elizabeth was perhaps the most highly trained, specialized city dog in the world. Elizabeth dutifully raised a paw, but gave her master a sideways look that hinted at disapproval for putting her through such pedestrian paces. If he had said "Elevator," Elizabeth would have trotted out into the corridor and leapt at the down button on the wall until the light came on. Eighteen months out of the country would not have dulled her city skills.

By the time Gail rose to her feet, Oscar had managed to contort his face into its closest approximation of suaveness, and began to ask polite questions about Gail's life during his absence. Gail had not changed much during the interval, except that she looked weary, and her monosyllabic answers were each preceded by a sigh.

"Look at you two," Fable interrupted. "What do I detect here? Is that lightning I see crackling between you?"

"Aw, Brian," Gail sighed. "Stop."

"No, no, I see it." Fable raised his hands like a film director and framed the couple between his thumbs. "A romance for our times."

"Please," pleaded a reddening Oscar.

"I take full responsibility," said Fable. "The wedding, the honeymoon, the kids' education."

"He'll stop soon," Gail said to Oscar.

"Actually," said Fable, "Gail and I are engaged. Or have I told you that already." He gave Gail a proprietary squeeze.

"I didn't know. Congratulations."

"He's lying," said Gail. "I think."

"My intellectuals!" Fable was shouting. "Bring me my god-damned intellectuals!"

Oscar looked down at his dog and shrugged. He found that even in all the confusion his mind was still on Val d'Argent.

IV

"*YOU HAVE BROUGHT YOUR DOG?*" *WAS THE FIRST THING VERONIQUE* said when she arrived at the bit of beach that provided the easiest access to the Honclours Caves.

During his fourteen years in Elizabeth's company Oscar had learned not to react violently to any impoliteness concerning his dog, no matter how offended he might be. In any case he was struck dumb by Veronique's appearance; it required all his strength to fend off a budding panic attack as she crossed her arms at her waist and removed her turquoise thigh-length shift. Underneath she wore a matching bikini, the bottom half of which was cut in a way designed to accentuate the length of the wearer's legs—which in Veronique's case was entirely unnecessary but stunning all the same.

"Elizabeth loves to swim," Oscar was finally able to say, removing his own shirt one-handed. He did not tell Veronique that Elizabeth also liked to dive down and investigate coral reefs, poke about among the swaying aquatic flora, and chase schools of terrified tiger fish while barking bubbles. Veronique would see for herself.

Under a three-quarter moon, Oscar and Veronique donned masks and flippers, and slipped into the lapping sea. Elizabeth followed at a respectful distance, paddling doggedly. They swam out beyond the shoals, turned on their backs to take in the sights of stars and lighted cliff-side villas, then turned the corner to the mouth of the largest cave.

The phosphorescent Honclours Caves, only slightly marred by spray-painted graffiti, glowed softly beneath the cliffs. Many legends were attached to the caves, which were said to have stored pirate treasure, swallowed small boats, witnessed torture and human sacrifice. Their reputation seemed to have been borne out a decade ago, when the mayor's daughter had used the premises to experiment with hallucinogens and boys, to sunbathe provocatively in full view of passing fishermen, and finally to launch a skiff with her favorite boyfriend and disappear into the dawn, never to return. The caves were currently used during daylight hours for homosexual nude bathing, but by the bereft mayor's decree were supposedly off-limits to minors.

Oscar and Veronique swam side by side into the mouth of the main cave, where the water glowed blue-green. White webs of light shimmered beneath the surface like cracked glass. The lapping of water echoed off walls bearing swastikas and peace symbols, under sweating stalactites encrusted with colorful calcified goo. The swimmers trod water under the central dome, and turned to watch Elizabeth catch up with them. The dog made for a ledge under one wall, crawled out of the water, and shook herself briskly.

Oscar, who was practically senseless with happiness at being here with Veronique, removed his mask and snorkel. "Have you been here before?"

Veronique shook her head. Her green eyes were magnified to piscatorial proportions behind her mask.

"Dive down. There's nothing much to see, but it's spooky." Oscar paused to let his voice stop echoing. "There's a rock floor just beneath us. As soon as you get to the bottom next to me, look up again."

Veronique nodded. Oscar replaced his mask, indicated that he was ready, and dived to the bottom of the cave. Having practiced this maneuver before, he knew to roll onto his back and grab hold of a crack in the floor with one hand. He looked up and saw graceful Veronique following behind. He extended his free hand. Veronique reached out for it and Oscar gently pulled her down next to him. She put an arm around his neck to keep from floating away. Oscar gestured with his head that she should look directly upward. After a brief, dramatic pause, the luminous surface of the water was broken by Elizabeth's expert dive—front and back paws pointed, nose down, eyes wide and white.

V

"MY INTELLECTUALS!" FABLE WAS SHOUTING. "BRING ME MY GOD-damned intellectuals!"

Fable's intellectuals soon appeared, a trio of writers he had plucked from poverty so severe they were supposed to have been near death from starvation, huddled together in a rent-controlled studio in an unmentionable neighborhood. While deprivation had left its sallow mark on these men, they had profited enough in Fable's employ to have purchased clean, expensive versions of the starving-artist clothing they had probably worn in the first place. These writers were responsible, under half a dozen pen names, for some of the trendiest verbiage in the city. Fanaticized by their evident need for food and shelter, they had proven themselves capable of transforming the dullest interview—even in the recent case of a hopelessly exploited European art-film starlet—into a bitter overhaul of the human condition. Their ferocious book reviews gave no quarter to any but the most *engagé* or obscure authors, preferably from just deep enough in the developing or Iron Curtain worlds that their angst credentials were unassailable; young people's music was grossly overrepresented between the *Lowdown*'s covers, discussed so frantically and passionately that a reader unfamiliar with Western society would have taken writhing young musicians as the nation's religious idols; adolescents' films were written about with similar devotion. For a long time Oscar had assumed that the *Lowdown* was a quite brilliantly satirical magazine, but he had not dared to ask.

Fabel's intellectuals greeted their employer with unconcealed gratitude, submitted to his pokes and jabs and touslings, nodded furiously when he asked them if they were as god-damned happy to be here as he was.

When the time came for them to say hello to Oscar Lemoine, they practically bowed to the floor in awe of the cartoonist. Oscar shook the writers' hands in turn and tried to memorize their real names. He had been away so long he knew no one on the magazine but Brian Fable and Gail Gardener: eighteen months was a long time in New York.

"Great," said the tallest of the writers, a specialist in city politics named Martin Arlington.

"Deep," said the writer next to him, a book and film reviewer named Marcus Barnard, who prided himself on once having written an unpublished review longer by half than the slim volume it had eviscerated.

"Sick," said the third of Fable's intellectuals, a particularly battered-looking young man named Harold Hampsten, the *Lowdown*'s unchallenged expert on trend, modern art and night-life, which he claimed were "three facets of the same jewel."

"Thank you," said Oscar, and looked down at his feet. Oscar was aware that people often mistook his shyness for a kind of arrogance, because they could not reconcile his usually diffident personality with the aggressive, scandalous cover art he produced for the *Lowdown*. He struggled to raise his eyes and smile warmly at Fable's intellectuals, who seemed to be waiting for him to speak.

"Have you met my dog?" he decided to ask them.

They seemed to find this amusing, at first, then they shook their heads in unison at the mysticism embedded in the question. They nodded hello to Elizabeth, still pondering what they took to be Oscar's Wildean *bon mot*.

Oscar wrestled himself into composure, and thought of something constructive to say: "I love what you write, each of you." This was untrue; the little he had read of their work tended to frighten him. They were reckless in thought and word.

"Aren't they terrific?" said Fable. "The men they called Indispensable."

"But you, you," said Martin Arlington reverentially. "What you are doing is—"

"Epochal," said Marcus Barnard. "Epochal, is what it is. You've struck a blow against—"

"Here, here," interrupted the third writer, Harold Hampsten, producing a brown envelope from a deep pocket in his black leather jacket. "Look what I found." He opened the envelope and removed a cardboard-backed drawing. "Do you recognize this?" The excited writer handed over the drawing.

"Well, yes, I do," said Oscar. "Of course I do."

"The very first Oscar Lemoine cartoon," said Hampsten proudly. "You must have been fifteen years old, am I right?"

"Yes, I'm sure that's correct. For my school newspaper. I haven't seen that drawing in ten years."

"May I see?" asked Gail.

Oscar fidgeted while she examined his first published drawing. It portrayed an angry-looking, uniformed prep-school boy standing in the headmaster's office. The stern headmaster sat behind his desk, holding a riding crop in his right hand. The boy rubbed his buttock as he spoke: "Well, in that case, my *parentis* are *loco*."

"Very nice," said Gail.

"Do you really think so?" asked Oscar, looking down at Elizabeth for a moment as if his dog might be able to confirm this appraisal of his work. "Just a cartoon, really," he said. "I don't do much of that anymore."

"Will you sign it for me?" asked Hampsten. "I have a pen."

"Of course," Oscar said. He had gained some experience with autographs during the short period of glamour that had preceded his exile, and quickly signed the drawing "To my steamed colleague, from the man who toons cars, Oscar."

Oscar handed over the drawing and smiled, but his thoughts were elsewhere.

VI

ELIZABETH NOSED THROUGH THE GLOWING GREEN WATER TOWARD Oscar's outstretched hands. He caught her in one arm and turned proudly to Veronique, who released Oscar's neck and clapped her hands through the water in slow motion. They rose to the surface together, and Elizabeth paddled off toward the back of the cave.

Oscar spat out the mouthpiece of his snorkel. "She wants to go to the bath cave. It's a little scary at night. We have to swim down to the entrance, then about ten feet through a tunnel. Shall we go with her?"

Veronique nodded eagerly, so they swam along in the wake of Elizabeth's small, sealike head. At the back wall of the large cave, where the water foamed against the rocks, Elizabeth disappeared beneath the surface.

"She knows the way," said Oscar. "Give her a minute to get through the tunnel."

When Elizabeth failed to resurface, Oscar counted to three on his fingers so that Veronique could take her last breath at the same time as he did. He dived down vertically, with Veronique following behind him, and quickly found the entrance to the tunnel. He crouched next to it and waved to Veronique for her to precede him. Long and slim, she had no difficulty pulling herself inside and swimming out of view.

Only the fact that he had practiced swimming through to the bath cave on dozens of occasions during daylight, and the need not to lose face in front of his new friend and his dog, prevented Oscar from turning back halfway through the tunnel. He was not a natural spelunker—in fact he was claustrophobic, and not just dark but dimness made him come all over queer. He swam and crawled through the tunnel using slimy outcroppings of rock to pull himself along. He imagined Elizabeth and Veronique moving through here, in total darkness, and was amazed.

The bath cave was so called because it resembled a Roman bath. Under a domed, smooth ceiling, half a dozen distinct bath-shaped depressions surrounded the deep central pool. The youth of Val d'Argent, before and after the mayor's unenforceable edict, had found it an ideal place to indulge in all that was illicit.

When Oscar rose to the surface, he found Veronique and Elizabeth catching their breaths against a recessed rock passageway that led to the central domed bath. A strange light flickered around the corner—not the normal chemifluorescence of the caves, but the flickering yellow light of candles. Oscar put a finger to his lips, indicating to Veronique that someone else must be using the caves, and swam away to take a look.

When he peeked around the corner into the baths, Oscar knew that what he saw would linger in his memory for quite a long time. Three girls in bikinis were seated at a table on a broad ledge beside the main bath. Next to the table stood a gray-haired man, liveried and immaculate, attending to the uncorking of wine. With a white-gloved hand he filled the diners' glasses, placed the bottle in a silver bucket, then addressed himself to preparing crêpes on a small propane stove. The gray-haired man delivered a muffled toast, and the girls giggled. The smell of crêpes filled the cave.

Veronique swam up behind Oscar and took in the sight in the bath cave with a startled gasp, and aspirated a mouthful of seawater in the process. Her coughing fit alerted the diners to the presence of spies, which Oscar imagined was particularly annoying for the participants once such an elaborate party was in full swing. Veronique clung to Oscar's shoulder while she finished coughing; the gray-haired man peered into the darkness; Elizabeth barked once, sharply. The gray-haired man, clearly visible in the candlelight, shouted into the echoing cave.

"I say! I say, you there!" The man was tall, thin, and erect of posture. He spoke with an English accent. "You there, go on, out!"

"He can't see us," whispered Veronique. "They probably think we are children from the town."

"I've see that man around, haven't I?" asked Oscar.

"Yes, of course, that's Neville," said Veronique. "Very amusing. Hansie invites him to our parties."

"What about the girls?" Oscar wanted to know.

"I don't know them. Maybe visitors from a boat?"

Oscar and Veronique stopped whispering, and Elizabeth did

not bark again, so that only the grumbling of interrupted voluptuaries echoed under the dome.

"Are they gone, Neville?" asked one of the girls.

"Have you gone?" Neville asked the darkness. Oscar and Veronique chose not to reply. "They're gone," Neville decided. "Nasty little beasties."

Oscar and Veronique watched as the man tried to decide how to re-create the mood of what looked every bit like a potential orgy. More wine was poured, crêpes were served and eaten. The gray-haired man removed his white gloves, then his trousers, and sat down again. Oscar clung to the rock; Veronique clung to Oscar; Elizabeth swam around in tight circles, pouting.

"We shouldn't be watching," whispered Veronique, as it became clear that a certain amount of further undressing was likely to occur.

"Oh, yes we should," said Oscar. "It's my job. Researching the human form."

"Of course," said Veronique. "I forgot. I will research with you."

Beneath the reverberations of the considerable noise the man and his girls began to make, Oscar and Veronique were able to converse in low voices. Oscar told Veronique how impressed he was with the Englishman's logistical expertise: Veronique replied that Neville had undoubtedly instructed servants and porters in scuba gear to lay the foundations of his evening in the Honclours Caves. Oscar said that his magazine would be interested in a scoop of this kind, since Neville and perhaps even the girls were likely to be unutterably famous, but that it was not his job to dredge up that kind of story. He said he was surprised that German and British paparazzi had not surfaced in the bath caves to photograph such a decadent tableau.

The three girls were young and lovely; Oscar guessed from the sounds they made that Neville had kept them well supplied with wine. Neville approached the post-prandial re-creation with the deliberation of an officer drawing up plans of battle. He placed more candles in nooks and crannies of the cave wall to light their scene to the best possible effect.

Oscar shook his head with disapproval—although he was not sure he disapproved—just in case Veronique took offense. At this early stage in their acquaintance Oscar did not want such a seemingly well-brought-up girl to get the idea that he had deviant tendencies. So Oscar clicked his tongue and shook his head, but when he looked over at Veronique, who had put an arm around his waist to hold her head above water, he was amused and relieved to see her eyes wide in appreciation, her lips parted in happy surprise. Veronique liked watching orgies.

VII

"DO YOU THINK I SHOULD GIVE ANOTHER INSPIRATIONAL SPEECH?" Brian Fable asked impatiently at the *Lowdown* party. "I think I should give another inspirational speech. Much to do, long way to go, that sort of thing."

"No more inspirational speeches," said Gail Gardener. "People are inspired enough. We don't want them to start breaking things."

The party had reached that crucial stage where without supervision it could quickly collapse into tabletop dancing, spouse-swapping, exhibitionism.

"In that case I will simply join the fray." Fable made a motion of rolling up his jacket sleeves, then paused as he remembered something. "Oscar. One bit of business. Won't you join me in the boardroom? Don't worry, everyone, I'll give him back momentarily. I have to give him a ton of money." He guided Oscar away by the elbow.

"Come, Elizabeth," said Oscar. He bowed good-bye to Gail and Fable's intellectuals.

"Trouble," said Fable, when he had shut the door behind them.

"Oh?"

"Yes. But first, your pelf." He extracted a white envelope from his jacket. "There's a gigantic check in here. Don't become a drug addict."

Oscar opened the envelope, scanned the enclosed check (which was decidedly not gigantic, but Fable always spoke this way), and stuffed it in his back pocket.

"Do you like money, Oscar?"

"Oh yes, I like money fine."

"Good. I'm trying to earn you lots of it."

Oscar had been given two incentives to stay with the *Lowdown* after the success of his first covers: a small stake in the magazine, and the additional salaried post of religious editor. The former had been moderately remunerative of late; the latter had resulted in two religious columns under Oscar's byline, both reading simply "No news yet." It was a very popular column.

"Again, welcome back," said Fable, more seriously. "I can't tell you how good it is to see you. You're staying this time, I hope. We don't want you losing touch."

"I'll be here several weeks. I'm not sure if I'm ready to move back yet. I want to see my brother, catch up with old friends, watch television. Now what did you say about 'trouble'?"

"*Orthoducks*," said Fable.

"Hmm. Lawsuits?"

"No, no. Just bad feeling."

Orthoducks was the title of a cartoon serial Oscar had written and drawn, which depicted a family of Hassidic ducks and told their story of domestic tensions in modern Manhattan. The saga of the *Orthoducks* had featured in each of the last six issues of the *Lowdown*, substituting for Oscar's religious column. Oscar had received an unprecedented volume of hate mail.

"Surely that's just my problem," said Oscar. "I can handle it. It's all very innocent."

"You know that, and I know that. But the wind on the street is that we're an anti-Semitic organ. These rumors start, and you can't believe how hard it is to defend yourself. Are you Jewish at all, Oscar? It might help."

"Sorry. That is, I never asked. One of my stepmothers, maybe."

"Could you draw something flattering, then?"

"It isn't funny to flatter people, is it? And as religious editor, I consider it within my purview to satirize a city sect. Anyway, I don't see the problem. We have bags of mail saying people think the *Orthoducks* are hilarious—or cute, anyway."

"Gah, no, don't say that. That's the worst thing you can say. You know the tune. The worst defense is denial."

"Oh, for God's sake."

"I'm serious. You have no idea. I'm getting heavy bids on the rag from *Nazis*."

"Come on."

"Well, you know what I mean. Unwholesome types. Anyway, what with that and the nudes, our image is in tatters. We're risking alienating our core readers. So I'm told."

The "nudes" were Oscar Lemoine's trademark, and they were what Fable's intellectuals referred to when they called his work "epochal." The *Lowdown*'s success undoubtedly rested on these works, and on the controversy and litigation that had followed on the heels of their publication. It amazed Oscar that people could be so offended by a little fun. He had never meant deliberately to scandalize anyone, he had simply employed his knack for caricaturing the human body to enunciate as wickedly as possible his opinion that people in high places should literally be exposed—especially evil or preposterous people, but just about anyone would do.

The nude-caricature genre was not exactly a widespread medium of expression, but it came naturally to Oscar Lemoine, and he had made it his own at an early age. After his sell-out inaugural cover of the dancing, naked Mafioso, Oscar had turned his brush on a religious broadcaster prominent at the time. Because the electronic minister was still alive, the magazine's editors knew the cover was guaranteed to result in the free publicity of outrage; after long consultations with Fable's attorneys ("Fable's Stable"), they pronounced it fit to print. They hoped to weather the inevitable public outcry with supercilious quotations from the Bill of Rights. In any event the minister was far too preoccupied with touchy legal matters pertaining to a paternity suit, and did not pursue the issue.

It would never have occurred to Oscar that his nude-caricature covers were obscene or libelous. He tended to take the oft-touted liberties of his country quite literally. He had only the vaguest understanding of his victims' legal recourse, and as a cartoonist he had always operated under the assumption that any product of his imagination was a piece of intellectual property that he could trade or sell without interference. Noble as it might have been, this belief had not prevented Oscar's expulsion from boarding school for a comparatively mild but nonetheless nude caricature of his music teacher.

It came as a revelation to him, therefore, when his second *Lowdown* nude caricature caused such a stir. Oscar thought the drawing was straightforward enough, portraying as it did nothing more than a realistic likeness of the religious leader's head, perched atop a revoltingly flabby body. But two embellishments appeared to be what offended some people: the Bible perched coyly on the preacher's jutting hip, and the absolutely mammoth collection of genitals that spilled out of the picture like meats in the window of a Bavarian butcher.

Everyone at the magazine at least pretended to support Oscar's work in the early days, even as his art grew increasingly gruesome and overtly anatomical. Politicians, film stars, prominent businessmen and even a thoroughbred racehorse soon graced the *Lowdown*'s cover, each with devastatingly exaggerated private parts. Most of the drawings, Oscar would have argued, were flattering to the subject. To those readers of an artistic bent, Brian Fable might have argued that the *Lowdown*'s covers had achieved a pinnacle of bad taste that no self-respecting twentieth-century intellectual could avoid defending as genius. The *Lowdown*'s founder had discovered, quite by accident, the graphic embodiment of his magazine's title. The reproductive organs of world leaders and other very famous individuals turned up on its covers in various states of decay or arousal, magnificence or paltriness—especially the mayor's.

A further key to the magazine's success was that it contained nothing but pseudo-highbrow features and reviews by Fable's intellectuals—which Oscar mistakenly took to be satirical—without the merest tinge of pornography or irreverence that its cover might have suggested. The cover sold the magazine, the content kept it trendy and vaguely respectable, and advertisers had their pick of diverse demographic targets. The notoriety of Oscar Lemoine nudes and the success of the advertising slogan GET THE *LOWDOWN* meant that Brian Fable was able to repay his backers after the first six months.

"You don't mean to say you're stopping the nudes?" Oscar asked Fable in the boardroom, as the muffled sounds of music started up beyond the door.

"Oh, don't get me wrong. We stick with the nudes, natch.

Keep 'em coming. It's the *Orthoducks* I'm really worried about. Very touchy."

"I have just two more installments. They're all done. We can't leave the fans in the dark. Everyone wants to know what happens to the Ugly Orthoduckling."

"Does he turn into a rabbi?"

"Of course not. That would be offensive."

"What, then?"

"He falls in love with his sister and they have to kill themselves."

"What a relief."

"I have a new religion column I want to show to you."

"'No news yet'?"

"A longer one," said Oscar. "I've been dipping into the literature and I have developed a kind of instructional angle for the column."

"Yes?"

"I call it 'Nun of the Above.'"

"Illustrated?"

"Naturally."

"You make me proud."

Oscar was honestly glad to see Fable again. There was something endearing about the man's energy and enthusiasm, his utter lack of subtlety, his eagerness to show people that if he himself happened not to be creative, he certainly knew how to manage those who were. Had he drawn a nude caricature of his friend and employer, Oscar would have portrayed Brian Fable with a transparent blond bubble of a head atop his spindly frame, posing as a baton-wielding maestro conducting an orchestra of responsive dollar bills.

"I could kiss you," said Fable. "You don't know what fun this has been. What the hell kind of fun could it have been in hiding? Word is you want to be known as a recluse. Tell me you aren't going back. We need you here."

"I haven't made up my mind."

"What," Fable wanted to know, sweeping an uncoordinated arm before him, "could be more fun than this?"

VIII

AFTER TEN MINUTES WATCHING THE MODEST ORGY IGNITE WITHIN THE bath cave, Oscar and Veronique had discovered the aphrodisiac properties of voyeurism. Elizabeth was the only creature in the Honclours Caves without a partner, although even in her fertile youth she had never been terribly interested in that kind of behavior. To pass the time she swam around the perimeter of the pool, her wet, ratlike face poking up into the candlelight.

Oscar thought it was safe to say he had never been happier. He supported Veronique by her waist, and cheek to salty cheek they watched the bath-cave frolickers, as if they were characters in a film projected on the cave wall. Only when Oscar developed a sore neck from clinging to both Veronique and the mossy rock did the trio swim back through the tunnel and into the sea.

Oscar knew from experience that after a late-night swim with a potential girlfriend it was important to eat goat cheese and cold cuts and buttered toast, washed down with the most arid of white wines. Clothed and dried, he escorted Veronique along the beach road to the Café Floride, one of the five or six places on the harbor where this kind of sustenance was available until nearly daybreak. The ever-cheerful waiter André greeted them with kisses and handshakes, and even brought Veronique a spare jacket so that the couple could sit outside. They sat side by side on a padded iron bench with their backs against the front window of the café, and watched the colorful strollers returning from dinner to their homes or yachts. Veronique knew most of the *habitués* of the Val d'Argent seafront and acknowledged them with her uncanny smile. Even Oscar was able to wave casually at two or three of the passersby.

Conversation was unnecessary at the Café Floride because there was so much to see, so much to savor. The prominent sounds were the clank of halyard against mast, the burp and whine of motorbike, the swish of breeze through palm. Added to the usual seaside smells were wafting perfume from stylish women walking by, and the briny scent of oysters and mussels packed in ice and seaweed on stalls near the entrance to the restaurant. Oscar quickly lapsed into his sensual café daze, and in half an hour said only three words to Veronique: "Oysters, my dear?"

The tireless André seemed to take genuine pleasure in the happiness of his clientele. He brought more wine unbidden; he chatted only when chatted to; he responded to praise with a bashful bow from the waist and a humble hand to the chest. His body language made it clear that he found Veronique to be the most gloriously beautiful woman ever to grace the undeserving Café Floride. Behind her back, in Oscar's view, he raised his eyes heavenward at the luck of any man who dined with her.

"Say, look," said Oscar at last, yanked out of his trance by an approaching group of people. "Isn't that the man from the caves?"

Sure enough, it was Neville, the English orgiast, accompanied by his friends from the Honclours Caves. They walked unsteadily in their baggy cotton clothes, collided gigglingly with one another, made histrionic apologies to the pedestrians they drove from the pavement. The girls really were awfully young.

"How can he behave this way?" Oscar asked. "Isn't he afraid of reporters? Oh, no, here he comes."

Neville lurched toward their table and stared at Veronique with wild blue eyes.

"Veronique, *darling*," he said. He turned to Oscar and pursed his lips. "And I know I've seen *you* before."

Oscar cringed and made his body huge on the bench, where there was just conceivably room for one more person.

"Do run along," Neville said to his companions. "I've found friends. I'll catch you up later, have no fear."

The girls waved good-bye and continued on their way.

"*Touristes,*" spat Neville, pulling up a vacant chair and settling down next to Veronique. "Oh, André, how nice to see you."

André smiled and cocked an ear, waiting to take an order he seemed to know would come in English.

"Would you be so kind," said Neville, "as to bring me one of your little coffees? And a great big brandy right alongside? Think yoh."

André nodded and sped away. Neville flattened his unruly wet hair with his palms.

"Been for a swim," he said. "And you, you naughty little things—what have you been up to? Tell me your name?"

"Lemoine, sir," said Oscar.

"Oh, yes, I remember now. I know what *you* do."

Oscar wanted to say that he knew what Neville did, too. "And this is my dog, Elizabeth," he chose to say instead.

"Yeh-oh," said Neville, only just able to make himself look at the dog. "Indeed."

Oscar supposed it was only fair to have his café daze shattered by Neville, having himself barged in on such a cracking party earlier in the evening.

"And my name is Neville," said Neville. "No doubt you already knew that."

"Yes, sir," Oscar admitted. "I knew."

As his coffee and brandy arrived, Neville grumbled something about the wages of fame. Oscar was glad to see that Veronique appeared to be enjoying their visitor.

"You must tell me what Hansie is up to," Neville said to her. "Or should I just pretend I never asked?"

The meaning of this was lost on Oscar. He assumed that by nudging and winking Neville meant it was what Hansie was up to that he shouldn't have asked about.

"He is away," said Veronique. "Just for a night or two. Always the same, business, business."

"I really think Hansie ought to slow down. He's a million years old, after all. What possible pleasure can he derive from *business*, at his age?" The very idea of work was obviously unpleasant for Neville to contemplate, and his ensuing monologue confirmed that the newly diligent Britain had become uninhabitable for a man of his leanings.

"Frightfully industrious, your Hansie," said Neville. "Always was."

Veronique explained to Oscar that Neville and Hansie had known each other for "a very long time," emphasizing the phrase so that it obviously encompassed the Second World War. Her remark allowed Oscar to calculate that Neville and Hansie were at least sixty-six years old, and the German looked considerably older than that. Neville, on the other hand, exuded a youthfulness through his watery blue eyes that could only be explained by an utter lack of stress in his life, combined with the kind of pulse-quickening exercise he had been enjoying in the Honclours Caves.

Neville talked on, unfocused even by the infrequent query from Oscar or Veronique. Oscar tried to concentrate on what the Englishman said, but found himself lost in a forest of dropped names, places, outrages. Neville looked like someone who had weathered his share of rumor-driven scandal, but he slandered with the best of them. Veronique, at least, seemed to know what he was talking about; Oscar merely pretended.

". . . but of course I am out of touch these days. Sad old devil, I am. Do you feel sorry for me?" He addressed this question to Veronique with sparkling blue eyes and great good humor. Nothing sorry about Neville, was what his expression said.

"Nonsense," said Veronique. "And all of that talk reminds me—you will be at our house on Saturday. You can catch up with everything if you feel so out of touch. Besides, Hansie says he hasn't seen enough of you lately."

Oscar was struck by how differently Veronique behaved in Neville's company. She sat up straight in her chair and exuded a poise and sophistication for which she had no use when alone with Oscar.

"Of course you will come too," she said to Oscar, brushing his hair from his brow and smiling at him.

"Naturally. I should be delighted," said Oscar. He blushed as soon as he heard that his response had come out sounding like a deliberate aping of Neville's accent. "What I mean is, you bet."

"I do so look forward to having a chat with you, Mr. Lemoine," said Neville. His formality was peculiar, considering their respective ages. "There have been far too few artists in Val d'Argent of late. In fact since before the war. I used to come here as a child, mind you, and . . ."

Oscar was glad to hear Neville veering off into yet another reminiscence, which saved him from having to explain that he was not really an artist—not in the sense Neville probably meant. Oscar was as proud of his work as the next man, but a monthly nude caricature and the occasional cartoon did not exactly rate an easel in the atelier of the Greats. To explain this to Neville would have meant adding that Elizabeth wore the artistic mantle in the family (even her immature works were far more in keeping with the current artistic *Zeitgeist* than Oscar's). To say so would have served only to confirm in Neville's mind that Oscar possessed the artist's unstable temperament.

". . . a good deal more Sancerre than sincere, if you must know the truth about him," Neville was saying, in his entertaining way, describing someone inconceivably famous. "But I do go on so." Neville pushed back his chair and prepared for departure. "I must let you young people carry on alone. The waterfront at this hour is no place for a tragic old cripple." Neville stood and bowed, then skipped away down the broad esplanade in a lively gait, less that of an old cripple than that of a teenager celebrating first love.

"Amazing," said Oscar. "What a full day he's had."

Veronique shrugged, and hitched up her shift so that she could cross her legs. "Hansie is very amused by him. They reminisce about the war together. You will not believe it, but our Neville was terrifically courageous. So was Hansie, of course, but in a less . . . *romantic* way."

Oscar was sure he didn't want to know about Herr Dohrmann's behavior during the war, at least not yet. He suggested instead that a chill had descended on the harbor, that they ought to be going. André appeared in time to insist that Veronique return the jacket on some other occasion, and to accept the gigantic tip such gallantry is likely to elicit.

Whether alone or with a friend, Oscar always enjoyed the late-night hike uphill to his house. The steep and crumbling asphalt road retained its heat throughout the night and warmed the cypress-scented air. Elizabeth trotted ahead along the familiar route, while Oscar and Veronique followed arm in arm. Together they negotiated the hair-pin curves that carved past the lesser houses occupying the lower half of the hillside. The lights of the town glowed warmly in the valley below, and along the horseshoe harbor. When they passed through the gates of the villa with which Oscar's guest house was affiliated, Elizabeth ran ahead out of hunger and possibly discretion, leaving Oscar and Veronique to fall into each other's arms even before they had reached his cottage, stumbling through the moon shadows like a pair of wounded soldiers helping each other back to their trench.

Oscar ushered Veronique inside, gave her a tour of his not-so-humble home, took her out on the terrace under the stars, and kissed her. Every move he made was still consciously executed, for if he had allowed his instincts to take over he would have fallen to his knees and wept with joy. Even as he kissed Veronique he opened his eyes and craned them toward the stars on the horizon and repeated over and over to himself that he simply could not believe his good fortune.

"Wait, stop," said Veronique.

"I beg your pardon?" Their lips were still touching.

"I have to go."

Oscar wanted to explain what he had been about to do when she had said "Wait, stop," which would have involved a certain amount of hot-tub stoking, nectar uncorking, pillow fluffing— hours and hours of extended pleasure. Instead he carried on his role of manly aloofness, and expressed his regret for what might have been merely by holding her hips and swiveling her closer for a good-night kiss.

"I will get you a taxi," was all he said. "What a wonderful evening we've had."

IX

"WHAT COULD BE MORE FUN THAN THIS?" FABLE HAD JUST ASKED AT the *Lowdown* party. Oscar thought of his first night with Veronique, but did not say so. "I think I ought to drink something so that I can say hello to these strange people."

"Ah," said Fable. "The man they called Bashful. I'm glad you're coming out of your shell. It's time for you to live, my boy."

As he mingled among the slobbering drunks who were his colleagues, Oscar kept an eye out for the blondeness of Gail Gardener. His intention was to show Gail that the Oscar Lemoine who eighteen months ago had been incapable of speaking to her without tics and spoonerisms had returned from abroad simply bursting with urbanity. He might even drop a hint that he had fallen in love over yonder in Europe.

There she was, over by the plastic rubber tree, or rubber plastic tree, smiling as usual but seeming to cringe at the same time, clutching her elbows over her chest as an overly friendly *Lowdown* employee poked at her with an ink-stained index finger. Oscar knew it was time to intercede, but first he had to dispense with an autograph-seeking woman who was unknown to him but appeared to be the spouse of one of the *Lowdown*'s now dangerously inebriated advertising crew.

"From the *Lowdown*'s humble top drawer," Oscar signed. When he handed the autograph back to the woman, she inspected it skeptically, then asked, "Could I have a sketch of the Ugly Orthoduckling, too?"

"What do you think, Elizabeth," Oscar asked his dog. "May she have a sketch of the Ugly Orthoduckling?" Oscar paused for a response. Elizabeth seemed to chew over his question, then looked up and panted energetically. "Elizabeth says of course you may," said Oscar, and used a fine-point marker to dash off a sketch of the Ugly Orthoduckling, wearing his little Hassidic outfit, thick black-rimmed glasses and phylacteries.

"Come, Elizabeth," said Oscar, bowing to the grateful woman. "Let's find Gail."

Oscar and Elizabeth weaved between the revelers, most of whom, like the man talking to Gail, seemed to have affected Brian Fable's locker-room poking and jabbing and tousling as a form of communication. Oscar covered his head with his hands, ducked down, and rushed through the crowd to the rubber tree where Gail stood.

"Running the gauntlet?" asked Gail.

"They're getting sloppy, aren't they. Are all the parties like this? This is my first real *Lowdown* bash."

"Yes, always. Do you know Travis?"

"We haven't met." Oscar appraised the earnest young man in wire-rimmed glasses.

"Travis Hall," he said. "Copy editor. I hyphenate your adjectival phrases in the *Orthoducks* strip. Shake." (Oscar shook his hand; Elizabeth raised her paw.) "I wish we saw more of you around the office, Lemoine. It's getting grim. Routine."

"I've been away, working alone. That's *my* grim routine."

"At least we see your mail," said Travis. "What a hoot." Fable had pinned some of Oscar's juiciest hate mail to the main bulletin board in the editorial offices. "I especially liked the woman who said there were no pens and ink in hell. How does she *know* that?"

Oscar shrugged.

"And who'll be alienated this time? Homosexuals? Battered women?"

"The cover is top secret, as usual. But the penultimate *Orthoducks* installment is likely to set people scribbling."

"I love the *Orthoducks*," said Gail Gardener. "They're adorable."

"Tragic ending, I'm afraid."

"No."

"Hmmm. Incest and death."

"Very appropriate," said Travis. "Oh, no, look. People are starting to dance."

"I hate it when this happens," said Gail. "They'll be on the desks in a minute."

Travis shook his head. "You know the party's out of control when Fable's intellectuals take off their berets and start doing the Charleston."

"They don't wear berets, do they?" asked Gail.

"Figuratively, sure they do."

"If someone steps on Elizabeth there'll be hell to pay," said Oscar, surprising himself with his macho choice of words. He had loosened up considerably. Gail leaned distinctly in his direction, and distinctly away from the aggressive and rather smelly Travis Hall.

"Do you dance, girl?" Gail asked Elizabeth. "Do you?"

Elizabeth did all a dog can do to roll her eyeballs. She looked up at her master as if to say, "I'm warning you . . ."

Oscar sighed. "Dance," he said.

Elizabeth reared up and placed her front paws in Oscar's hands. She stepped to the left, stepped to the right, stepped backward, stepped forward, wiggled her hips, then dropped her paws back to the floor. "Good girl," said Oscar. "Sorry about that."

"You must spend all your time training that dog," said Travis. "Fable says she can dial a telephone."

"Not too loud," said Oscar. "She'll call the fire department."

"You're joking," said Gail.

"Absolutely not. That is the least of her talents. She is a superb painter. She held quite a successful exhibition back in France."

Gail giggled, as if this could not possibly be true, but when she saw Oscar's face she realized he was serious.

"Really?"

"Sure." Oscar put his index finger in his mouth and wiggled it, demonstrating the way Elizabeth wielded her brush.

"You're *awful*," said Gail, which Oscar took as a compliment, much the way he had grown accustomed to being called "sick."

"No fair whispering," said Travis, who seemed mightily put out by the transference of Gail's attention to Oscar, and who must have assumed the giggling and finger-wiggling had something to do with a lewd remark which he would have preferred not to miss.

"Is it my imagination, or is the party thinning out?" Oscar asked. "Are people beginning the long stagger home?"

"So it seems," said Gail.

"Travis!" came Brian Fable's voice from behind Oscar. "The man they called Irreproachable. And the only one who can spell streptococcus. How are we?"

"We're fine."

"Step this way, step this way. Have a word with me." Fable was full of winks for Oscar and Gail.

"That was sort of nice of him," said Gail, when the men were out of earshot.

"Was it?" said Oscar. "I mean, was Travis bothering you? I didn't notice. I mean I didn't—"

"Do you feel like going to another party?" asked Gail.

Exhausted as he was, Oscar wanted to be polite to the stalwart Gail. "By all means," he said. "Come, Elizabeth."

There was alcohol in the streets. Men in business suits and

loosened ties lurched out of taxis, propped themselves against their colleagues, weaved along the sidewalk, doffed invisible hats to lampposts. Cursing homeless drunks laid their cardboard and cellophane beds in alleyways, retched against skyscrapers, kicked at shards of broken bottles. Beer cans lay crushed in the gutters, overflowed from wire-mesh trash cans, rolled from opened taxi doors.

In their vomit-scented cab, the perky Gail was full of questions. Where did Oscar's cartoons come from? Did he always use his own ideas? What was the genesis of the nude caricature?

"I have always drawn cartoons. I was asked to leave school at sixteen—after and because of my first nude."

"You never went to college?" Gail crinkled her nose.

"Well, as I used to tell my Ivy League brother, you don't have to go to Harvard to learn what *autodidact* means."

The uncomprehending Gail continued to ask questions. Her blond head bobbed and bounced as the taxi rocketed southward over crater-sized potholes.

"I have a confession to make," said Gail. "When I saw your first cover—when I actually had it in my hands? I didn't *get* it. I thought it was—"

"Obscene?"

"Right. I've come around, now. I think I understand."

"Don't strain yourself. It's only shock value, after all."

Gail used a lurching, evasive action of the taxi to lean her head against Oscar's shoulder, and she kept it there. She gazed up at him, if Oscar wasn't mistaken, adoringly. Oscar was uncomfortable with the young woman looking up his nose. He sniffed and turned his head away. This was not at all what he had had in mind.

"Do you think Brian meant it when he said we were engaged?"

Oscar blinked. "Is there the slightest possibility that he did?"

"I think so, yes," said Gail, obviously thinking as hard as she could.

"I'm not the right person to ask," said Oscar, reasonably. "I'm not known to be perceptive, and I've been away a long time."

"I'd like to know if Brian wants to marry me. Could you ask him for me, do you think? Because I would really like to know."

"I could do that, yes. Are we almost there, wherever it is we're going?"

Oscar had begun not to like Gail Gardener. Two years ago he had admired her quite a great deal, from afar.

"We're going somewhere so we can show them how your dog can dance," said Gail.

"Oh no we're not. Elizabeth is not a circus animal. Besides, she's exhausted."

"Whatever you say." Gail didn't seem put off in the slightest by Oscar's stern tone of voice. Oscar was irritated that she seemed oblivious to what by his standards was a temper tantrum. "We'll go to my apartment." She leaned forward and gave new instructions to the driver.

Oscar wanted to tell Gail that it had been a long, tiring day of travel, that he should be heading to his hotel. Instead, he found himself being dragged out of the taxi with his suitcases, onto the street, and into Gail's apartment building. Exhausted as he was, Oscar was incapable of the impoliteness that would have been involved in refusing a nightcap with Gail Gardener.

Five minutes later he had a glass of whiskey in his hand and was being told by a stark-naked Gail, in the living room of her health-hazard hovel, that her old boyfriend liked taking naughty pictures of her. Gail asked whether Oscar would like to see them.

"Very much," said Oscar, who was simultaneously annoyed and embarrassed. When Gail turned her back on him to dig into a drawer for the photo album, Oscar fixed a demented expression on his face and used it to glare at her naked backside. He was going to have to learn to be a better judge of people.

Gail returned with the album and let Oscar peruse the nude photographs. She stood in the center of her living room and mimicked the poses. Elizabeth sat in an armchair and watched with furrowed brow.

"How do I look?" Gail wanted to know. "I know you're an expert."

"Terrific," said Oscar, looking down at the photographs.

"Not there, here," said Gail. "In real life."

Oscar looked up. "Ditto," he said.

"That's nice to know. I'm pregnant as anything, but don't tell anyone." Gail began moving her body in various suggestive and revolting ways, each swivel and twist bringing her closer to the seated Oscar. "You could use my body for one of your covers."

"Ah," said Oscar.

Now he felt gloomy. An abrupt departure might have been the correct move, but Oscar's upbringing had not equipped him with an ability to hurt friends' feelings. A few escape routes presented themselves to him: a statement of principle regarding *Lowdown* colleagues; feigned illness; a sudden display of effeminacy.

What he chose to do instead was a peculiar reversal on the age-old practice of getting women drunk so as to have one's way with them. He advised Gail that in her condition she should not be drinking, then grasped the whiskey bottle firmly by its neck and set about pretending to get so drunk that he would not have to sleep with her.

X

IT WAS EARLY SUMMER IN VAL D'ARGENT, BUT CLUMSY WEATHER HAD enveloped the coast in fog and chill. For two days, daybreak had comprised nothing more than a slow and vague accretion of light, sunset only a pale suggestion of what it might have hoped to be. The bay, when it could be seen at all through the persistent fog, glowered blackly beneath rain clouds so heavy they dragged their skirts in the spume.

Oscar Lemoine sat outside on the veranda of his rented guest cottage, a blanket around his shoulders, waiting for breaks in the weather that might afford him a glimpse of the sea. The coffee mug in his hand warmed his stiff fingers. Elizabeth lay at his feet, adoring as ever, lapping water from a glass bowl.

The gloomy scene might easily have suited Oscar's program, because he had come to Val d'Argent for the peace of isolation and the luxury of uninterrupted work. Four of his five senses would have been satisfied by the salty air, the scowl of the climate, the strong black coffee, the lounge chair beneath his body. His one remaining sense might have been especially pleased by the songs of shivering birds, the distant wash of surf and spray against the rocky shore, or even the occasional hum of sports-car tires on the wet road outside his driveway, which wound up the steep road leading to the even more impressive villas farther up the hill. Might have been, that is, without the presence of the team of laborers whose pneumatic drills had first plunged into the asphalt outside his front gate just as Oscar had tried to fall asleep after his long night of spelunking and romance with Veronique. Undaunted by the appalling weather, the workers blasted tirelessly into the road; they relieved one another at the controls of the pneumatic drills and a mechanical claw; they dug wide and deep. After three and a half days of destruction they had managed to exhume a short length of antique piping, and to accumulate a pile of mud, rock, and asphalt as tall as a man and twenty yards long.

Oscar had come to know the rumble and ring of their machines as if it were the instrument of his own trade. It was a complex sound, at once broad and piercing. He had abandoned his previous efforts to escape the noise, and chose instead to face the din outdoors, as if challenging it to drive him mad. He had long since given up any idea of work, and his drawing pad lay unopened on the drafting table in what would ordinarily have been a quiet study, but was now a reverberating torture chamber. In the face of this quite amazing aural onslaught, Oscar tried to force himself to imagine a cartoon involving such a scene: an elderly British couple at a seaside resort, for example, displaying their indomitable good cheer by remarking to each other that without the pneumatic drills it would seem somehow *too* perfect to be true. Oscar mentally tore this sketch and several others into tiny pieces, and flung them into the brimming wastebasket of his mind. He told himself that he had plenty of time, that he could work at night if necessary, and that the relief of being so far away from home ought to compensate for the minor inconvenience of heavy artillery outside his driveway. He leaned over to pat Elizabeth on her shiny head, told her she was a very good girl, and apologized to her for the noise.

There was no relief when the workers took their morning coffee break, for the teenaged son of Oscar's landlords had arrived for the long summer break: French father, German mother, pyromaniac son. Anton, as the child was known, literally burned off his hormonal overload by setting trees and shrubs ablaze, and buying as many explosives as his considerable allowance could purchase. Oscar had once caught him throwing shotgun shells straight down between his own feet, hoping they would go off. On this day it sounded as if Anton had decided to explore the pleasures of underground dynamite testing, and even the roadworkers seemed worried by the dull explosions rolling out from behind the gates of Anton's villa.

A reprieve would come in the early evening, when Oscar was due at Veronique's house for an informal cocktail party. She had confirmed the invitation over the phone, and said that Oscar ought to meet "Hansie." The cartoonist considered this only proper. He had not seen Veronique since their first night together, but as far as the optimistic Oscar was concerned mutual love was not entirely out of the question. Oscar had always prided himself on his ability to impress girlfriends' parents or guardians, and eagerly looked forward to a second, more intimate meeting with the imposing German he had taken to be Veronique's father.

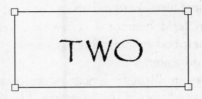

TWO

I

OSCAR WAS RELIEVED TO BE ON THE MOVE IN NEW YORK CITY'S
bleary dawn. He had left the unhappy Gail Gardener asleep on
her pull-out bed, too confused and exhausted by her worries to
speak, except to mumble that Oscar's boss, Brian Fable, was
undoubtedly the father of her fetus. Elizabeth trotted along
happily beside her master, who was encumbered by his worldly
possessions and the extra baggage of a throbbing, jet-lagged
head that felt as if it might in fact be (he apologized to himself
for thinking of this) full of boiling pus. Oscar avoided the
human and material detritus of the previous night's outdoor
drinking, steered clear of bodies, skipped over broken glass, and
skirted patches of pooled human urine and vomit. As always in
this city, he gagged frequently. He tried gamely to whistle to
himself, then remarked to Elizabeth that there was nothing like
a brisk walk to clear the scum from the mouth and throat and

the boiling pus from the cranium. Elizabeth moved with her tongue hanging close to the filthy sidewalk, and did not reply. Oscar took some satisfaction in the knowledge that while he stretched his lungs and drained his brain, dozens of colleagues and acquaintances were scattered about the city, lying naked or half clothed in fetid bedrooms on sweaty, yellowed sheets, every cell in their bodies screaming, as starving plants are said to do, for air and water.

Coming upon an all-night grocery store, Oscar stopped to admire the latest edition of the *Lowdown*. His cover cried out from the crowded racks: the colorful nude caricature of Bunny Fenton, TV reporter *extraordinaire*, displayed in exaggerated glory her marble bosom, her sequoia legs, her bonfire hair. Oscar took a copy of the magazine from the stand and analyzed it as objectively as he could. He had never let anyone tell him whom to use as a subject for his cover caricatures, but Brian Fable had more than once suggested that a few more attractive women would be welcome. When selecting the alluring Bunny Fenton, Oscar had been acutely aware of bowing to Fable's admittedly astute marketing advice: the huge numbers of people who wanted to take girlie pictures home, but were too inhibited to make a public purchase of these materials, were given a great excuse to do so by the trendy *Lowdown*. Still, Oscar was proud of the finished product, which he could not imagine was erotic: good old Bunny Fenton, ace journalist and millionaire, twirled golden tassels from dollar-sign pasties, in opposite directions; she ground her golden hips and snapped her long-nailed fingers; her cheekbones shone around the grin of a casino jackpot winner. Here was a number that would sell. Oscar bought an extra copy, then heaved his belongings out onto the sidewalk where he could flag down a taxi.

Barely twelve hours in the city, and Oscar felt ruined. Ah, but the Domino Hotel would take care of that. Just uttering the name of that ancient and hospitable institution as he gave his taxi driver instructions, made Oscar feel warm and comfortable again. Oscar had stayed there when his father's second divorce made living at home a bit too cramped; he had lost his virginity there, in Room 1107, courtesy of an adventurous girlfriend and his older brother's credit card; he had attended dozens of rendezvous in the twenty-four-hour Domino Bar, home of New York's most obese bartender, the ageless Miles Ortier. Oscar could honestly say that when in New York he *always* stayed at the Domino, although he had stayed there only three times.

The first sign that something was wrong at the Domino was that a uniformed porter dashed from beneath a garish yellow awning to relieve Oscar of his cases. The Domino had never believed in this service in the past, much less in sheltering its entrance with an ostentatious awning. The second sign that all was not right at the Domino came when the officious little man at reception almost—almost, but not quite—objected to Elizabeth's presence in the hotel. Perhaps he was a dog lover, or a bender of rules; or perhaps he had read in Oscar's expression a threat on his life if he turned the aging labrador away.

Oscar had booked his room under a pseudonym—death threats were quite flattering, really, but a precaution here and there seemed sensible. Because Brian Fable knew where Oscar was staying, a stack of mail awaited him at the reception desk. After sending his luggage and dog off to the room with a porter, Oscar took his mail and walked across the unpleasantly redecorated lobby toward the all-night bar, hoping that Miles Ortier was the one fixture the Domino had left intact.

"*Oui, monsieur*, and what can I get for you?" asked the mincing man-child behind the bar.

"Miles. You can get me Miles Ortier."

"Ah, Monsieur Miles, I am afraid he has gone away."

This was profoundly depressing news, almost as depressing as the bogus accent put on by the would-be television actor who had taken Miles' place behind the bar.

"A drink for you zen, *monsieur?*"

"*Non merci* very much." It was just after six o'clock in the morning. "I just wanted to say hello to Miles. What's your name, then?"

"Jacques," said the new bartender, unconvincingly.

"Okay, Jack. I'll be seeing you."

The disgusted cartoonist retreated from the Domino Bar and hopped aboard a mercifully unmanned elevator. He reached out to press a button before he noticed that there were no buttons to press. The upholstered, *fleurs-de-lis* walls of the elevator were bare of controls.

"*What floor please, monsieur?*" asked a canned voice as the elevator doors closed. The voice seemed to emanate from a speaker in the mirrored ceiling.

"Is that you, Jack?" asked Oscar.

"*This is Philippe,*" said the voice. "*What floor, please?*"

"Eleven. That'll be *onze* to you, Phil."

"*Merci, monsieur,*" said the voice.

The elevator ascended.

"Can you see me, Phil? Or only hear me."

"*I cannot see you, monsieur.*"

"Then how did you know I was a *monsieur* and not a *madame?*"

"*I saw you board zee elevator, monsieur.*"

"So you can't see me at all now?"

"*Non, monsieur.*"

Oscar spent the rest of the ride to the eleventh floor making Quasimodo faces at the ceiling of the elevator.

"Thanks, Phil," he said, as he strode out into a corridor redecorated to resemble the Hall of Mirrors.

By now he had not the slightest expectation that Room 1107 would look anything like it had ten years ago on the night he had misplaced his virginity. Elizabeth greeted him at the door with a jet-lagged wag of her tail. After petting his dog, Oscar pushed past her to inspect his room. The most shocking difference was that what had been a more-than-adequate skyline panorama now amounted to no more than the glass wall of a skyscraper directly across the street, which gave the effect of rubbing noses with someone wearing reflecting sunglasses.

Oscar turned on the television, his first glimpse of the box since leaving New York. He sat down on a bed that, come to think of it, might very well have been the same one he had employed so life-alteringly a decade ago. The picture rose colorfully to the screen and there, in all her glory, was the voluptuous Bunny Fenton herself, the object of his current cover, interviewing a holistic dietitian on a morning news program. Oscar had modeled his nude caricature of Miss Fenton on magazine photographs, and because he held the latest *Lowdown* issue in his hands he was able to compare his drawing with the television image. He decided that if anything her appearance on the television was more of a caricature than his artwork. He turned off the sound of the interviewee's inanities, and addressed himself to his mail.

Oscar frisked the bulkier letters for signs of explosives, because a recent issue seemed to have caused some consternation among rather militant fans of an assistant secretary of state whose grotesquely misshapen body had adorned the *Lowdown*'s cover. (Oscar had captured the little man at the height of a naked jeté, waving a thin red-white-and-blue streamer in an infinity sign over his head, his prickly and minute genitals poking from between his legs like stunted cacti.)

Oscar read his mail distractedly, his tired mind on the more pleasant recollections of his recent past.

II

THE DREARY WEATHER LIFTED SHORTLY AFTER NOON, AND BY THE TIME
Oscar arrived at Herr Dohrmann's house the seaside cliffs
gleamed beneath bright sunshine. Isolated from the main
collection of villas nearer the center of town, this mansion
presided over its own sandy cove, which was reached by mossy
and precipitous stone steps. The grounds also overlooked a mini
fjord suitable for swan diving and the mooring of guests' boats.
One such vessel, a blue yawl flying a Union Jack, now occupied
the fjord. A crew uniformly dressed in white shorts, white knee
socks, and blue-and-white-striped sailor shirts busied itself with
the scrubbing of teak and polishing of brass on the decks of the
grand yacht.

Showing great foresight, Oscar had not brought Elizabeth
along. His intuition had warned him that someone of Herr
Dohrmann's status and national origin was likely to own a
canine or two. Elizabeth was a strictly nonviolent dog, as far as
Oscar could tell, and attack dogs had a way of taking advantage
of her Gandhian pacifism. When several muzzles full of lethal
fangs sprang at Oscar from behind a chain-link grill just inside
the gates to Herr Dohrmann's driveway, he congratulated
himself on having left Elizabeth safely at home with her paints
and brushes.

Oscar always felt at a disadvantage at the few super-rich
gatherings he had attended because he had difficulty distin-
guishing between servants and European royalty. He usually

went by the rule that servants wore formal evening dress, and princes dressed down. His rule proved reliable when an impeccably attired and distinguished gentleman wearing white tie and tails relieved him of his lightweight jacket and offered him a glass of champagne from a silver tray.

Oscar spent a lonely couple of minutes on the front lawn engaged in a frenzied pantomime of pretending to recognize close friends somewhere in the distance, while all around him total strangers hugged and kissed and fawned over each others' physical beauty. Oscar smiled insanely and sipped at his champagne glass and even went as far as to wave jovially over the heads of a nearby cluster of ever-so-beautiful people as if he had just spotted his own brother moving through the crowd. He decided that if Veronique failed to appear in one minute he would find the friendly butler, retrieve his jacket, and beat it past the Dobermans to the gate.

It was Neville who came to Oscar's rescue.

"I don't know about you, Mr. Lemoine," said Neville, ambling up to Oscar's side wearing a green silk ascot tucked into a yellow polo shirt stitched with a golf-club insignia, "but I find that champagne flows in direct proportion to conversation—rarely in sufficient quantities and almost never of sufficient quality. Have a scotch."

Oscar accepted a glass from Neville, so that he now held a glass in each hand. "Call me Oscar. I don't even know your last name."

Neville related his full name, but because he seemed to be swallowing scotch and chewing ice cubes at the same time, it sounded to Oscar like "Neville Hacking-Cough," and this was how the cartoonist would remember it.

"Help me, sir," said Oscar. "I don't know anyone here."

"Awaiting our hostess, are you? Ought to watch your step there, my boy, if I may presume to give a recent acquaintance some advice. I couldn't help noticing the other night that the two of you were, shall we say, close-knit? Thin ice, dear boy."

Oscar could not imagine what the problem could be, and said so.

"Goodness, you Americans certainly are a progressive lot, then," said Neville Hacking-Cough.

"She's no minor, Veronique."

"Of course not, no, that isn't exactly what I meant. Goodness. I meant that our host, Herr Dohrmann—and I must say I rather take his side in the matter—is possessive to the point of obsession."

"I can understand that, sir." Oscar had already convinced himself that Veronique's mother—Herr Dohrmann's late wife—must have met an end so cruel that Veronique was her father's only solace in a world unfair enough to rob him of the woman he loved.

"Oh, can you? Well then surely you will tread cautiously. I have certain allegiances to old Hansie, in a peculiar sort of way, and if I suspected anything untoward—by my standards, which I assure you tend toward the libertine—I would be unable to restrain myself from informing my friend about what was taking place behind his back."

"I understand completely, sir," said Oscar. "I can handle it. I might as well just tell old Hansie the truth. He's going to have to come to terms with losing Veronique to someone someday anyway, whether to me or to someone else. Right?"

Oscar couldn't understand why Neville looked so aghast at a perfectly reasonable statement of rational intent.

"Really, my *dear* chap. Surely even in America this . . . this *overtness* simply isn't on. A bit of rumpy-pumpy when no one is looking is one thing, but in broad daylight, to steal a man's—ah but look, here she comes now."

Oscar had only a moment to ponder Neville's peculiar outburst, which seemed doubly odd to one who had witnessed the Englishman misbehaving so recently in the Honclours

Caves. Oscar chalked it up to some curious English trait having to do with keeping even mild impropriety closeted, and reminded himself huffily that a country where Elizabeth was unwelcome without prolonged quarantine must have some very strange ideas indeed.

Veronique's appearance quickly erased these thoughts from Oscar's mind, and Neville's warning was forgotten. All around her stood women who had labored with their elaborate costumes to stand out in the crowd, while Veronique wore a plain white sundress and let her beauty speak for itself. Seeing her, Oscar was exhilarated and frightened at the same time: exhilarated because he had so enjoyed the few hours they had spent together the night of their swim in the Honclours Caves; and frightened because Veronique did not appear at first to reciprocate his facial expression, which he could feel was one of unadulterated infatuation. Oscar's first problem arose when he found that the momentum of his relief in seeing Veronique had propelled his arms outward for an embrace, and that she seemed to be recoiling from them, to the point that Oscar had to take two full strides downhill across the lawn before he was able even to grasp her shoulders.

By the time he achieved contact, they were moving at a considerable speed, one forward, the other backward, and an objective observer might have concluded that the young woman was shying away from a lunging assassin. To the extent that he was able to make a conscious decision during this embarrassing *pas de deux*, Oscar thought it best to see his original intention through to its conclusion, which was to plant several kisses on Veronique's suntanned cheeks. This required an extra step downhill in the retreating Veronique's direction, and extra concentration so as not to spill either of the drinks he now held before him, all the while attempting to fix an expression of complete serenity on a face that should have been wracked with confusion and humiliation.

People stared. Like pedestrians momentarily bobbing for position as they approached each other on the street, Oscar and Veronique could not agree on a way out of what had become something of a tango, or more accurately a tango in which the male partner appeared too drunk to lead properly. In the end it was Veronique who broke the cycle, far down the lawn toward the cliffs overlooking the mini-fjord, so that Oscar was able at last to throw his arms around her and plant a kiss on her cheek. In his relief at having achieved part of his original aim, even at such expense, it took him a few seconds to notice that he had spilled both of his drinks down the backs of Veronique's calves, and given pleasure to a large audience of sybarites. People applauded.

If the situation was defused, it was because Veronique managed to communicate to her guests through sign language that the American cartoonist was the worse for drink. Oscar saw this, and could do nothing to dispute her implication. He thought he knew when he had committed a gaffe, but in this case he failed to understand the root cause. He blamed his own social clumsiness, and apologized to this effect while Veronique blushed straight through her impressive tan. A moment later she glided away toward more socially adept guests near the main house, leaving Oscar to trudge back uphill alone to Neville, his only ally.

"We'll get you a new drink," said Neville Hacking-Cough. "Never mind. Artists are expected to behave this way."

"I don't understand," said Oscar. Neville waited for him to go on, as if this were not the sum total of what Oscar wished to say. He was awfully disappointed that after such a promising start the other evening he might already have ruined his dream of fabulous romance with Herr Dohrmann's gorgeous daughter.

"All's forgotten, I assure you," said Neville. "Everyone's mind is on the diving."

"I beg your pardon, sir?"

"The diving contest. An annual event. I do hope you'll join in. Even I, at my advanced age, will enter. I perform only one dive, a rather rickety swan, which I have been practicing for fifty years. Not so limber as I used to be, but the competition this year is abysmal."

III

OF THE TWENTY-FIVE LETTERS OSCAR OPENED IN ROOM 1107 OF THE newly redecorated Domino Hotel, half were well-reasoned briefs arguing that he had no right to be doing what he did for a living; a few more were less cogent attacks on his character; three told him he would burn in hell for his caricatures of cult leaders; three asked for signed covers; two contained semiliterate death threats. Oscar swallowed two aspirin and read the juicier letters again. "You can't hide," was the simple message of one of them, written in a scrawl that was familiar to Oscar, as was the signature, "Elkin (The Eliminator)." Elkin had been more specific in the past about the ways in which he hoped to torture Oscar to death. "And your little dog too," Elkin had sometimes closed, indicating, unnervingly, that he had seen Oscar and Elizabeth together in the flesh. Another of the regular threats came from a woman who actually signed her name "Mrs. Arnold Peele," and who had ended her latest letter with the sentence, "If my husband and I weren't Christians we would shoot you dead."

Oscar was unconcerned. He had searched out the advice of experts and been told, in effect, that he was not important enough to assassinate, that a lunatic hoping to go out in a blaze of glory was not likely to empty his chambers on a mere cartoonist, and that in general written death threats were the only outlets such cretins required. If anyone killed him, death would come unannounced.

Oscar looked up from his mail to see the glorious coiffure of Bunny Fenton, whose gaudily made-up eyes stared out at him almost accusingly from the silent television screen.

"Bunny, Bunny, Bunny," Oscar said aloud. "Have I wronged you?" He thought not.

Far more worrying to Oscar at the moment was the thought of meeting his brother later in the week. George Lemoine was three years older than Oscar, and so different from the cartoonist as to cast doubt on their mutual parentage. Not by nature a soul-searching sort, Oscar nevertheless worried that his relationship to George had been the root of certain as yet unresolved anxieties; he made this judgment based on the sweaty palms and butterflies that accompanied the prospect of seeing George again.

George Lemoine had always been the comfortably superior human in Oscar's large extended family, and growing up as the great one's only sibling had worn on Oscar in all the characteristic ways. It began with George's being supernaturally good-looking, and stretched on through a list of impossible virtues, including modesty. It was out of the question that anyone should resent the charmed life of a man so self-effacing, so humble, so magnanimous. Here was a man who excelled at all he attempted, who attracted women across crowded rooms as if they were drawn by a miraculous vision of paradise, whose overall prowess elicited nicknames such as "King George" as a matter of course, and yet who remained so annoyingly generous and lovable that even an introverted, jealous, inferior younger brother could never summon so much as mild dislike for George Lemoine. Oscar did not have to know about or even believe in psychoanalysis to understand that the path of his life had been affected at every stage by a fear of having to follow in the wide swath cut by the golden blade of his older brother's good fortune.

That was the old George Lemoine, at any rate. The old George Lemoine had waltzed back to the inevitability of financial gain as a twice-boiled egg from Harvard and its business school, and for nearly five years was duly apologetic to friends and family because he earned the salary of thirty hardworking men. No one held this against him, least of all Oscar, who profited from his older brother's windfall by gaining food, shelter, and even the occasional cash payment when work was particularly unforthcoming. The old George Lemoine kept his mind and body fit, worked obsessively and honestly, and drank too much only once a week. The old George Lemoine's youthful features slowly lost that young lion's look of having just showered at the squash club, and began to solidify into the face of respectability itself. The old George Lemoine had memorized a vast store of witty and persuasive responses to those who dared suggest that he and people like him were going to cause an economic apocalypse that would drag the nation and perhaps the world straight into hell. Oscar did not join in these debates, because no matter how often George tried to explain his daily occupation, Oscar had never quite been able to grasp precisely what his brother's work entailed. He knew only that it was abstract, that it required all of George's waking hours to accomplish, and that he and his colleagues were making a fortune. Oscar chalked up his inability to understand his brother's profession to a lack of higher education. It all made even less sense when one of George's more flippant friends summed it up as "Breaking other people's eggs to make *our* omelette."

On the personal side, the old George Lemoine maintained quasimonogamous relationships with excellent women, conducted for the most part via the telephone, and dissolved them on the best possible terms. While others like him complained of stress and a lack of time to themselves, George heroically decreed that to his ears all such whining was profane in the context of an unfair world of which he and his acquaintances were by far the most fortunate members. Young, free, rich, American, the old George Lemoine would pronounce: count your lucky stars and stripes.

In the meantime Oscar had searched desperately for an identity, which he found in the dubious form of *Lowdown* cover caricaturist. The old George Lemoine greeted his younger brother's minor success with some paternal condescension and the suggestion that even in his mid-twenties it was not too late for Oscar to become an architect. Sadly, and like so many of his contemporaries, George equated usefulness with income, happiness with good credit, and self-esteem with a vaguely defined concept called "power."

At around the same time that Oscar decided the furious city was too much for him and planned to beat a retreat to Val d'Argent, George began to show signs of mortality. The first symptom was a bagginess to his face and a bulging of his girth that would have been unnoticeable in anyone but a man of George's previous fitness. He started to show nervousness and something of a temper. He missed dinner engagements with his younger brother without offering excuses. On the few occasions when he did oblige he drank red wine until his earlobes turned crimson, and he became first confrontational, then altogether uncommunicative. He grew openly critical of Oscar's doting on Elizabeth, and of Elizabeth herself, when it was George who had picked the pup out of a litter for Oscar's thirteenth birthday. He complained about his thinning hair as if it were a fatal disease. He spouted absurd rhetoric about survival of the fittest and the wretched peons who had failed to make the grade. Twice Oscar had to enlist the help of other guests or doormen to bundle his increasingly heavy brother into cabs.

Oscar had left for Val d'Argent with George's deterioration very much on his mind, but had soon been reassured by mutual friends that the bad patch was over, that George was back to his old self and going strong. It was a strange experience for Oscar to worry about George—as opposed to the usual recoiling in awe—but his mind was set at ease by the short letters he received in George's own hand, which indicated that all could not be better, that as a bonus big brother had fallen in love with the woman of his dreams, and was engaged to be married.

IV

WHILE ACROPHOBIA DID NOT NUMBER AMONG OSCAR'S NEUROSES, HIS first instinct after Neville Hacking-Cough told him about the contest was to leave the cliff-diving to the experts. But upon reflection, and after a couple of generous refills organized by his new English friend, he told himself that a man bent on creating an extroverted personality needed precisely this kind of exercise in reckless abandon to prove that he was one of the lads. Soon he had formulated a new plan, which was to steel himself with drink and enter the contest with the intention of winning it. He imagined himself performing a caricature of a dive, appealing to the judges' sense of humor, and winning not only the contest but Veronique's renewed respect.

Several drinks and stuffed mushrooms later, and Oscar felt like a new man. Other guests had come up to meet him and

Neville, and seemed especially interested now that the *Lowdown* was on sale in Val d'Argent's main newsstand, merely due to the cover artist's temporary residence in the community. At least one copycat magazine had started up in Paris, they reported, and had survived the visit of ominous American lawyers dispatched by the now-legendary Fable Enterprises Inc. Oscar listened to this news while keeping one eye on Veronique, who circulated on the far side of the lawn without once meeting his eye. It really was mighty peculiar, Oscar thought, that a young woman of Veronique's obvious worldliness could be so cowed by her father. It was as he mulled this over that Oscar realized he might have stepped into something a bit more serious than your run-of-the-mill fatherly possessiveness: Oscar had learned that people's private lives were roughly six times more complicated and unhappy than they appeared on the surface, an equation that would lead even a cautious man to think that Herr Dohrmann was pathologically cruel to his daughter. Add to that old Hansie's age and nationality, and all sorts of scenarios burst into the imagination. But never mind, he told himself: the new Oscar Lemoine faced such a situation head-on, head high, headfirst.

Oscar did his best to concentrate on what people around him were saying, until an announcement came in three or four languages for all guests to assemble on the steps to the fjord to watch the cliff-diving contest. With one mind, Neville and Oscar took another belt each of the nearby scotch, and retreated to the pool house to change. There, a horrified and above-all American Oscar was issued a black bikini "swimming costume," as Neville called it, that might have served David well against Goliath, but that hardly jibed with the cartoonist's concept of public decency. The other men in the pool house chatted to one another, and two of them combed their pubic hair into curls over the waistbands of their swimsuits. Oscar spent a few moments pep-talking himself into donning the sling-shot suit, and after having tucked and folded himself into the flimsy costume he decided rather self-righteously that the Mediterraneans who invented such a garment must have been as ill-equipped as their classical statues. As a nude caricaturist this sort of anthropometric information was of the utmost importance to him.

"I have to tell you they take their cliff-diving quite seriously," said Neville. "They go in for a bit of pomp and pageantry. Although it is still light we will be led out by a ceremonial torchbearer, single file. The judges will be aboard my yacht."

"Oh, that's your ship, is it?" said Oscar.

"Well," replied Neville, "technically she belongs to my wife."

Neville began to perform stretching exercises in the cramped quarters of the pool house. He was in superb condition: what little flesh he had hung like a loose T-shirt on his aging skeleton, but his overall form compared favorably with most of the younger men surrounding him; his deep knee bends showed off sinewy thighs and a taut midsection. The white hair on his chest only accentuated a dark brown tan that even the knowledgeable Oscar would not have thought possible on an Englishman's skin.

Oscar stole a casual glance at himself in a full-length mirror mounted near the showers on an off-white stucco wall. He would not have been at all displeased with his reflection—which he had exercised into something far more attractive than his formerly patchy and pasty city body—had the tan lines created by his own more conservative swimming trunks not made it appear that he wore a pair of white boxer shorts beneath his borrowed G-string. His only solace lay in the fact that he was not a hairy man, and found it unnecessary to groom himself in the manner of his more hirsute cocompetitors.

There were seven contestants in all, including Oscar, the youngest of whom was a skinny adolescent who had been honored with the assignment of carrying the torch. Oscar's attempts to inject some backstage gallows humor into the situation were met with the kind of cold stares he associated with professional athletes, which made him feel deeply uneasy. They marched out to the swimming pool in silence, the torch was lit, and in lock step they proceeded toward the cliffs. Warm applause greeted their arrival. The torch was passed from the adolescent to Herr Dohrmann, who passed it down the line of guests, one to the next, until it arrived on the dock below. From there the torch was ferried to Neville's wife's yacht, where it was affixed to the bow. Aboard the yacht were the five guests who had been chosen to act as judges, each of whom held a stack of numbered cards with which they would broadcast their scores to the crowd.

Oscar noticed all of this with an increasing sense of being out of place. His mild drunkenness was aggravated by the act of looking down at the water from such a terrific height. He no longer wondered why the contestants took the event so seriously, for it was undoubtedly dangerous. Having mistaken Neville Hacking-Cough's offhand description of the event for an invitation to amusing party games, rather than for the mortal challenge it plainly was, Oscar found himself standing atop the rocky cliff in a line of seasoned high-divers, knees trembling, gut aflutter, staring down eighty feet past his toenails to the blue-green water below.

Like all men who possess an ounce of self-respect, Oscar knew that a life in a wheelchair was infinitely preferable to the slightest display of cowardice. There was no question that he would soon hurl his precious body over the edge of the cliff, just as his predecessors in history had charged against artillery on command, parachuted behind enemy lines, agreed to step outside of bars to be pummeled by pugilistic rivals. Realizing this immutable fact of his near future, Oscar concentrated his thoughts on the dive he would perform.

"Visualization," he thought. "That's the ticket."

He visualized himself departing from the clifftop with arms spread wide, head arched back, chest thrust out, slowly arcing toward the water like a badminton shuttlecock, extending his arms and breaking the water with less splash than a longbow's arrow.

"Only one dive each," Neville whispered. "Did I mention that?"

"No, sir. What a pity."

"The more difficult the better, but I've found that just as in Acapulco they reward the swan rather heavily if it is executed with purity of spirit."

"I can't thank you enough for inviting me to join you, sir," said Oscar.

"Oh, yes, it's jolly good fun," said Neville. In his intensity he had missed Oscar's sarcastic inflection.

Neville had begun breathing deeply and expanding his well-proportioned chest. With deep-set eyes the color of the sea below he stared out at the horizon and gathered his concentration. The first candidate, the torch-bearing teenager, approached the highest point of the cliff where a block of cement marked the launching pad. Oscar feigned indifference to the fate of the courageous child by craning his neck back and forth as if loosening the last tight joints or muscles in an otherwise perfectly tuned body. In fact his eyes were locked on the skinny boy, hoping to learn something from the execution of his dive. The boy paused for several seconds on his perch, rubbed his hands together before raising his arms eaglelike to shoulder level, lifting his head, and flying off the cliff with a surprisingly abrupt spring of his legs.

"One, two," Oscar counted.

The boy's legs had come slightly apart and he seemed to struggle to keep from flipping too far backward.

"Three, four."

The boy slammed into the choppy water with both legs bent at right angles from the knees. The cautious audience held its applause until the child surfaced and delivered the obligatory wave of the uninjured. The boy swam toward the steps as the judges' scorecards were raised from shipboard. Threes and fours, Oscar noted, which seemed a bit ruthless when the diver was only a child. They meant business here at Herr Dohrmann's house.

During the first diver's swim back to the steps, Oscar spotted Veronique standing at the very bottom of the steps. This ruled out any lingering hope he might have had that escape was still possible. She stared straight at him, no mistaking it even at this distance. Oscar tried to read the expression on her face, unreliable as this was from so far away, and decided that her broad smile was one of love and encouragement. Out of old Hansie's line of sight, she seemed to have reverted to her former self. Oscar forced a smile back at her in case her eyesight was good enough to make it out, while hoping that she could not see well enough to notice the quaking of his legs.

The second diver had taken his position on the cement block. He was a sturdy young man of about Oscar's age, with muscular thighs and slightly more cleavage than might have been becoming. His fierce Mediterranean profile twitched in anticipation of his feat. It did not take an *aficionado* to know that this fellow would shun the swan in favor of a certain number of tightly tucked revolutions, and Oscar winced involuntarily at the prospect.

Over the side went the burly man, who tucked and flipped once even before he began to lose altitude.

Flip, flip, flip, flip, went the diver.

One, two, three, four, counted Oscar.

Splash, went the diver.

Cringe, went Oscar, for the man had landed still folded up like a hunchback, squarely on his backside.

There was a long silence this time as the audience waited for the diver to emerge from the froth of bubbles his clumsy entry had aroused. When he did so his wave was as halfhearted as the applause was condescending. They were a bloodthirsty lot. The judges lazily flipped their scorecards as if unwilling to waste their professionalism on a mere thrill-seeker, and awarded the stocky diver a high score of three and a low score of one. The adolescent was still in the lead.

Oscar was now seriously worried that visualization alone might not guarantee his survival. His two goals were to dive with dignity and to save his life, in that order, but the two examples he had seen did nothing to make him feel that either aim was likely to be achieved. As he watched the third diver attempt a pike-position triple somersault and go crashing into the water like a piece of military equipment dropped from a transport plane, he began to experience a combination of nerves and nausea that he thought might prevent him from remaining upright much longer. The fourth dive was slightly more reassuring because the man's out-of-control spin and extension coincidentally ended in a knife-blade entry. This gave Oscar the germ of an idea, which slowly took root as he watched the fifth diver's backward layout finish in a relatively harmless but unintended feet-first splash: Oscar should simply attempt to look interesting in flight and take his chances on landing.

It was Neville's turn, and the Englishman approached his dive as if this were the way he made his living. His bushy white eyebrows descended from his brow toward a nose scrunched in utter intensity; he walked with the exaggerated stride and pointed toes of a ballet dancer; his belly was sucked in beneath his rib cage to accentuate his slimness of hips and broadness of breast. Oscar was left standing alone.

Neville took his time, let the sea breeze play in his white hair, raised his arms, unfurled delicately articulated fingers. His every gesture heightened the audience's expectation. At last Neville sniffed aristocratically, bent slowly at his ancient knees, and flung himself toward the sky.

If the cliffs had not been rushing by, an observer would have been unable to say that Neville was airborne, so perfect was his arched body in flight. His swan dive was of one piece, without the slightest lurch or sway, and culminated in a double-fisted entry into the fjord that was more disappearance than splash.

The applause this time was immediate. Neville sprang from the water and waved in one triumphant motion, a wave obviously not intended to reassure the audience that he was unhurt, but to acknowledge the ovation that he knew would await him on the surface. He was awarded one eight, three nines, and one perfect ten from a judge who leaned over and took a swipe at the member of his panel whose scorecard showed a mere eight points. The thrilled onlookers clapped and yelled Neville's name as the hero swam strongly to shore. They probably would have raised him to their shoulders and carried him up the switchback steps if there hadn't been one diver remaining.

One lonely, terrified diver.

From where Oscar stood, entirely alone, the sounds of jubilation below were muffled by the wind and by the bubble of his own pulse. He tried his best to imitate Neville's stately carriage as he walked the few steps to the concrete platform. He watched as one by one the spectators turned their gazes from the bottom of the steps, where Neville had begun to towel himself dry, toward the top of the cliff. Not more than a handful knew who Oscar was, and he decided most would have assumed he was a ringer brought in at the last minute to give the great Neville some semblance of competition.

But I am not a ringer, thought Oscar. I am not a diver, I am a cartoonist. I paint pictures of naked people for a living.

It occurred to Oscar, as he stole a dizzying peek at the

rock-lined sea so very, very far below, that he ought to express something of himself in his dive. He was patently incapable of attempting any version of the dives he had seen so far, least of all Neville's regal swan. He needed to tell the audience who he was, and in the few seconds he had to think about it he decided that, like his dog Elizabeth, he was a simple painter. Addled by fear and vertigo, his thoughts led him to two conclusions: that for practical purposes he had an audience of one, Veronique; and that his dive must represent a recognizable nude caricature.

Think, think, think, he thought. Thinking, he thought of Rodin.

With one hundred impatient eyes upon him, Oscar stripped off his borrowed G-string, cast it to one side, stood proudly for a few seconds so that not one member of the crowd could fail to note his dangling dignity, then leaned forward into a crouch with the back of one hand pressed to his chin in the famous pose of Rodin's *Thinker*.

V

OSCAR'S RENDEZVOUS WITH HIS OLDER BROTHER HAD BEEN POSTPONED four times due to George's grueling and unpredictable schedule, but at last all had been arranged. In a display of conspicuous waste and luxury that surprised the formerly frugal cartoonist, Oscar casually asked the doorman at the Domino Hotel to call him a taxi for the short journey uptown to his brother's apartment. It was hot for late October, and Oscar did not wish to perspire in his one and only suit, a charcoal affair he had worn imagining that semiformal dress was appropriate once brothers were both gainfully employed adults. He spent the bumping, lurching cab ride rehearsing all of the nice things he would say to George, and trying to suppress uncomfortable memories of meetings at his brother's apartment in the past: Oscar had established a pitiful routine of falling in love with all of George's girlfriends, *seriatim*, dating back some fifteen years. In more recent times it was all Oscar could do to get through one of George's dinner parties without falling to his knees in a confession of lifelong devotion to his brother's latest find. At the end of such an evening Oscar would collapse into the elevator and claw at his reflected face in the mirror and stumble out into the steaming Manhattan streets looking for a cab not to carry him home but to throw himself under. George had once asked his younger brother if he didn't think people noticed that he was carving his own tongue on his plate. Those were the days before Oscar became mildly glamorous himself, but still he lived in fear of being introduced to yet another of George's wonderful companions. The news that George had found the woman of his dreams was not reassuring.

George lived exactly where he was supposed to—on the Upper East Side; his new doorman wore the requisite gray uniform with braided epaulets, and the demeanor of a suspicious customs officer. He checked Oscar's name on a clipboard, telephoned upstairs, said "So you're the brother, are you?" but still looked on warily as Oscar made his way to the elevator. During his ascent, Oscar enjoyed a long enough ride that he could muse over the fact that in this town he spent a great deal of time grooming and calming himself in elevator shafts. The elevator opened on a corridor that smelled of new paint and old-lady's perfume, and that offered enough mirrors during his walk to George's door that he could inspect himself again from every conceivable angle. He looked fine: wavy brown hair glazed attractively by French sunshine; blue eyes accentuated by a dark tan; a recent shave expertly done, if he said so himself. He paused before his brother's door, raised his hand to knock, and prepared himself for a manly hug.

The door was opened not by Oscar's brother George, but by a stout woman of about forty-five wearing a caftan the color of dried blood and a good deal of noisy brass jewelry that dangled from her ears, neck, and arms. Her blue-black hair was drawn straight back from her broad forehead, and then reappeared slung over one shoulder like the tail of a mink stole. Without a word, but with further tinkles and clinks, she motioned for Oscar to enter by extending a pudgy arm toward the vestibule. Once inside Oscar introduced himself cautiously to the woman, having more than once in his life been embarrassed by shaking hands with servants. A smell of spicy food more or less jibing with the woman's appearance reached his nostrils from the kitchen down the hall, so that Oscar was able to assume with some confidence that this must be his putative future sister-in-law.

"I'm so pleased to meet you," he said.

"I'm Sheila," said the woman. "He's in there." She pointed noisily toward the living room.

"I can't wait to see him," said Oscar. "I've been away for quite a while." He smiled at Sheila with all sorts of *bonhomie*; she looked skeptical, much the way the doorman had.

Oscar rocked back and forth on his heels and continued to smile, thinking he could live with this woman as a sister-in-law even if she did not exactly match his preconceived idea of George's ideal woman. He was waiting for her to lead him into the living room, and was taken aback when she turned and shuffled off to the kitchen without another word.

"I guess I'll just go right in, then," said Oscar, with so much forced enthusiasm that his grin felt like a rictus. He hoped Sheila's apparent rudeness didn't mean he had come at a bad time. Oscar drew back his shoulders, stood as tall as he could stretch, and marched down the corridor toward the living room with the same maniacal baring of teeth still fixed to his face. He strode in like a politician to a podium, only to find the room empty. Nothing here had changed—all was still chrome and glass, deep pile and black leather—except that a general mustiness hung in the air and the carpet was mottled with faded stains, which Oscar took to be just two inevitable symptoms of a drawing room's maturity.

"Little brother," came George's voice. "I'm out here on the balcony. What a sunset."

Oscar walked to the far side of the room, parted the curtains, and found his brother reclined in a deck chair surveying a skyline backlit by an invisible sun whose rays refracted gaudily through a gauze of radioactive-looking haze.

"Sorry I can't get up," said George, as the brothers shook hands. "I've done this." He rapped on a plaster cast that encased his foot and lower leg. Part of George's gregariousness had resulted in a long history of doing himself bodily harm. He had always been the one to climb the tallest trees, ski the steepest runs, slide headfirst for home—and the first to splinter bones.

"Water-skiing?" Oscar asked. "Basketball? Skydiving?" George had broken bones in all of those ways in the past.

"Not this time," said George.

"What, then?"

"Just missed a step at the office, actually. Snap. Very silly." George shook his head. "Have a seat, Oscar."

Oscar sat down in the other chair on the narrow balcony, separated from his brother by a low glass table. On the table rested two oversized brandy snifters and two bottles of red wine, one of which was nearly empty.

"That glass is yours," said George. "Help yourself."

When they had each sipped at their wine and smacked their lips, they paused before talking to smile and appraise one another in the twilight. Oscar was stunned by what he saw, and sipped again at the bulbous glass of wine to conceal any sign of surprise that might have leaked into his expression. This was George, all right, his older brother George, but his formerly lean and distinctive features were now couched in a layer of padding around his face and neck as if he had suffered innumerable bee stings. The lower buttons of his white shirt were stretched to the snapping point over a dome of belly on which George now rested the base of his glass. George had gained at least thirty pounds. This in itself was not fatal, but even in the twilight Oscar thought he could detect the telltale spots of hair-transplant plugs on his older brother's thinning scalp.

"Don't you look sharp," said George. "Have I ever seen you in a suit before?"

"Probably not. I'm sorry about this. I never seem to dress appropriately."

"You look good, Oscar."

"Thank you."

This was Oscar's cue to say something patently false about George's appearance, but instead he sipped at the quite delicious wine and pretended to have found something fascinating to look at on the skyline.

"Just look at that," he said. "What a wonder, Manhattan."

The ghastly, glowing smog had turned a darker shade of menace. Police sirens, the native bird-call of the city, whined and whooped in the canyons. Traffic helicopters buzzed the island's clogged arteries.

"I never get tired of it," said George. He seemed really to mean this. "You get the feeling, way up here, that everyone's trying to climb the ramparts. I have to keep boiling oil pouring over the sides."

"Right you are," said Oscar, thinking what a horrible thing that was for his brother to say, but wishing to be diplomatic. "I

suppose you're still really slogging away at . . . at . . ."
Oscar could never remember the name of his brother's firm.

"Never more so. Do you realize—" he began, pouring himself
more wine.

Oscar was now treated to part of George's old soliloquy on
the subject of the fierce battle being waged by all competent
men that had produced, with Darwinian ruthlessness and
infallibility, an elite species of mover and shaker that lived
within a few blocks of where he sat. It was almost as if he
continued from where he had left off at their last meeting.
George seemed to see himself sitting at the delicate controls of
a perfect machine that only his vigilance and expertise could
keep in tune. That he earned a fortune was only right, really,
when lesser beings depended on his watchfulness and skill for
any happiness at all to trickle their way from on high.
Fortunately for Oscar, who in his ignorance of things financial
was incapable of conversing on this subject, George was
interrupted before he could really begin by a singsong "Hell-
oh-oo!" behind the curtains.

"That," said George, "will be Rachel. Honey? Is that you?
Hey, baby, don't be shy."

Rachel? Oscar thought. What happened to Sheila? Oscar
braced himself for the appearance of another potential sister-
in-law, and for inevitable infatuation.

The curtains parted behind the darkened balcony, and from
the sleeve of light emerged a pale and slender figure who
stepped unsteadily into their midst. Her paleness was accentuated by her choice of a black dress and tights, and by the
tininess of her body and head. It was now too dark to get a good
look, but when George leaned back in his deck chair and
flicked on the balcony light, Oscar nearly exclaimed at the
sight of her, for here, really, was a *child*. A curtain of straight
black hair was parted over her thin white face. Feathered

earrings poked out from behind her hair, reaching almost to her narrow shoulders.

"Come sit on my lap, baby," said George.

VI

NAKED AND HUNCHED IN HIS THINKER'S POSE, OSCAR ENJOYED A sublime moment of rashness and committal. He studied his toenails and sensed the quiet tension of his audience. He lowered himself into a tighter coil, closed his eyes, and sprang away from the cliff. In the air, he folded his legs back into a half-kneeling position, and maintained the pose even as he felt himself tumble forward, over and down. He sensed two revolutions and a full sideways twist before suffering an explosive impact centered directly between his shoulder blades.

From the pressure in his ears he could tell that his entry had been at least clean enough to send him deep down into the fjord, although he was unable to judge which direction was up. He relaxed amid a swirl of froth and waited patiently for the salty Mediterranean to hoist him to its surface. As his body turned upright he had time to realize that he was uninjured, not even stunned, and that he could rise from the water to the ovation that was surely his due. His head bobbed into the evening air. He raised his eyes to the cliffs and waved victoriously, only to discover that he faced the wrong side of the mini-fjord. From behind him came exclamations of relief in several languages, and the international language of laughter.

Oscar turned around, still waving, to see a most diverse

selection of poses on the staircase: heads held in hands in sympathetic pain; hands over mouths in shock; frowns from those who disapproved of suicidal dives on private property; mouths agape with laughter. At the bottom of the steps stood Neville Hacking-Cough, a towel around his shoulders, applauding with hands raised high but shaking his head at the young cartoonist's foolhardiness—and keeping a competitive eye on the judges aboard his wife's yacht. As Oscar stroked slowly for shore, he was astonished to see the judges conferring among themselves before delivering their individual verdicts. He stopped swimming near the hull of the yacht and glared at them so that they would know their egregiously unethical behavior had not gone unnoticed. One by one they raised their cards: eights and nines—a transparent conspiracy to keep their star diver in the lead. Oscar made for the pier thinking that corruption ruled the world.

It was important to appear nonchalant as he was helped, naked, from the sea. Neville handed him a towel and shook his hand.

"Fearless," said the Englishman. "Your dive showed great pluck."

Pluck you, Oscar wanted to say, for getting me into this. But at least the desired result had been achieved, in that among Oscar's well-wishers was a newly amicable Veronique.

"It wouldn't have been so funny if you had killed yourself," she said. "We have had injuries before, you know."

It was all Oscar could do to keep from breaking down in tears at the sight of Veronique up close.

"I wouldn't have done it if you hadn't been watching."

"Shh, not so loud. He is right behind me."

"Who? Oh, *he*." Herr Dohrmann stood a few feet away on the pier, chatting with Neville Hacking-Cough. The scar on his left cheekbone traveled in a tidy crescent from the corner of his dead eye to the corner of his mouth. With his expert powers of physical observation, Oscar thought he could detect certain features of the German's physiognomy that had been transferred to his stunning daughter: the greenest of eyes, of course, but also the curved upper lip, the small pointed chin, the minuscule ears—all of these they had in common.

"You seem worried," Oscar said to Veronique, attempting gently to touch her forearm but missing when she jerked it away.

"Of course I am," she said.

"Should I have a little talk with him?"

"You? Are you suggesting that *you* should have a talk with *my*—"

"Wait," interrupted Oscar. "Here he comes."

Herr Dohrmann was a large man with a barrel torso and knobbly legs with the varicosities tanned out of them. His left leg appeared slightly atrophied, which accounted for his pronounced limp. His leonine head was a jumble of windswept white hair and leathery folds. His scar turned white and angular when he smiled.

"Young man," said the German, taking one of Oscar's small artist's hands into both of his swordsman's paws. "You were magnificent. You should get a medal. I'm afraid our judges didn't know what to make of you. It was naughty of Neville to include you, but I think you showed him, ja?"

"Thank you, sir," said Oscar.

"Wonderful. You are a friend of Veronique's, then? Is that what you are?" Herr Dohrmann let go of Oscar's hand and put an arm around Veronique's shoulders.

"That's what I am, sir," said Oscar. "My name is Oscar Lemoine. I met Veronique at a party—"

"Ja, yes, I remember. I remember your little black dog who swims."

Oscar wanted to launch into a lengthy autobiography and a description of his suitor-suitability, but Herr Dohrmann excused himself to attend to the further entertainment of his guests.

"Now that wasn't so bad, was it?" Oscar said to Veronique.

"I suppose not. He is too egotistical to be suspicious."

"How odd that he should—oh, never mind. There are all sorts of things we have to do, Veronique."

"What do you mean?"

"I thought a little picnic out on the islands, just to start."

"We will have to take precautions," said Veronique, glancing over her shoulder to see that Hansie and Neville were well out of earshot.

"Well, yes, of course. That's right. You let me take care of the 'precautions.'" Oscar winked.

"Tuesday will be fine," said Veronique.

"Tuesday it is. There are some small cliffs out on the islands. I can practice my dives for next year. But won't I see you before then?"

"He will be here." Again she glanced over her shoulder.

"Does that really make a difference?"

This question seemed to anger Veronique. She leaned forward until her mouth was just beneath Oscar's dripping jaw, and hissed: "I like you, Oscar. I do. But if you are not going to be careful and do things my way, I'm afraid I will have to—"

"Gotcha," said Oscar. "Just relax, I'll see you Tuesday."

Consummate hostess that she was, Veronique was able to regain her composure instantly. She waved at someone on Neville's wife's yacht, she adjusted one of the straps of her dress, and ascended the stairs to the main house alone.

The eavesdropping, gossip-hungry Neville Hacking-Cough was quick to join Oscar once Veronique had departed.

"Not taking my advice, I see," he said.

"I can handle it, sir," said Oscar, who had already decided that, despite Veronique's insistence, the best way to proceed was to get things out in the open with Herr Dohrmann. Oscar thought a man-to-man talk was in order.

VII

"COME SIT ON MY LAP, BABY," OSCAR'S BROTHER GEORGE HAD JUST said.

"I'd rather have a glass of wine and stand up, okay?" said Rachel, whose voice sounded older than she looked. She looked thirteen.

"Well that's fine then. Suit yourself. I want you to meet my brother, Oscar."

Oscar felt a scene coming on. He could see himself, the new Oscar Lemoine, standing up and spewing his outrage at the decadence that seemed to have taken control of his formerly decent brother's life. I come back here to see you, he wanted to say, and what do I find? I find a fat man with what looks like an ultraviolet tan and plastic hair sewn into his head and a broken limb he probably got stumbling drunk out of a cab at five in the morning, and . . . and a little girlfriend young enough to be his daughter down whose gullet he pours very, very good wine. *That's* what I find.

"So, Rachel," Oscar said instead. "It's nice to meet you."

"Nice to meet you, too," she said, sweetly. She was a pretty girl, with an open smile, Oscar thought—but *really*. "I'm older than I look. Aren't I, George."

"She's older than she looks," Oscar's brother agreed. "She's seventeen."

"Eighteen on Thursday," said Rachel.

Oh, well, that's all right then, thought Oscar, who was revolted. He could feel that his eyebrows had narrowed, his upper lip had furled, and his chin had receded toward his own chest, so that he was looking at George in the way that an interrogating police officer might look at a prisoner whose confessions were simply too vile to be believed.

"Oscar was just going to tell me everything," said George. "How's our native France?"

The Lemoine brothers always referred to that country as "our native France," not only because of the French derivation of their surname and their long-dead French grandfather, but because as small children they had lived in Paris during their father's convenient predivorce business posting.

Oscar launched into a vague geographical description of Val d'Argent, then on to a romanticized version of his first hard-working year there, all the while running his mind through a series of outbursts that might be suitable to the discovery that his brother consorted with minors.

". . . reading a great deal, working well in advance of deadline, walking my dog," Oscar was saying. Then he looked at his lap and added, bashfully, "And of course, falling in love."

"Hah!" said George, leaning over clumsily in his cast to slap at Oscar's knee. "You don't say. Why didn't you bring her with you?"

"She isn't here, she's a world traveler. I'm not exactly sure where she is. It's all slightly complicated. In fact I can't really tell you the details."

"What? Secrets from King George? You know this isn't permitted. Give, O."

"Maybe later," said Oscar, casting as polite a glance as he could toward Rachel. "It's highly personal."

"You're ashamed of her."

Oscar tried to convey with a mischievous little suck on his

wineglass that Veronique was no ordinary girl. And besides, you pathetic bastard, Oscar wanted to add, as Rachel finally complied and sat on George's lap, she is an *adult*. Instead Oscar helped himself to more wine, hoping its effects might spur him on to a voicing of his deep disapproval.

Actually, it was not really disapproval that made him so angry, but disappointment. He thought he had finally reached the stage where he could have greeted George's ideal woman with equanimity and brotherly appreciation. He had come prepared with his own story of romance, so that together they could rhapsodize about the savior that is love. To find George in the arms not of the suitable and excellent wife-material he had expected—or even Sheila, for that matter—but in the company of a piece of cast-off teenaged high society, had caught Oscar unawares. Now he thought he knew what it meant to be piqued.

"Tell me all about her," said George, nuzzling the wine-sipping waiflet on his lap. "Your great love, I mean."

Oscar loosened his tie and continued to frown. He gulped his wine as if he were finishing off a pitcher of iced tea after three sets of tennis.

"A French girl," he said. "Way over my head. Elegant as can be." *Mature*, he wanted to add, and *legal*. "Her name is Veronique, and we have lived an adventure together."

"Gaw," said George. "Heaven."

"It would take days to tell you the story."

"I don't have the time. At least tell me what she looks like."

"If you saw her you would want to kiss her neck."

"Good. Very nice."

Rachel seemed to like this conversation. She crossed her skinny legs and threw an arm around George's shoulders, but didn't take her eyes off Oscar. Her teeth were quite attractive. Her little feet were shod in black ankle booties with upturned toes.

"Are you going to get married?" Rachel wanted to know.

"That's unlikely."

"I've been giving marriage some thought," said George. "Haven't I, baby?" He gave the girl a squeeze. Rachel nodded, unenthusiastically.

Oscar found this preposterous and irritating. Never had he been forced to such an extent to skate over the questions he really wanted to ask. And what method of birth control do you use? Do your parents neglect you to such a degree that a live-in arrangement with an overweight financial high-flyer is acceptable to them? Do you confer with girlfriends between classes at your progressive prep school about how old and rich your lovers are? He thought that if he managed to imbibe five more glasses of wine he would be able to make a proper statement of his general disdain for their arrangement.

Someone like Rachel was not part of a life trajectory that for thirty years had been as predictable and inexorable as that of a fired cannonball. George's woman was supposed to be roughly half-a-dozen years his junior, bedecked with academic degrees (but naturally interested mainly in motherhood and household management), physically attractive on a nearly impossible level without looking gauche, mischievously overt about her powerful sexuality when in the right company, and of course rich as a queen. Oscar had never met nor heard of such a woman, but had never lost his faith in his brother's ability to find or create her. George had never failed before, after all.

"I suppose I ought to ask about our parents," Oscar suggested.

"Bad idea," said George. "Mayhem."

"I guess I just wanted to know if any new marriages were on the horizon. Or litigation."

"None that I know of, on either count. Hate fills the air. Hey, but aren't the Lemoine boys well adjusted, Rachel? You have no idea, the scars." He tickled Rachel's rib cage as if she were a five-year-old awake past her bedtime. She squirmed and giggled, but continued to stare straight at Oscar with dilated eyes in a manner that had become disconcerting in its flirtatiousness. George seemed not to notice this as he briefed his younger brother on the old news that their parents shared nothing in common any longer save for an appointments secretary whose main task it was to see that they never appeared at the same party.

"All is as it should be, in other words," Oscar said. "I am overjoyed." For twenty years the Lemoine brothers had built up a convenient world view that saw the nuclear family and long-term wedded happiness as minority perversions. It was not lost on Oscar that this could help explain why George had turned to such a drastically unconventional romance, but this made the fact of "Rachel" no more palatable to him.

Rachel helped pour George more wine. She kicked her little feet and giggled at nothing. Oscar searched his raging brain for small talk. George was better at this: "Where's your mother, Rachel?" was his unexpected question.

Mother? thought Oscar. *My brother lives with his nymphet and his nymphet's* mother?

"She's in her room. She always takes like forever," said Rachel, employing the jarring syntax that seemed to have infected an entire generation.

Oscar tried to calm himself and analyze the situation. He had almost, but not quite, reached the conclusion that Sheila must be Rachel's mother, when the curtains were disturbed and yet another figure stepped onto the balcony.

"Ah," said George. "At last. Oscar, I want you to meet Diana."

This introduction was spoken with such formality that even the maladroit Oscar was capable of realizing that here, finally, was George's fiancée. Oscar leapt to his feet, a maneuver that would have come off more gracefully in a larger space; and he would have said hello in a normal voice if both his knees had not struck the low table as he stood up.

"*Arg,*" said Oscar. "How nice to meet you."

"Diana Burke," said Diana Burke, a compact woman who did not at first appear old enough to be the mother of a seventeen-year-old daughter. She squeezed by George and Rachel and leaned against the balcony's railing, as if after all her hard work pulling herself together she had to pose for the company's appraisal.

Slender and perky, Diana Burke gave Oscar a friendly look and launched immediately into polite interrogation. This is okay, thought Oscar. I can live with this. He came to this conclusion despite his inherent mistrust of divorced people, and Diana Burke, without question, was a victim of marital meltdown—a condition Oscar felt he could recognize at fifty paces. He quickly regained his composure, as well as his seat, and rubbed his bruised knees while awaiting further acquaintance with the dark-haired Diana.

"Splendid," she said, as if trying out the word for the first time. "Isn't this splendid."

"Yes," said George and Oscar in unison.

Oscar busied himself with mental calculations of Diana Burke's likely age, impolite as this was, and reached two conclusions: that Diana Burke was thirty-eight years old; and that Diana Burke considered this to be a sufficiently old age that cosmetic surgery had been in order. There was no denying it. Someone had taken away part of her face, the part a student of human features like Oscar would have termed "character." A photograph of Diana Burke and her daughter Rachel, taken from a discreet distance, would no doubt elicit clucks of amazement at their similarity from society's sippers at the fountain of youth, but even in the fading light on the terrace the older woman's skull-like countenance lacked a natural expression. Someone's scalpel had taken away the main physical outlet of Diana Burke's personality. Oscar wondered if it were sufficient reward that instead of people automatically thinking "She's not young any longer," they thought "She's had her face removed."

The rest of Diana Burke's personality remained in good order. Oscar warmed to her quickly, even as he pitied her her loss of face. Oscar appreciated good manners wherever he found them, and Diana Burke possessed good manners in abundance. Her recent history was swiftly and elliptically related: divorce two years ago from a man who in four or five choice and indirect words she managed to portray as unfaithful, cruel, and rich; a year of travel and retrenchment while Rachel lived with her father (here Diana Burke's cosmetic surgery failed her, for she really could have used the aid of facial muscles to convey to Oscar that when she said "traveling" she actually meant intensive psychiatric treatment); six months retrieving her daughter from her ex-husband's clutches and dipping her toes back into society; six months living with and learning to love George Lemoine.

Oscar took in what he could understand of Diana Burke's narrative with suitable expressions of sympathy and admiration for her strength and determination. He watched George's face out of the corner of his eye and saw love there. This is okay, he thought again. I can live with this.

A jangling of bangles announced the return of Sheila.

"Dinner," she said.

Oscar and Rachel helped George to his feet. Like the good Ivy Leaguer that he was, George eschewed crutches in favor of a gnarled wooden cane with an ivory handle. "What a nuisance I am," he said, as if Oscar and Rachel were his grandchildren and he had come to their home to live out his days. "You're too good to me."

Standing erect, George was still as imposing as ever, but in a different way from the days when he had been arguably the city's most attractive man. His additional poundage made him look more like a slightly softened veteran of contact sports than the wine-guzzling paedophile for which Oscar had so recently mistaken him. Still, the extra flesh could not conceal his winning smile—or in this case his winning grimace of discomfort as he limped on his cast and cane toward the dining room.

Rachel seated George at the head of the table and stood his cane in a corner of the room. Oscar took his seat to George's right, across from little Rachel, leaving the seat closest to the kitchen for Diana Burke. A copy of the most recent *Lowdown* lay on the table within George's reach.

"I've been explaining to Diana and Rachel what it is you do for a living," he said, picking up the magazine by the corner of the cover, as if it were someone's used handkerchief. "Gaw, poor old Bunny Fenton."

"She's probably flattered," said Oscar, who was ashamed to use his most mundane excuse in front of his brother. Oscar had hoped to learn a heartlessness in Val d'Argent that was commensurate with the savageness people saw in his drawings; instead he had grown more convinced than ever that, far from being savage, his *Lowdown* covers exuded nothing more than a love for humanity qualified by standard doses of envy and mistrust of authority. "Anyway it can't do her ratings any harm," he added. Oscar had learned to mention his victims' likely material gain, which in New York never failed to stop any such debate in its tracks.

Little Rachel had taken the magazine from George, and appraised Oscar's nude caricature of Bunny Fenton with a scowl. "How did you learn to do *this?*" she asked.

"He's done it forever," George answered for his younger brother, a remark that, while well-intentioned, still overlooked the decade of diligent and sometimes costly study and apprenticeship that had brought Oscar to his current level of ability.

"This is what she looks like?" continued Rachel. "I mean like they're *huge*."

"It's a caricature," said Oscar, refraining from correcting Rachel's grammar. "I use my imagination, and I exaggerate everything."

"So I see."

Sheila emerged from the kitchen through swinging doors with a veritable caldron of soup in her asbestos-gloved hands. Her cheeks were reddened by steam and effort. It was impossible not to like someone working so hard at something as fundamentally useful as hearty soup.

"Bisque," said Sheila. "Hope you like it."

Oscar wanted to stand up and give Sheila a hug; instead he played with his soup spoon as she ladled the exquisite mixture into all four bowls in turn.

Once everyone had been served, George gave a perfunctory toast to the return of his little brother, then quickly launched into a disquieting outline of his next day's itinerary, which would begin with a breakfast meeting in Philadelphia and end with a banquet in Boston. Oscar was left with the impression that if George was unable to instill in his adversaries a fear of the bowel-voiding variety, the economies of the free world faced a possibly fatal spasm of chaos. It would be in all the newspapers, George assured his guests, but of course he could offer no specifics. His earlobes had already turned the color of the wine.

Oscar listened patiently and pretended not to notice that Rachel would not take her eyes off him. When he felt her foot meeting his beneath the table he did not look at her. He sat up straight, wound his ankles round the legs of his chair, and thought of Val d'Argent.

VIII

OSCAR LIMPED HOME FROM THE HIGH-DIVING PARTY, THINKING OF
Icarus. His neck and shoulders and groin were sore, his ears
were plugged with seawater, and his lower back had a few things
to say about daredevilry. Despite these complaints his spirits
were high, because he had accomplished his mission in such
controversial style. Life was a simple matter of meeting individual crises of greater or lesser importance with as much careful
forethought as time allowed, combined with a willingness to go
for broke.

He returned to his house to find Elizabeth asleep on the floor
next to a finished painting, exhausted by her labors. She
dragged herself to her paws and wagged her tail in greeting, but
wore the downcast expression of an art student whose work was
about to be appraised by a professional. Oscar picked up the
stretched canvas and held it at arm's length. Elizabeth had
always done her best work in acrylics, and in this case she had
outdone herself. True to her exhaustive training, there wasn't a
pawmark on the canvas, and even the floor near where she had
been working was clean. The painting itself was another
example of Canine Expressionism, a school of art that held
cleanliness in the workplace above all other considerations, but
otherwise had much in common with most of the Abstract
Expressionist works dating back fifty years. The painting in
Oscar's hands, which he decided to call *High Dive*, employed
Elizabeth's two favorite colors—black (the color of her coat),

and pink (the color of her tongue)—in approximately twenty brushstrokes. Elizabeth had been trained to execute her works starting at the top of the canvas and moving steadily to the bottom, to avoid stepping in her own paint. She had started *High Dive* with a broad black stroke, a broad pink one next to but not touching it, like two-tone eyebrows. In her impatience to finish—she no longer had the endurance of a young artist—she had repeated the same strokes all the way to the bottom of the canvas where they began to mix in a noisome confluence that was, Oscar thought, particularly appropriate to her age. Because such paintings amount to nothing in the absence of someone who makes a living talking about them, Oscar imagined a learned voice speaking of Elizabeth's deep preoccupation with good and evil, and the stunning simplicity with which she elicited a feeling of straddling polarized moral choices that finally blended into the dismal lot of man and dog.

"Give me your paw, Elizabeth," said Oscar. "You haven't signed your beautiful painting."

IX

"I HAVE TO TELL YOU A HORRIBLE STORY," SAID GEORGE, AS SHEILA emerged once again from the kitchen with enough beef stew to feed Rachel's high school. George had already had too much to drink; he had spilled some of his soup onto the tablecloth and looked likely to do the same with his glass of wine. "Here it is. Horrible. Coming out of the office a few days ago, before I did this,"—he reached down and knocked on his cast—"I decided

to go around the corner for a drink . . . and, you know, a bite to eat. Shortcut, through the alleyway. A guy is standing in the alleyway, and I'm ready to knock his head in if he tries anything. He's small and he's wearing an overcoat on a hot night. He tells me to stop and I kind of loom over him so he gets the idea I've been beating up muggers since before he was born, but I see he's holding a what-do-you-call-it in his hand. A thing. A *hypodermic* needle." George drained his glass. "I step aside and he cuts me off. He starts waving the thing, the *syringe,* and says he's going to poke me with it unless I fork over the old wallet. 'I *shit* you,' is what he says, but I get the idea. The syringe has *blood* in it, Oscar. Blood and *AIDS*. So what does George do? He's done this thing before, you know. Twice in that same alleyway, King George has broken the wrists and ribs of crazies with knives. But he remembers that both times he was cut. Cuts you survive, obviously. But a needle . . ." George refilled his glass. "I retreated and made a show of reaching for my wallet. I took out the wallet and showed it to him and started taking out the money. I had about seven hundred dollars in there. I started throwing the money at him bill by bill. Twenties, tens, fives. I left a trail between me and the little junkie. I thought this would make him stop to pick up the money so I could kick him in the head. Instead he lunged at me and I ran backward out of the way, still tossing bills. I yelled at him that I had thrown down all my money, so he stopped and went back to get it, still waving the needle at me so I wouldn't follow him. I went to find a cop so we could go back and maim the little creep, but I found a cab first and decided to go home. I still had four hundred dollars left."

Young Rachel had listened to this narration with a forkful of stew poised in the air and a look of disbelief and amazement. Diana seemed to have heard it all before.

"So what you are saying," said Oscar, "is that you were robbed at *needlepoint?*"

"Oh, very funny. He could have stabbed me and given me, what is it, acquired insufficiency syndrome. No one at work would believe that's how I got it. You shouldn't joke about that, Oscar."

Oscar wondered why it was that George's first worry about such a grotesque condition was that it wouldn't go over well with his colleagues.

Oscar wanted to be polite and include the women in the conversation, but Diana was content to allow George to hold forth, while Rachel appeared not to have a concrete thought in her head. "God," was one of the things she said frequently, along with little puffs of incomprehension.

While Sheila cleared the table George lit a cigar, which Oscar had never seen him do before. He was drunk in a way that was also unfamiliar to Oscar: his syntax had come unhinged, he repeated himself, he grumbled about life's little problems as if he were an emperor displeased with the progress of distant wars. Oscar finally managed to interrupt, and began to tell the story of his Val d'Argent high-dive, just to inject a little pep into the conversation. Rachel's eyes lit up as she heard him describe the scene, so he addressed himself mostly to her. He had just told her about stripping off his miniature bathing suit when he looked over and saw that George had fallen asleep with his cigar still burning between his fingers.

"George," said Diana, not sharply.

His eyes blinked open, but it took him a moment to surface. When he realized where he was he excused himself and blamed it all on stress. No one can possibly understand, he told them, the strain of a job like his. "Take tomorrow," he said to them, and repeated the description of his next day's duties in Philadelphia and Boston. Again the point was made that, without heroic measures on George's part, a financial shock-wave would circle the globe leaving catastrophe and ruin in its wake. Nothing would ever be the same again if King George failed in his mission.

"Speaking of which," he said, emitting the tiniest of belches between his fingers, "I should go to bed before I drink too much. Don't get up. Just my cane, please, Rachel." George limped out of the room without another word or even a glance at his younger brother. He bumped first one then the other shoulder in the doorway. He muttered curses to himself until he had rounded the corner and could no longer be heard.

Oscar exchanged a meaningless look with Rachel and Diana. Sheila came back from the kitchen with a fresh pot of coffee.

"I don't see why we shouldn't have a little more coffee together, eh girls?" said Oscar, with exaggerated cheerfulness. "Won't you join us, Sheila? I'll help with the dishes later."

Oscar loosened his tie, unbuttoned his shirt collar, and stretched a false smile onto his face.

X

ON A HOT LATE AFTERNOON IN VAL D'ARGENT, OSCAR SAT ON HIS terrace and looked out over the tops of the cypress trees bordering his swimming pool to the road, where two nuns in blue habits had stopped to chat with a woman pushing a pram. All three carried loaves of bread. The nuns poked at the baby in the pram, who held a small heel of bread of its own. Both nuns wore glasses, and must have looked to the baby like a pair of goggle-eyed eels lunging at him out of the blue.

On the sea a golden carpet of sinking sun shot across the

water, speckled with the multicolored sails of catamarans returning to the central beach from a race. To Oscar's right, the hairpin turns of the road descended into the small town that had almost become a suburb of the port city farther along the coast. Cars were parked in a long line along the seaward side of the road, and the weekend crowds now climbed the cliffside steps from rocky beaches to their vehicles, preparing to fight their way through the town's traffic back to the main road.

Under the shade of a beach umbrella, Oscar sketched the foundation of his newest nude caricature. Elizabeth dozed on the cool tiles nearby, wearing her little navy-blue beret. The workmen and their pneumatic drills had gone away; Oscar's young pyromaniac neighbor Anton had been defused and taken to the beach for the afternoon. The loudest noise to be heard was the scratching of Oscar's pencil on paper.

The subject at hand was unknown to Oscar, just another run-of-the-mill billionaire tycoon. A package of photographs and biographical information had arrived from the *Lowdown* a few days before. The man looked so much like an elephant—a long snout surrounded by baggy gray folds—that Oscar was tempted to draw him that way, but this was not Oscar's style. He did not draw elephants as men, and he did not draw men as elephants. Besides, elephants were likable creatures. He had decided to draw the tycoon in all his immensity, and to make his corpulent body transparent; inside the man's stomach would be visible the industrial symbols of his insatiable corporate appetite—mills and aircraft, oil rigs and printing presses—leading through a realistic digestive tract toward stainless-steel plumbing between his legs, leaking toxic waste. That ought to do it, Oscar thought.

Oscar loved his work. He tried to strike a balance between his natural tendency toward perfectionism and a rigorous schedule of self-imposed deadlines that ensured productivity. There was nothing Oscar enjoyed more than his evening walk to one of the harbor restaurants and a relaxed meal after a good day's work. Apart from food and art supplies, he was happily self-contained in his house on the hillside.

At the start of his stay in Val d'Argent Oscar had traveled by bus once a week to the city to buy art supplies, but had since arranged for everything he needed to be delivered to his house. Often it was the art-supply storeowner himself who handled the delivery—a dapper Frenchman named Berlinger who enjoyed a single glass of beer on Oscar's terrace each time he visited. Monsieur Berlinger never overstayed his welcome, leaving after finishing his beer with many apologies for having interrupted Oscar's important work. He had not asked outright to see any of Oscar's caricatures, but he had seen several of Elizabeth's creations and had been impressed to the point of offering her an exhibition in town. Monsieur Berlinger had seen a lot of modern art in his day, and not for a moment did he so much as hint that a work could be diminished merely because it had been painted by an animal. Oscar told Monsieur Berlinger that a retrospective might not be out of the question, since Elizabeth had accumulated perhaps two dozen presentable paintings.

"We need to give her a last name," was Monsieur Berlinger's only suggestion. "You cannot simply say 'It is an original Elizabeth,' can you?"

"Bête Noire," said Oscar. "An original Bête Noire."

THREE

I

ᴛʜᴇ ꜰᴏʟʟᴏᴡɪɴɢ ᴍᴏʀɴɪɴɢ ᴏꜱᴄᴀʀ ᴛʀɪᴇᴅ ᴛᴏ ᴘᴜᴛ ᴛʜᴇ ᴜɴᴘʟᴇᴀꜱᴀɴᴛ dinner with his older brother out of his mind. Feeling guilty about not having put pen to paper since his arrival in New York, Oscar deployed his and Elizabeth's art supplies so that master and dog could work together in their hotel room. He was interrupted by more telephone calls than he had received during an average month in Val d'Argent: Fable called from his car; Gail called from her bathtub; two of Fable's intellectuals called from the *Lowdown*; Veronique called from Paris; George called from an airplane over upstate New York; Rachel called from George's apartment. Each call was disturbing in its own way.

Through static and interference, nosing through traffic on the F.D.R. Drive, Fable managed to convey the usual sense of crisis and imminent downfall at the *Lowdown*. The Bunny

Fenton caricature had drawn fire from feminists, and Fable was more paranoid than ever about the *Orthoducks* strip. People with credentials were up in arms. Oscar tried to reassure his boss by explaining that the long-awaited Jesus caricature would be finished in plenty of time for the special Christmas issue, and of course the "Nun of the Above" strip was well under way.

Over the sound of lapping soapy water, Gail Gardener reiterated her desire that Oscar ascertain Fable's true intentions regarding marriage and fatherhood, not necessarily in that order. Oscar choked back his disapproval and promised to investigate at the first appropriate opportunity. He hung up the phone wondering why Gail sounded angry rather than apologetic.

Fable's intellectuals wanted to talk about life, one at a time, to nominate candidates for future *Lowdown* covers, and generally to enthuse about their new lives as takers of the city's pulse.

Veronique only wanted to say hello, did not have time to say where she was at the moment, and could not yet say whether she would be able to join him in New York; hearing her voice caused an onanistic delay in Oscar's morning proceedings.

George Lemoine's airborne call was crystal clear, and he started by describing the view from his plane. He went on to apologize for having fallen asleep at the dinner table, and hoped to be in better form next time. "You have no idea, the stress," he said again. He made no mention of, and in fact did not seem to remember, the supposedly earth-shattering nature of his day's business. "Oh, and Oscar," he said. "I'm sorry about Rachel— don't worry that she seems to be a bit of a flirt. It's just a stage she's going through. It happens all the time."

Rachel's call soon followed; the girl wished to meet Oscar secretly as soon as possible for "some serious talk," a prospect Oscar did not relish.

He hung up after this last conversation with a shudder and a shrug of his shoulders at Elizabeth. He telephoned the reception desk and asked not to be disturbed for the rest of the day. He finished arranging his drawings, hoping that a few hours' work would take his mind off the problems and intrigues of the people he had met since coming to New York. He kept an eye on the soundless television hoping for an appearance by the glamorous Bunny Fenton. He spent half an hour training Elizabeth to scan the dozens of television channels available at the newly high-tech Domino Hotel.

"Stop," said Oscar, an hour later. "There she is."

Elizabeth stopped changing channels.

"Volume," said Oscar. Elizabeth fumbled with the remote control and succeeded in raising the volume. "Good girl."

Oscar knelt down in front of the television and inspected the image of Bunny Fenton. She used her trained masculine voice to report on inexcusable abuses of public funds by clearly unworthy people whose only defense was a claim that they lived like barnyard animals. In her lightweight trench coat, chalk-blue cowl-neck and pearls, Bunny Fenton solemnly faced the camera and shared in her viewers' disapproval of these rather unclean blots on the landscape of New York. Not the sort of people she would want living downstairs in her apartment building, she seemed to be saying. Back in a moment, Bunny told Oscar, to talk of more pleasant things—namely the personal miseries and Bel Air house-hunting travails of a recently divorced film actress.

Oscar spent the commercial break unwrapping his major work-in-progress, the definitive nude caricature of the famous religious figure, Jesus Christ. He had found this painting to be his most difficult yet, if only because of all his subjects Jesus was the one who had most often been portrayed unclothed, and by some fairly accomplished artists at that. He was glad the customs official at the airport had not seen this particular series of drawings. Oscar had worked on sketch after sketch of the man's grotesquely contorted facial expression, which was one of almost supernatural revulsion, twisted and horrified, like that of a monk being forced to watch sadomasochistic pornography. This was supposed to convey Jesus' reaction to the modern consumer-driven celebrations of his birthday. The face was recognizably that of Jesus, tatty beard, crown of thorns and all. Oscar had sketched the body separately, in various poses, but was still not satisfied that he could tastefully represent the holy privates. It wouldn't do to abandon his trademark in favor of a loincloth, but with all the controversy surrounding his previous works he had begun to suffer something of a block. It was one thing to offend one person—the caricature's victim—for the amusement of thousands; but to offend thousands for no good reason was another matter. He arranged all of the Jesus sketches on his bed and stood back to appraise them. He chewed on his pen and hoped for divine inspiration.

Just as Bunny Fenton returned to his television screen following a flood of advertisements, a knock came on the door of Room 1107. Oscar couldn't remember having summoned room service. Elizabeth growled softly. Oscar opened the door rather absentmindedly, aware that this was a city where robbery and death rarely paused to knock, and felt himself being pushed back into his room by a bejeweled fist. The woman attached to the fist wore dark glasses and a trench coat, and had enough blond hair to coif a pride of lions. Here was the glamorous Bunny Fenton, in the flesh.

II

THE TWIN ISLANDS OFF THE COAST OF VAL D'ARGENT WERE KNOWN AS
Tristan and Isolde. Oscar knew enough to leave port before
dawn, even on a weekday, to ensure sole possession of the most
desirable cove. He and Elizabeth met Veronique at the Café
Floride, where the loyal André awaited them with the basket of
picnic supplies Oscar had ordered the previous day. Pyromaniac
Anton's parents had agreed to lend Oscar their launch in
exchange for a gruesome caricature sketch of their son. Oscar
and Veronique puttered out of the harbor as the first tinge of
daylight reached the horizon. Elizabeth stood proudly in the
prow like a figurehead.

Tristan and Isolde were forty minutes away at low speed.
Oscar and Veronique sipped the hot coffee that the thoughtful
André had provided in a thermos, and huddled together in the
stern of the launch. The black sea grew paler as daylight
expanded overhead, and by the time they reached the shallows
surrounding their island they could make out anemones
and coral, sandbars and fishes, and one surly octopus. As
Veronique was the more accomplished seafarer, Oscar turned
over the controls so that she could maneuver the craft alongside
the rickety pier without causing damage or embarrassment.
They left the launch, climbed a sandy path, and hiked for ten
minutes to the far side of the island. There they clambered
down a craggy precipice to a sheltered cove that would see most
of the day's sunlight.

Elizabeth was the first to take a swim, while Oscar and Veronique ate chocolate-filled croissants and finished the last of the coffee. Oscar went about chilling the wine in an eddy, setting the pâté, cheese, pickles and hearts-of-palm in the shade, arranging towels to face the sun. Clothes were folded and set aside, oil was applied to flesh, and the pair reclined naked in the sun.

Oscar lay on his stomach and speculated in a shallow way about Veronique's life. He thought it must be exhausting being a socialite, which is why he had decided to take her to such an isolated and restful place. He asked her questions and watched her mouth as she replied. She spoke entertainingly about the far-flung places she had seen in Herr Dohrmann's company. When Oscar revealed to her that he had grown up in New York, Veronique told him how much she loved it there.

"Ah, New York," she said. "My favorite. It is the only place for Christmas. The lights, the excitement, better food than Paris. You are so lucky to have lived there."

She went on in this vein without using either of the two adjectives Oscar employed most frequently when describing his hometown, namely "foul" and "degrading." His most recent memories of Christmas in New York were of trudging through appalling cold in his stinking overcoat, sidestepping deranged mendicants. He had probably brushed past the mink-coated Veronique on her way to the ballet, cursing her under his breath, siding with the shouted insults of paranoid-schizophrenics.

"You're right," said Oscar, playing with warm sand. "A fantastic city."

Veronique raised herself onto her elbows and looked out to sea.

"Aren't you worried about your dog?"

"Can you see her?"

"No."

"She'll be fine. She likes a long swim. Probably exploring the island. Elizabeth loves it out on the islands."

"You're going to burn yourself, here."

"Probably, but I have to catch up sometime." Veronique had quite a brown bottom.

They swam. They frolicked in the tideless sea. They put on clothes to eat and drink with dignity. Elizabeth returned from her circumnavigation of the island in time to be fed pâté and bottled water. Oscar was so lost in pleasure, so deep in his sensual trance, that when Veronique said "You must miss New York," he thought he would break a rib laughing.

III

"SO, HERE YOU ARE THEN," SAID BUNNY FENTON, REMOVING HER sunglasses and glaring at him with eyes of artificially accentuated blue. "You *bastard.*"

Oscar cocked his head and smiled. Elizabeth trotted over to be introduced. "Relax," he said. "Meet my dog, Elizabeth." He could tell that this confrontation was going to require every bit of the social savvy he hoped he had acquired in Val d'Argent.

"I don't care about your dog," said Bunny Fenton.

"You cannot possibly mean that, ma'am," said Oscar.

"Shut up. I just wanted to see you, you bastard."

"Could this have anything to do with—"

"You're damn right it has." Bunny Fenton backed up her statement by waving a tattered copy of the *Lowdown* in Oscar's face. It was odd seeing the woman standing in his room and flickering on the television screen and waving two-dimensionally in the air all at the same time.

"How did you find me? How did you get in here?"

"I'm a reporter," said Bunny Fenton. "I can find anyone. I can get in anywhere."

She began to stride around Oscar's hotel room, still waving the magazine, making direct comparisons between the cartoonist and the offspring of Elizabeth's species and gender. Oscar waited for her to calm down. This did not happen immediately because Bunny Fenton had paused to look at the drawings spread out on Oscar's bed.

"Jesus," said Bunny Fenton.

"Correct," said Oscar.

"No, I mean you are one sick son of a—"

"Look, we've been through all that. How would you like it if I called room service and got us some coffee. Then we can have a little talk."

It was too late for that, though, because the formerly fierce Bunny Fenton had collapsed into Oscar's chair and begun to sob into her crumpled *Lowdown*.

IV

OSCAR LEMOINE, ADULT CARTOONIST—SUNBURNED, EXHAUSTED BY THE tiring business of frolicking in sand and sea—steered the boat back into the harbor of Val d'Argent with Veronique under his arm. They had spent a beautiful day together, even if her behavior so far had shown a paradoxical love of exhibitionism and fear of the most common end-result of heterosexual intimacy. It crossed his mind that she might be hiding from another suitor in town, but he lacked the nerve to broach this question.

They dined inconspicuously behind palm fronds and out-croppings of synthetic rock at the Restaurant du Rocher, where Oscar did well to conceal the terrible pain of his scorched buttocks. Halfway through their salmon mousse (wrapped in spinach leaves, garnished with baby shrimp and slivers of avocado), while deep in conversation about food, the dense foliage behind Veronique's head was parted to reveal the smirking face of Neville Hacking-Cough, who said in a comical accent, "This your car, then?" Oscar had heard Neville introduce himself to people this way before—the question seemed to be the punch line of a terribly funny joke known only to Neville and his intimates.

"Sorry to frighten you, my dear," he said in his normal voice. "You naughty girl. Hallo, Monsieur Lemoine. I couldn't possibly join you—no no, couldn't possibly. All right, if you insist. I've asked our man for a drink."

Neither Oscar nor Veronique had yet said a word, but Neville seated himself between them and launched into the tale of the first time he had sipped a glass of brandy, the point of the story being that the snifter had been handed to him by Winston Churchill. "Frightfully memorable thing he said to me that day," said Neville. "Forgot it on the spot. The dear man was gassed to the follicles, of course. Something prescient about the Cold War, I believe. Ah, here's my beverage. You're looking pink, my boy. Tell me about America."

"It's—"

"Do you know that your young President Kennedy was practically old enough to give me fatherly advice? I was closer to his brother, of course. . . ."

Neville continued to drop names like hydrogen bombs until Veronique asked him please to shut up.

"You young people," Neville said, instead of stopping, "live entirely without moment. My generation lived with upheaval, with . . ."

"Did you come here to lecture us?" Veronique interrupted. "Or only to spy?"

"Now speaking of spies," said Neville, "I'll never forget the time Anthony—"

"Neville," scolded Veronique.

"All right. Yes, if you insist. I made inquiries at the Floride. André was most helpful. I believe I succeeded in reconstructing your day. I admit it—I am insatiably curious and always have been. If someone is misbehaving beneath my pleasure dome, I want to know about it."

"No misbehaving here, sir," offered Oscar.

Neville turned on him with an expression of such pouting, pitiful sarcasm that Oscar actually flinched. Neville threw up his hands in a gesture of surrender, raised his white eyebrows, shook his head. "Far be it for me—or is it *from* me? In any case I am not the one to judge. . . ."

"Oh do stop," said Veronique. "Can't we be friends?"

"Yes, let's," said Neville, who had finished his drink and seemed to be suffering from its effect and that of its numerous predecessors. "Let's just be friends and *forget* about Herr Hansie, shall we, just *forget*—while we're gallivanting around the inner islands and sipping wine behind the tropical plants, just *forget* about your—"

"I beg you," said Veronique, "to stop."

Neville sulked. Oscar exchanged worried looks with his girlfriend. The miniature waterfalls of the Restaurant du Rocher gurgled and purled.

"Never mind," said Neville with false cheer. "Never mind. Pretend I never said anything. Who listens to ancient people anymore? Do you know that before he died, Somerset—that is, *Willie . . .*"

Oscar and Veronique finished their meal while Neville rattled on about some of the better advice he had received as a young man, all from the mouths of greats.

V

OSCAR STUDIED THE UNEXPECTED SCENE IN HIS HOTEL ROOM: BUNNY Fenton weeping over the *Lowdown*; Bunny Fenton's television voice overdubbing scenes of palm trees and red-tiled Spanish mansions; and Elizabeth, who melted at the slightest sign of human distress, sniffing comfortingly at one of Bunny Fenton's golden ankles. Oscar called room service and ordered coffee for two, then sat on the corner of his bed nearest to where Bunny Fenton sat sobbing.

Oscar was not discerning enough to know if Bunny Fenton wept out of anger or sadness. He told himself to take his time, to analyze the situation, not to leap to apology. Unprepared as he was for a confrontation with one of his caricature subjects, he had long since decided to meet such an eventuality with a forceful attitude of attack-as-best-defense. All he had done, after all, was to offer to the public his own version of Bunny Fenton's stately bosom and peachy pubic region—a fictionalized account, as it were. For the sake of the *Lowdown* lawyers, Oscar could not let her know that he disliked hurting people's feelings; any hint of weakness on that count would amount to begging for a lawsuit, and if Oscar had learned anything at the *Lowdown* it was that rich people sued, and sued often.

It was with some satisfaction that Oscar allowed these thoughts to turn in his mind; it showed a new maturity that he hadn't thrown himself to his knees and pleaded for forgiveness at the first sign that Bunny Fenton might not share the *Lowdown* readers' sense of humor. He crossed his legs and half-yawned and stared at the ceiling, as if such a demonstration of female emotions interrupted him every day, and only his superhuman patience prevented him from calling the hotel bouncers. Elizabeth coiled herself on the floor and cocked her sympathetic head to one side, just as she did on the rare occasions when Oscar was bedridden with flu or hangover. Coffee arrived with the usual ceremony of the newly renovated Domino Hotel, and Oscar could tell that the young waiter was surprised to see Bunny Fenton sitting on one side of the room while her voice emanated from the television on the other. The waiter departed with exaggerated gestures of having seen nothing, heard nothing.

Oscar offered Bunny Fenton a napkin, which she snatched out of his hand as if he had been brandishing a weapon. She blew her nose and wiped her eyes, which was all very normal, but then Oscar watched in amazement as she plunged her hands into her purse and extracted various articles of facial reconstruction and began to rebuild the same icy eyes and fiery hair that glowed from the television across the room.

"There," said Oscar hopefully. "All better?"

"Like hell," said the so-far foul-mouthed Bunny Fenton.

"Oh, come on," said Oscar. "Be reasonable. Laugh a little. Everyone else does."

"They do, do they? They laugh?"

"Sure." Oscar thought he was getting somewhere here.

"Have you put a lot of women on your cover?"

"Plenty. Half, probably."

"All with these?" she asked, lifting the *Lowdown* cover and pointing at Oscar's representation of her own tasseled breasts.

"What, tassels?"

"You know perfectly well what I mean."

"Well, yes, of course. That's the whole point."

"And you just make it up, do you?"

"So far, yes, I have not been on intimate terms with any of my subjects."

"I should say not," said Bunny Fenton, who seemed to be struggling to hold back another wave of tears.

Oscar poured coffee while Bunny Fenton tried to compose herself. He was getting bored with this conversation. He had feared at first that someone of Bunny Fenton's career-mindedness might have been offended on feminist grounds because she was portrayed as a striptease artist, but this did not appear to be the case. She seemed preoccupied only with the golden tasseled breasts.

"Coffee?" Oscar offered, as gently as he could.

"I ought to throw it in your face," said Bunny Fenton, but she accepted the cup without resorting to violence.

Now it was time for Oscar to react in the way he had planned all along. Time for manliness, time for standing up for one's beliefs. He stood up and spoke as forcefully as he knew how.

"That'll be about all the time I have for you then, Miss Fenton," he said. "You can't expect to barge into a man's room and hurl incoherent insults for more than a few minutes before he gets impatient with you. Now that you have threatened to scald my person with coffee, I think perhaps it is time you left me alone to my work." Oscar gestured at the bed covered with nude Jesus caricatures.

"You make me sick," said Bunny Fenton, in tears again, standing shakily and spilling coffee.

"Please, just get out," said Oscar, warming to the tone of voice he imagined his brother would use at particularly sensitive meetings. "Go on," he said, like a sheriff to a saloon brawler, "out you get."

Bunny Fenton whirled around; Oscar was whipped across his left cheek by a wave of her impossible hair, then again for good measure by her right palm. "Don't you *dare* touch me," she said.

Elizabeth leaped onto the bed, careful not to tread on Oscar's work, to get a better look at the evolving fracas.

"And don't you *talk* to me that way," countered Oscar, feeling that it was still incumbent on him to hold the line. "I don't care *who* you are, you don't barge into a man's hotel room uninvited and use childish language and tell him not to *dare* when he asks you to leave. Now out!"

This was a deeply satisfying speech for Oscar. He thought he had come a long way. When he was hit in the face by a flung copy of the *Lowdown*, he felt he was justified in continuing along the same lines.

"Is this what they're looking for in reporters at your ghastly network? Sheer bad manners?" Oscar was flushed with fulfillment. "They've hit a gold mine in you, obviously."

Bunny Fenton stood near the door; her shoulders heaved.

"Is this how you get interviews with the bitchy and acquisitive? Do you *cry*? Do you stamp your little *feet*?" Oscar shook his head and mock-spat as if Bunny Fenton were simply the most pathetic bundle of fur and flesh he had ever encountered. "You really ought to be ashamed, you know," he concluded, crossing his arms and making it clear that she should now depart in disgrace.

Bunny Fenton bit her upper lip. She blinked back another surge of tears. Her crinkled chin trembled. When she finally managed to speak her syllables were aspirated. "*I* should be ashamed? . . . I just wanted to tell you . . . if you had given me a chance . . . I just wanted to warn you . . . that you might be more *careful* in the future." Oscar made an expression of impatience, and flicked his eyebrows at her to tell her to get on with it.

She got on with it. "Does the word 'mastectomy' mean anything to you?"

Bunny Fenton opened the door and charged down the hallway. Oscar turned and looked at his dog.

VI

THE ANTICLIMACTIC—OR RATHER NONCLIMACTIC—HOURS OSCAR HAD spent with Veronique were beginning to take their toll on his psyche. There was no satisfactory explanation that Oscar could see for what amounted to adolescent games, unless it was the possessiveness of her appalling German father. He had begun to wonder, by the time he had survived the relatively chaste if unclothed day on the island, and yet another difficult night seeing Veronique off in a taxi, if he had the courage to see the operation through. Still, this aspect of his new affair did not diminish Oscar's strong feelings for Veronique. He thought and daydreamed about her with inconvenient regularity.

His work suffered. He wanted to draw only lifelike pictures of Veronique's body, hardly a suitable model for his overdue caricature of the American billionaire. He sketched her from memory and pined after the results. He considered, then rejected, the idea of presenting her with a full-color nude of himself in a state of gigantic arousal.

Oscar gnawed on the pleasant but still uncomfortable memory of their two evenings together. Last time a point had been reached—a very specific point—where Veronique protested that self-control was in order. "What do you think you're doing?" she had asked, when Oscar attempted, however gently, to force the issue. Oscar had sat up and stared for a full minute at the horizon—they were stretched out on a blanket on Oscar's terrace—mentally pinching himself to be certain that she had actually uttered such a preposterous question.

Oscar mulled this over in his study, dabbing absentmindedly at the industrial intestines of his transparent billionaire. It was a scorching midday in Val d'Argent; Elizabeth panted in a cooler corner of the room, curled up on the tiles. "What do you think you're doing?" Oscar heard Veronique say. "What do you think you're doing?" Oscar threw himself to the floor and performed fifty therapeutic push-ups.

Living alone, one is liable to become overanalytical. One talks to one's dog. Oscar asked Elizabeth a series of questions, trying to gain insight into the female mind. She waddled over to him with her belly close to the cool floor and lay at his bare feet, listening patiently.

"Clearly you aren't going to answer me," said Oscar at last. "I'll pack up and we'll go for a walk and a bite to eat. That's what dogs and people need."

Strolling downhill to the town center, Oscar raised his face to the hot sun and inhaled the familiar smells of cypress and pine, palm and sea. No one was out on foot at this time of day except for flocks of nuns making their way back from the shops to the small convent higher on the hill than Oscar's house. Oscar nodded hello to the nuns, who were perspiring through the hairlines of their habits with the effort of the climb. The underbrush and succulents on either side of the road made insect noises. At the roundabout that signaled the beginning of the town proper, smells of cooking food reached the walkers— steak and *frites*, sole and butter. Oscar and Elizabeth licked their chops and pressed on.

Once in possession of a newspaper and seated at the Café Floride, Oscar was finally able to drive away the mystery and frustration of his new love affair. He sat outdoors in a corner and held the newspaper in front of his face, fearful of any interruption by the leering Neville Hacking-Cough. Elizabeth crawled into the corner under the shade of Oscar's chair and made herself small. A capacity crowd under the restaurant's broad green awning kept André busy serving ice cream. Stunning Val d'Argent girls gossiped and giggled, gobbled and sipped.

It should not have surprised Oscar that Veronique and Herr Dohrmann arrived at the Café Floride for an early-afternoon snack and a sip of something alcoholic—they did so almost every day. But such was the state of Oscar's puerile infatuation that he had not admitted to himself that his constitutional amounted to nothing less than a deliberate effort to cross paths with his beloved. They arrived together in their sleek black convertible with Veronique at the wheel, and left the ostentatious car half on, half off the pavement with the typical nonchalance of the extremely, terribly, really frightfully rich. Sporting dark glasses and a white jumpsuit, Veronique flounced into the Café Floride as if fending off an invisible gauntlet of photographers. The brooding Herr Dohrmann followed behind, limping, slightly stooped, wearing a blue blazer and white turtleneck, instinctively raising a hand to mask his face from the crowd.

Oscar clutched the newspaper close to his face and felt his heartbeat lurch out of sync as the couple swept past him into the restaurant. Could this spectacular woman—the one who pulled up in a one-has-no-adjectives vehicle, who strode saucily along as if bombarded by photographic flashes, whose slender hips swayed like fronds, whose round brown bosom stared down the choking males who beheld it—could this be the same sweet Veronique who had rubbed coconut oil into Oscar's flaming buttocks only three days ago? This was precisely the question Oscar asked himself. She seemed to be two different women.

Oscar was able to watch from behind his newspaper as André ushered Hansie and Veronique toward a table behind the glass partition between the shady outdoors and the air-conditioned interior. He swiveled on his seat to keep his newspaper between himself and the highly visible pair, and made certain that Elizabeth was well concealed behind his chair. He felt a bump against the glass and knew that either Hansie or Veronique was now no more than an inch away from his left kneecap, through a pane of glass.

Oscar stared into his newspaper and forced himself to read the first words that came into view. They pertained to a local child-murder case with overtones of witchcraft. Even this riveting story could not hold his attention when he knew that by moving his head a few inches to the left he would stare either into the slashed leathery face of Herr Dohrmann, or into the ultra-green eyes of Veronique. He raised a hand to his face, pretending to adjust his hair, and slowly drew the paper to one side. He lowered his head, so that the first thing he saw was a potted plant just beyond the glass. As he lifted his gaze he saw with some relief that it was Hansie's blue-blazered back that faced him.

Veronique's eyes were lowered into her menu, which gave Oscar a chance to mold his mouth and eyes into an expression of relaxed but expectant curiosity, like a fisherman sensing the first intimations of a tug on his line. He told himself to appear blithely indifferent. He could see his reflection in the pane of glass, and reworked his posture so that he looked slightly less like a pitiful spy. Still Veronique did not look up. Poor, sweet Veronique, driven to virtual frigidity by a domineering father— such was Oscar's analysis, at any rate.

Veronique took her time with the menu, so that Oscar was able to observe the donning of Hansie's half-moon reading

glasses as he perused the wine list; Veronique's nervous twid-
dling with a tiny gold earring; Herr Dohrmann's mottled hand
as he turned the plastic-coated pages; Veronique's pursed lips as
she narrowed down her choice of food. Oscar knew he could
not hold such an exceedingly suave pose forever, and had
almost reconsidered his strategy when Veronique looked up to
announce her decision to Hansie. He saw her speak, saw her
eyes wander lazily over Hansie's shoulder and into Oscar's own
eyes, saw her reaction of surprise dissolve into a minor coughing
fit to distract Hansie and prevent him from turning around.
Hansie's suspicions did not appear to have been aroused, or at
least he was preoccupied with the long and well-argued wine
list, so that Oscar felt comfortable staring straight through his
own reflection at Veronique and even launching a silent air-kiss
with puckered lips he hoped would do justice to an Italian film
star.

Now this is very strange indeed, thought Oscar, when he saw
to what lengths Veronique's face and body went to discourage
him from drawing attention to his presence: a shaking of her
head that was no more than a nervous shiver; a flick of her
fingers as if she were shooing away a cockroach; and most of all
a pair of glaring, irate ultra-greens that honestly called daggers
to mind. Veronique's gestures served to paralyze the already
bewildered Oscar, who could react only by solidifying his
evidently inappropriate look. During the confusing few seconds
that followed, Oscar experienced the nauseating sensation of
having a great number of his preconceptions about the state of
his relationship to Veronique ground into small and meaningless particles. He was an ogler outside a restaurant, like fifteen
other men in his section of the café who had not taken their
eyes off Veronique since she had jounced out of her sports car
a minute ago. She did not know him. He was a stranger
behaving rudely.

Veronique had started to make another series of motions

with her head and eyes, as Hansie's attention was given over to ordering food and drink from trusty André. A jutting of her chin, a warning in her ultra-greens, this time carrying a meaning somehow different from her original and all-too-clear "Get lost." Oscar squinted and leaned forward and raised his one free palm, intending to convey the sentence "I don't understand," which as usual was the truth. He could plainly see that Veronique's new meaning was simply "Look out!"

"The heat," said a voice nearby. "Unbearable."

Oscar managed to say "Oh, hello, sir," to Neville Hacking-Cough, without quite falling over backward in his chair.

"People watching, are we?"

"I guess so."

"I was stretching my legs on the jetty, spotted you here on my way in. What a life you lead, dear boy. Toss a bit of paint on paper, then down to the seashore for a breath of air and a snack care of—oh, André, how nice to see you."

Oscar had managed to turn toward Neville while simultaneously interposing himself between the Englishman and the couple indoors.

"Just a coffee for me, André," Neville was saying, as he seated himself. "Oh, and, well, since the wife isn't here, how about one of your splendid martinis, the ones that catch fire in direct sunlight?" André rushed away. "It is my belief," said Neville, lifting his face to the sky, "that the color of one's drink should match the color of the hour: clear martini at sunny summer noon; white wine at twilight; red at sunset; darkest brandy after nightfall." He looked back down at Oscar. "Anything in the papers, young man?"

"A murder or two."

"I meant about *me*."

"Not that I saw, sir."

"I'm surprised you were able to concentrate, what with all the people to look at."

"Hmm?"

"Don't think I didn't notice, my boy. You have the best seat in the house."

"Oh, you mean—" Oscar pointed behind his newspaper at Veronique and Hansie, "you mean *them.*"

"Yes, *them* is precisely what I mean. Like everyone, you seem to be something of a stargazer."

"I was just sitting here, I promise. They walked right by me." Neville had a useful smirk at his disposal. "Tell me something," he said, as André returned with his drinks. "Just who, exactly, *are* you?"

Oscar smiled apologetically at André as he deposited the coffee and martini on the table. Once the waiter was out of earshot, Oscar had a chance to absorb Neville's rather philosophical question. As usual, Neville was in no mood to wait for a reply.

"What I am getting at," said the Englishman, plucking the olive from his drink with slender tanned fingers, "is your *affiliation.*"

"I'm not sure I understand, sir," said Oscar, who was proud of his general lack of attachments.

"Let me try to be clear," said Neville Hacking-Cough, popping the olive into his mouth so that when he spoke he was anything but clear.

"You'll have to repeat that, sir," Oscar said, once Neville had swallowed.

"I am not trying to be unfriendly. I like you. You dived bravely from the cliffs. And you must think I am an awfully strange old man to keep popping up this way." Oscar only half nodded. "But—and I don't know any other way of putting this—I wouldn't say, really, that you quite know your, er, *place.*"

Who *am* I? thought Oscar. What is my *affiliation?* Do I know my *place?* Was this some sort of ontological quiz?

Impatient as ever, Neville continued without waiting for a reply. "I really think this is probably very American of you, actually, to play dumb this way. That's what Americans do, isn't it? They seem so naive, so innocent, so—"

"Ingenuous," said Oscar. "We're all ingenuous, sir. Every single one."

"Temper, temper," said Neville, who had correctly perceived a timbre of sarcasm in Oscar's American accent. "I merely wished to reiterate my warning of a few days ago. What you are doing is irresponsible. Do you realize I am having to keep my voice down because they are *right there?*" Neville jabbed a finger at the interior restaurant.

A terrible thought had dawned on Oscar. He stole a look over his shoulder, through the window, and saw Veronique patting Hansie's hand, looking into the old man's eyes. He turned around and faced Neville once again as the truth burst before his eyes like fireworks. Oscar decided he needed the social equivalent of reading glasses; he suffered from interpersonal myopia. Neville had tried to warn him—how many times now? And only right, too. Oscar would have done the same thing. It was a stunning experience to be released from the darkness of his misunderstanding, to see what had been in front of his nose since the beginning: Neville himself was the mystery suitor, the cause of Veronique's surreptitiousness and indecision. How obvious, and how sad, that Neville was in love with Veronique.

Oscar checked himself just as he was about to say "My God, what a fool I've been," and said instead, "I suppose I should have known."

"What, are you saying you *didn't* know?" Neville had finished his martini and winked at André for another.

"Of course not, how could I?"

Neville Hacking-Cough thought this over. "She never told you?"

"I never asked."

Of course by now Oscar had begun to look upon Neville as a rival. He sat up straighter in his chair and tried to look haughtier-than-thou, which was quite impossible when sitting across from a silver-haired, bullet-eyed English aristocrat, but Oscar gave it his best.

"This is most disturbing," said Neville.

"I agree."

"Really most disturbing. I don't suppose there's any question of your being deterred?"

"No, none," said Oscar. He thought this was the right thing to say to a rival. And just because Hansie and Neville were friends, who was to say Oscar was automatically out of the running? People weren't very straightforward here in Val d'Argent, was what Oscar thought, but he was damned if he would be anything but honest about his own intentions. "None whatsoever," he said, even more forcefully.

"You are making a serious mistake, young man," said Neville, scolding as only the gray and elderly can.

Oscar could at least be satisfied that he held one trump card, which was that only he knew that Veronique had seen Neville's shameless cavorting in the Honclours Caves. Even if she were so open-minded or twisted that Neville's age was not an issue, could Veronique possibly be attracted by so recklessly promiscuous a man? Surely not.

"It is my decision, sir," said Oscar, feeling manlier by the minute.

Neville sighed with what might have been resignation, but was not. "Just look around you, dear boy," he said. "What do you see?"

Oscar shrugged. "Boats?"

"Girls," said Neville. "Look at all the beautiful girls." Oscar looked at all the beautiful girls. "Do you see how marvelous they are?" Oscar nodded; they were marvelous. "Now why not devote your energies and attentions to one of *them*? A good-looking lad like yourself? Wouldn't that simplify matters? You really are out of your depth, if I may say so."

"Say what you like, sir."

The exasperated Neville finished his second drink, then reached into his pocket for money. "It doesn't really matter, all this free advice I'm giving you." Neville stood up, then leaned down and spread his tanned fingers on the table. "You will fail in any case. Good day, Mr. Lemoine."

VII

LIFE'S LITTLE DRAMAS. OSCAR RETREATED FROM THE HALLWAY INTO THE room and sat on his bed next to Elizabeth, amid the naked Saviors.

"Oh, no," he said to his dog. "I feel terrible."

Bunny Fenton was still on the television, reporting the uplifting news that someone very rich was also very happy. Oscar could not take his eyes off her misinterpreted chest. He backpedaled along his bed, drew back the covers, and slid beneath them fully clothed, under his renderings of Jesus.

When his telephone rang, Oscar cursed the *faux-français* switchboard of the Domino Hotel. He answered gruffly.

"Who is it?"

"What's this 'No calls' stuff then, little brother?" said George Lemoine. "Shouldn't that be 'No calls except George's?' Luckily I still have clout at the Domino."

"Where are you?"

"I can't be too precise about that, Oscar. Top secret. I'm in the back of someone's limo, circling Boston." And drinking, Oscar surmised from his brother's singsong voice. "But listen, enough about me. I only wanted to . . ."

George repeated the apology for his behavior the previous evening, forgetting that he had already done so en route from Philadelphia. Oscar lay back on his bed and listened to his brother's rambling sentences.

"Hey, do you have a minute?" asked George, once he had finished promising never to fall asleep in public again.

"Sure."

"This is serious. I've made a decision, just this morning. Touching down in Boston, I decided."

"What did you decide?"

"I decided that I have to get married. That's really why I'm calling. I need your approval."

Since when, Oscar wondered, did George need his approval for anything?

"You've met her. Not under ideal conditions, of course, but still. You got a gander. I need to know what you think. Am I crazy?"

Oscar had to avoid voicing his first reaction, which of course was one of horror that George would want further to complicate his life with Diana Burke. With the direct question "Am I crazy?" still buzzing in his left ear, he had to choke back the automatic affirmative that would have been his natural response.

"Not that I know of," he said. "Of course I only had the merest glimpse."

"But what a doll, am I right?"

"Yes." George's was an apt enough description of the diminutive Diana.

"Hell," said George. "Traffic jam. I don't even know where we're going."

"Can't you find out?"

"My driver is about twenty feet away, behind bulletproof glass."

"I see."

"It's nice to have the kid brother back Stateside."

"Yes." Oscar could now clearly hear the sound of glass and ice cubes raised to George's mouth.

"I'm tired. I think maybe my seat pulls out into a bed. There's room, you know. Turn on the tube, stretch out, cop a nap . . ."

"Why don't you do that, then? Get some rest."

"Right. Well, thank you, then, little brother. I knew you'd approve. A match made in heaven. Maybe a little niece or nephew for you."

"We'll see."

George yawned, and signed off with a breathy "Good night."

Oscar replaced the receiver, thinking how quickly things seemed to happen here at home, and remembering the sense of panic that had sent him into exile. Remembering Val d'Argent, he decided that even deep humiliation crept up slowly in that more relaxed climate.

VIII

AFTER NEVILLE'S STERN WARNING AT THE RESTAURANT OSCAR KEPT TO himself and his work. He did not see Veronique again for more than a week, except in a series of almost pathologically steamy dreams. He spent his spare time arranging Elizabeth's retrospective exhibit with Monsieur Berlinger, and selecting a dozen or so of her most intriguing canvases. A consummate artiste, Elizabeth ignored the selection process and made it clear that an animal of her creative powers was above the mundane business of arranging a simple viewing.

Monsieur Berlinger agreed that Val d'Argent was a more suitable venue for Elizabeth's work than any of the places he normally booked in the larger city down the coast: she was known and liked by the community; most of her paintings had been inspired by Val d'Argent; and between them Oscar and Monsieur Berlinger could rustle up a handful of the richest people in Europe who might be convinced to part with the large sums her labrador paintings deserved to command.

Oscar packed each painting with care and stacked them in the front hall of his house. When he was finished he took Elizabeth out onto the terrace and explained to her that in exchange for all his hard work he wanted a one hundred percent commission on her earnings in perpetuity. The canine artist did not dispute this arrangement.

Now Oscar was rich, but lonely. He thought over what Neville had said about the countless desirables of downtown Val d'Argent, but could not agree that Veronique was replaceable. Certainly his admiration for her was no more than a couple of well-tanned skin-layers deep for the moment, but he found himself already reminiscing fondly about their infrequent hours together—the day Elizabeth helped introduce them at the party, the Honclours Caves, the Café Floride, Tristan and Isolde—and thinking that they tended to have a great deal of fun together. Oscar had come to feel that he was on a romantic mission of liberation. He had infiltrated the citadel, and all that remained was to free the imprisoned maiden.

But, predictably enough, he did not dare telephone Veronique—or at least every time he dialed her number he made sure to hang up after no more than a ring or two. He scoured the waterfront every evening hoping for another chance encounter, but for a week not even Neville Hacking-Cough was bumped into.

Oscar finally met Veronique again at a club called Le Village, where the trendiest young locals had congregated to hear the act of the week, a poetic French crooner and guitarist named Antoine. Oscar arrived early and stationed himself near the back so that he could both see the door and be protected at least in part from Antoine's droning voice. Antoine sang badly out of tune, which to the Val d'Argent audience was an indication of deep soulfulness. He sang songs about village life and love of one's mother. He was accompanied on acoustic bass by a tragic young woman whose painted fingernails were too long to make proper contact with the neck and strings of an instrument that dwarfed and overwhelmed her in any case. When she leaned over her microphone and sang her nails-on-blackboard harmonies, it was all Oscar could do to keep his teeth in his head. French people loved this music.

Oscar had nearly decided to leave when he spotted Veronique in the doorway, accompanied by a substantial entourage of colorfully dressed pleasure-seekers—guardians of the citadel, Herr Dohrmann's storm troopers. Veronique wore a snug sailor's shirt and what looked like satin trousers that were tight at the ankles above her high-heeled sandals. Those around her looked like various flavors of sorbet, and were showing signs of already enjoying themselves on an unimaginable scale. They tossed their heads and guffawed, shouted greetings to friends, called for drinks, and made so much noise that the hapless Antoine had to wind down his song about first love and take five.

Oscar suddenly felt physically puny and insecure. As a rule, the American cartoonist was uncomfortable in the presence of people who were so overtly in the throes of "fun," and never more so than now, when Veronique would not fail to spot him in the small crowd—alone, subdued, no fun at all. Oscar had to act quickly if he hoped to be successful in portraying himself as a fun-lover and liberate Veronique from her guards: it would require a shift from coffee to alcohol; a complete make-over of his facial expression into one of carefree abandon and scorn for those incompetents who failed to take supreme advantage of every *second* of their lives; and possibly an outburst directed at the musicians, just to make it clear that a man of his pleasure-quotient did not have to put up with inferior entertainment. It did not occur to Oscar that he ought to be himself.

Now that Veronique and her mostly male chaperones had arrived, the clientele of Le Village became more animated, safe in the knowledge that they were at the hub of Val d'Argent society. The waiters broke into a collective sweat as champagne was ordered from every corner of the room. Antoine and his girlfriend looked on apprehensively from the wings, doubtful that they would be allowed to return to the stage. Oscar clung to the shadows and ordered a local and nearly hallucinogenic beverage called Coeur de Lyon. An illegal member of the absinthe family, Coeur de Lyon was served in a bottle marked with the label of a common *pastis*. You really had to *be* someone to be served Coeur de Lyon, or like Oscar you had to have been told the password used at Le Village. Oscar had tried the drink only once before, under excruciating peer pressure, and from what he could remember of the experience he knew that two or three diluted ounces of the stuff transformed him into precisely the kind of boisterous bastard he hoped to become before Veronique picked him out of the crowd.

A waiter bearing Oscar's bottle of Coeur de Lyon arrived while Veronique and her glamorous guardians were still making the rounds of acquaintances seated nearer the front of the club. The waiter poured carefully, and stood back. With a suave but impatient gesture Oscar communicated to the waiter that he wished to be served something more along the lines of a triple. The waiter hesitated, perhaps fearing the destruction of club property, then poured away with a cautionary click of his tongue. One part water, one part Coeur de Lyon, and Oscar had before him a cloudy liquid the color of—as he had once heard Neville put it at a party where the beverage had been served—tubercular mucus. Oscar closed his eyes and gulped down the medicinal mixture, feeling terribly *louche* and existential.

His fire-breathing grimace to the waiter signified "Once again," and once again the waiter reluctantly poured. There was an anesthetic ingredient in Coeur de Lyon, so that the drink's first effect was a pleasant numbing of the lips. The second noticeable effect was an ominous warming in the belly like the welling of magma before eruption. Oscar paid his tab so that he would be free to move about the club—and because he suspected this might be his last chance to conform to society's preferred norms of behavior. He took a quick pulse reading for future reference, smoothed his hair with sweating palms, and stood up to step into a smoky blue spotlight as Veronique and her entourage neared.

Their recognition and greeting came off well, by Oscar's standards; he knew that jet-setters greeted one another in public like siblings separated by years of hardship and war. They whooped and shrieked and threw out their arms and pranced across the crowded floor, flung themselves into each other's embrace, kissed each other's coconut-scented cheeks, stood at arm's length and shook their heads in amazement at the sheer beauty they beheld, then repeated the shrieks and hugs and kisses for good measure. Oscar had never before been able even to pretend to greet someone with this amount of exuberance, but with a dangerous dose of Coeur de Lyon flooding his brain he was able to pull it off like a native Val d'Argentian.

Introductions were made in several languages. Oscar recognized many of Veronique's ornamental friends from the cliff-diving party, and they, in turn, recognized him. Most said they had since been worried about his physical well-being. One said he thought the judges had robbed him of rightful victory. Another suggested that next year an alternative diving competition should be organized for suicidally inclined nudists. A woman said, in German, that Oscar had a very large penis. Someone else said something in Italian, and Oscar pretended he understood by laughing and jabbing a fist playfully at the young man's shoulder. Soon he realized that he had been swept to the other side of the room in the tide of their friendly greetings, and was seated at a round table next to Veronique with the heavily accented password for Coeur de Lyon being shouted out recklessly by a German youth.

The men spoke animatedly in English. The women looked beautiful. There was no doubting who was the leader of this tribe, even though Oscar considered her their prisoner: although she did not often speak, every remark was addressed to Veronique. The same waiter who had served Oscar arrived with the falsely marked bottle. When he saw the cartoonist he flared a nostril and raised a despairing eye to the ceiling as he regretfully poured. Oscar smiled back at him wickedly and ordered him to leave the bottle on the table. He felt that he was probably going to die tonight anyway, and that he might as well go out seeing the colorful vistas of paradise the drink was liable to project onto one's eyelids.

Oscar did his best to hurl a few opinions into the conversation, which from what he could understand centered prematurely on skiing. He was asked if he was a skier, and if he would join them when the season arrived. Oscar shoved a hand into his shirt-front, *à la Bonaparte*, and said, "There shall be no Alps."

Oscar felt distinctly at the center of things, partly because he sat so close to Veronique, but also because as the only American at the table he found himself interrogated on all sides about his influential country. The French asked about film

Paul Micou

directors; the Italians wanted to know about film stars; the Germans needed their theories confirmed about the status of certain kinds of wildly expensive cars. In his present state, Oscar had something to say to everyone.

"What you have to understand," he said to the company at large, although it was not at all in Oscar's nature to be pedagogic, "is that while people like us all around the world are discussing America, Americans simply couldn't give a toss." Oscar had learned this expression from Neville Hacking-Cough, and though he knew its idiomatic meaning, he mistakenly believed that it derived from an arcane rule of cricket. He was beyond knowing what he said, much less the crude origins of the words he used to put his disjointed points across.

Oscar continued in this irresponsible and ill-informed manner, and thought that his soliloquy was going over well with the assembled jet-setters. Inexperienced as he was with mind-altering chemicals, Oscar became apprehensive when he felt the stirrings of an out-of-body experience, but he was not deterred. For the benefit of his own table he sang ("Darling, *Je Vous Aime Beaucoup*"). When Antoine and his disheveled sidekick took the stage once more, Oscar joined in the jeering that sent them scurrying back into the wings like cockroaches fleeing light. A member of Oscar's group took the microphone from its stand and brought it back to the table so that all of Le Village could be entertained by the cartoonist's rambunctiousness. Oscar put his arm around Veronique's shoulders, raised the microphone to his lips, and sang a perennial French love song. A spotlight was swiveled to highlight the romantic couple. The crowd joined in the singing, swayed in the hazy candlelight, begged for more when he was done.

It could not be said that Oscar was consciously aware of what was happening to him. He would recall most of his activity in nightmarish flashbacks spread over the next few days, assembling against his will pieces of the evening's puzzle that would form a practically cubist image of reality. For the time being life passed before Oscar's eyes in a swirl of disconnected scenes, requiring all his concentration merely to grasp one frame at a time: the singing of love songs; the tabletop Greek dancing with the German youth who had ordered the Coeur de Lyon; the misunderstanding with the management when the table gave way; further dancing on stage with the limber Veronique; a touch of delightful exhibitionism from another girl who shook and paraded herself along the lip of the stage; the abrupt and confusing exit through a fire door into a cobbled back street; the distorted faces of his companions in the streetlights as they rebounded off one another and produced champagne bottles and sent corks soaring into the starlit sky.

Oscar had not stopped to wonder who these people were, even as he ran naked across the beach with them and threw himself into the sobering sea; even as a girl stubbed her toe nearby and he tried to carry her from the water, only to fall backward with the naked girl flailing and yelping on top of him; even as Oscar himself was finally carried from the water in a fit of uncontrolled laughter by the German youth; even as he was buried in the sand by all of the naked people and threatened with death-by-rising-tide. Oscar laughed and wriggled and asked no questions.

The night grew increasingly complicated, and therefore more difficult to piece together later on. A certain amount of drunken driving followed Oscar's disinterment, along with fresh-water swimming, hot-tub soaking, speedboat racing, and a long period of total unconsciousness during which he may, for all he knew, have traveled great distances in a hot-air balloon. He would retain a fixed memory of finding himself alone with Veronique in the master bedroom of a yacht; of listening to her animated discussion of the brandies she intended to make him taste; of tasting the brandies; of reeling under their effects and the sick-making motion of the yacht; of being unclothed for perhaps the tenth time that night; of slipping and sliding on silk sheets and thinking that there must be a polite way to tell a woman that, while one considers this a truly magical moment, one is afraid one's imminent vomiting will spoil the occasion.

So much for the jigsaw of Oscar's big night on the town. He was next aware of his existence when he opened his eyes to hot sunshine and the reviving tongue not of Veronique, but of Elizabeth. When she saw her master awake, Elizabeth's expression changed from one of concern to one of censure. She seemed to know that his wounds were self-inflicted. Oscar raised his leaden head and saw that he lay in the center of his own driveway, near the gate, like a corpse thrown on an enemy's turf *pour encourager les autres*.

IX

"THAT'S VERY BAD," SAID WUNDERKIND BRIAN FABLE, REFERRING TO Oscar's run-in with Bunny Fenton. "We have to avoid this sort of thing. Couldn't you have . . . no, I suppose you couldn't." Predictably enough, one of the day's tabloids had carried a story, leaked by the unethical Domino Hotel room-service waiter, concerning Bunny Fenton's tearful confrontation with the cartoonist.

"The poor woman," said a chagrined Oscar Lemoine. "Can't you please slow down? You're making Elizabeth sick." Fable's powerful car, so often caged by traffic, hurtled down deserted Park Avenue well ahead of the synchronized lights. Elizabeth thudded around in the backseat.

"Just what we don't need, stories like this. And now she's likely to do her own story on it, maybe even reveal her illness and operation. Great self-promotion, sympathy ratings. You'll be crucified." With Fable it was always "we" in triumph, "you" in adversity.

Fable was in an even more irritable mood than usual because he had struck and injured a pedestrian earlier in the day, costing himself several minutes of precious time. "I hate it when that happens," he said. "Lazy people dawdling in front of cars. Lucky she wasn't killed."

"Lucky for whom?"

Fable ignored the question. "The ambulance took forever to get there."

Despite these remarks, Oscar did not consider Brian Fable to be a bad man. Stupid, maybe, but not inherently *bad*. He blundered about in his big car and every now and then someone misstepped and was crushed beneath his wheels. Powering around in this way since he was old enough to knock over a cocktail tray, Fable had met no resistance along the way more inconvenient than a law suit or flat tire—both easily overcome by ready money. Like Oscar's brother, Fable was an articulate spokesman in defense of those who were persecuted by the masses for appearing to have more fun and comfort than anyone else, when in fact they considered themselves *volunteers*, men who could just as easily buy islands in the South Pacific rather than burden themselves with the fine-tuning of mankind's socioeconomic progress.

"We have to talk," said Fable. "I mean really talk."

"Shoot."

"The *Lowdown* is sitting on a cultural fence," said Fable. "Or at least, that's how it has been put to me. The idea is—or, this is what my people are telling me—the idea is that we have to go one direction or the other. We have a choice. One way, the other way. We pick."

Fable was not the most well-spoken man in the world, but his inarticulateness in this case was partly attributed to the three red lights he ran waiting for the next series of greens to begin. His gangly legs and arms worked the controls of his vehicle as if he were running late for the last flight out of a city under nuclear attack.

"Give me a clue," said Oscar, gripping his door handle for support.

"One way, uhm, you know, stay the course, medium, I don't know, retrenchment, see it through. The other, the different way, maybe more of something else."

"Thank you, Brian," said Oscar. "Crystal clear."

"Sorry. I've got a lot on my plate. The *Lowdown* isn't exactly . . ." (here Fable narrowly avoided collision and caused a law-abiding driver to swerve) ". . . at the head of the list. I'm talking about pornography."

"Whose pornography. My pornography?"

"You haven't been reading the magazine."

"There's pornography in the *Lowdown*?"

"I'm told, they say, some say, that we're more or less sort of teetering toward a certain demographic kind-of-maybe *group*. I tried to tell you this the other night, I've been trying to tell you. We were really making inroads, but now you're being misunderstood."

"Are you selling the magazine, Brian?"

"Did I say that? Did I say that?"

Oscar tried to imagine Brian Fable's life during his absence. Here was a man who had no need to feign reckless abandon. During Oscar's time out of the city, while the cartoonist went studiously about the business of participating in irresponsible youth, Fable had been rocketing around this filthy city, barking into his phone, pouring out money to solve his problems and survive. Meanwhile, Oscar had it on fairly good authority, Fable had paused in his enterprises to impregnate the unfortunate Gail Gardener. This was a topic he hoped to bring up as soon as they reached their destination.

"Can I ask you a question, Brian?" Oscar asked, reaching into the backseat to calm Elizabeth with a tickle under her chin.

"Anything." .

"Where are we going?"

Fable thought for a moment. "Oh, well, back to your hotel, I suppose. I like to take meetings in my car."

X

OSCAR HAD NO IMMEDIATE PLANS TO GET UP OFF THE GROUND.

"I'm alive, and that's the important thing," he said to Elizabeth. "Don't look at me that way. This was all done for a good cause. I'm going to liberate Veronique from the citadel. I have breached the gates. I have ingratiated myself with her guards. All that remains is to take on the awesome Herr Dohrmann, who probably keeps her manacled to a wall and makes her sleep on a pile of straw. Like all good knights I have a rival, Neville the Aged, but he too will be dealt with ruthlessly. No ruth whatsoever."

Oscar babbled away and felt life return to his limbs. Elizabeth stared through the gates to the sea.

"I wonder how I got here," Oscar said aloud. "Veronique would not have deposited me here so callously. Was it one of my corevelers? Or Hansie himself? Whose boat was I on? And what about that slipping and sliding on silky sheets with the fair

Veronique? I find it hard to believe that I was a maker of love, don't you?"

Elizabeth looked as if she doubted it too.

"Not to worry, Elizabeth. It is fated."

Boom went one of Anton's bombs in the sprawling back gardens of his parents' villa.

Oscar heard the sound of tires slowing on the road outside his gate.

"Oh, no," he said, trying to open his eyes. "They've come back to finish me off."

But no, it was Monsieur Berlinger, in his rickety van, come to bring Oscar his art supplies.

"I hope he doesn't run over me," Oscar said.

Elizabeth stood up and barked, which alerted Monsieur Berlinger. The Frenchman leaped from his van, believing perhaps that his friend the American artist had died. He rushed to Oscar's side and leaned down into Oscar's field of view.

"It's okay," said Oscar in French. "I'm perfectly all right."

"You are not injured?"

"Strictly speaking, yes I am. I had a great deal to drink last night. I just woke up a few minutes ago."

"Oh la la," said Berlinger disgustedly. He was fed up with drunken artists. Perhaps that is why he liked Elizabeth so much.

"If you could just put the things in the house," said Oscar. "You know where they go. I think I'll just stay here for a little while longer."

FOUR

I

"WHAT HAVE THEY DONE TO YOUR HOTEL? IT'S REPULSIVE."

At last Oscar had contained Brian Fable in the Domino Bar, where he could pin him down for a talk. To center a conversation with Fable was nearly impossible without verbally shaking him by the lapels.

"Now try to grasp what I am about to say to you, Brian. It is important. I feel unclean even knowing about this, and I don't want to have to say it more than once."

"Shoot." Fable looked at his watch, tried to catch the bartender's eye, patted his breast pocket for important scraps of paper.

"Listen to me."

"You bet."

"Gail Gardener asked me to ask you if you were serious about marrying her. She claims to be pregnant. She says you are the father. That's all I have to tell you. Clear?"

"Oh, *fuck*," said Fable.

"Probably . . ."

Oscar tried to imagine himself on the receiving end of this news: the whimpering, the pleading, the gnashing of teeth, the selling of his soul to turn back the clock. No such reaction from Brian Fable.

"Stupid, stupid woman," he said. "Now who's going to take care of this?"

In Fable's world, evidently, Gail was on a par with the woman who had been careless enough to step in front of his speeding car.

"She can't prove it," said Fable.

"I think there are tests."

"Not a problem."

"But the poor—"

"It isn't going to happen. Listen, how about doing me this little favor. I'm sure she respects you. Will you just have a talk with her and say that I—"

"Absolutely not. Never."

"*Ingrate.*"

"Call her from your car, then."

"Aw, get *you*. You pop in here from your French paradise, you stir up this thing, and you can't even do your old friend one tiny favor. And you're getting sarcastic on me. The man they called Disloyal."

Oscar was having a bad time in New York. After little more than a week he had become embroiled in one public scandal and at least two private ones that he could remember. Fable began to list the ways in which Oscar was indebted to him—his job, his guest cottage in Val d'Argent, his very identity.

"But forget I asked," said Fable. "I'll handle it."

"Oh, no you don't," said Oscar, drawing on the steely

personality he thought he had forged in Val d'Argent. "You cannot possibly make me feel guilty. I quit, okay? No Jesus caricature for you this Christmas. No sirree. Wild horses couldn't—"

"I think I get your meaning, Oscar."

"You must see Gail all the time. Isn't it something you think you should talk about?"

"That's where you're wrong, pal. You think I hang around the *Lowdown* all day long? Things have changed. I keep my distance. I do not fraternize with employees. They live in constant fear of a surprise inspection. I think I've seen Gail twice in half a year. Once at the party—you were there—and once . . . well, you can imagine."

"Sure."

"What a big mistake she's making, involving you. It's a pitiful plea for attention."

"You make it sound like a suicide attempt. It's sort of the opposite, having a baby."

"Gah, don't say that word."

"I'm only supposed to be conveying a message to you. But I think I should add that she struck me as desperate. You mustn't treat this too lightly."

"Done." Fable looked at his watch. "There will be an abortion."

II

IT WAS EARLY AFTERNOON WHEN OSCAR STARTED TO CRAWL TOWARD his house on the hot gravel of his driveway; Elizabeth watched his progress from the shade of the front porch. Anton had finished defoliating his parents' gardens and had popped over to see what his American neighbor was up to. Anton wore a Hawaiian shirt and shorts, wraparound dark glasses, and over-sized black paratrooper boots. He stood over Oscar's worm-like body with a realistic-looking assault rifle cradled in his arms, and said something in German that sounded threatening.

"Leave me alone," said Oscar, although in French it came out rather more crudely.

Anton did not leave him alone. Anton was a sadist. Anton wanted to dance in circles around Oscar's helpless crawling body. Anton wanted to play out battlefield fantasies. He pointed his weapon at Oscar's head and made sound effects of devastating firepower. During the ten minutes it took for Anton to lose interest in torturing his nearly lifeless victim and run away, Oscar managed to crawl within a few feet of Elizabeth and shelter.

Oscar almost never lost his patience with Elizabeth, but at times like these, when she was so clearly posing as his conscience, he wished he spoke her language so that he could tell her to lighten up. As it was he was able to groan a few indecent words and phrases at her as he crawled past, hand over fist, and made his slimy way to the stairs. Stair by stair, left cheek close to the cool stone steps, Oscar hauled himself to the landing. Exhausted by his progress, he was reduced to moving like a giant tortoise, his flipper arms and legs propeling him down the hallway in increments of inches. He comforted himself with the realization that he would never, ever, have to pause for thought when asked to identify the worst hangover of his life.

First stop, the shower just outside his bedroom. He crawled into the tiled room, into the shower, and lay coiled around the drain. He rested for a quarter of an hour before lunging at the cold-water tap, which he was able to turn on full blast before collapsing back onto the cool tiles.

"Oh, my clothes," he gargled.

He undressed like an escape artist releasing himself from a straitjacket. When he opened his eyes he noticed an assortment of marks and bruises on his body that reminded him of further misadventures in the night; in particular the thin red stripe across his chest confirmed that he had, indeed, as he had vaguely remembered while lying in his driveway, supported his naked self against a shipboard stay while vomiting copiously into the oily harbor.

He lay in the stream of water and thought about beautiful paintings. Elizabeth dropped by to make sure he had not drowned. She poked into the shower stall and looked down her muzzle at her disgraced master.

Oscar thought he was having a premonition of a telephone call until he realized that his telephone actually was ringing. He did not even consider letting it ring unanswered, despite the effort that would be required to answer it. He was eager to learn more about his night on the town, and convinced that Veronique was the caller. He struggled blindly out of the shower and staggered down the hall to his bedroom. Elizabeth trotted ahead.

He crawled into his bedroom at labrador level—around the

bed, over to the table near the window—and lashed out at the telephone until the receiver fell onto the carpet within his grasp. He found it easiest simply to lie on top of the receiver with his ear pressing it to the floor.

"So," he said into the phone, mightily pleased that Veronique had decided to call him as soon as she recovered, and grateful that whatever it was that he had done to her had not ruptured their friendship forever. "All rested, are we?"

"Mister Lemoine," came the familiar voice. "Neville here. I do hope I'm not disturbing your work."

"No no, " said Oscar. "I was just knocking off for the day." Oscar held onto the receiver and dragged himself to the wall where he could attempt to sit up and reach his bed.

"The reason I'm phoning is that old Hansie rang me a few moments ago. It appears that Veronique has gone missing. I didn't say anything to him about you, of course, fair play and all that, but I confess that a, er, *sighting* was made late last night. I thought you might have some intelligence in the matter that I could pass on to my very worried friend."

"A *sighting*, eh? You were on patrol, were you?"

"Taking a stroll, dear boy. A particularly boisterous group trundled past me. I noticed that the men appeared to be carrying a dead body, which aroused my curiosity. On closer inspection I saw that it was *your* body, and because I am speaking to you now I can safely conclude that you were not dead at the time. Veronique was also in the group, looking marvelous even in a state of some drunkenness. Very unlike her, actually."

"And she isn't at home?" This worrying development had nudged Oscar back into consciousness, so that he was able to pull himself into a quasisitting position with the aid of a chest of drawers, close enough to his bed so that soon he would be able to fall back into the desired prone position.

"No, she is not. And I'm sure you will recognize that in the circumstances it would behoove you to tell me everything you know. Hansie is frightfully worried about kidnapping."

It was going to be embarrassing for Oscar to tell the truth, which was that he had only the vaguest recollection of the last time he had seen Veronique. Besides, he was not certain he could trust that his rival, Neville the Aged, was leveling with him. Nevertheless he intended to do what he could to help, because it was truly disturbing that Veronique had not gone home: this could mean she had spent the night with any number of the citadel's guards.

"I can't deny that I was with Veronique and her friends at some point last night," he said, stalling for time, struggling to sit up.

"Of course not. The question is, what have you done with her?"

"Now just hold on a second, Neville," said Oscar, falling with a grunt onto his bed. "You aren't suggesting—"

Oscar was interrupted by a long brown arm that flopped onto his chest. He gasped and turned to see Veronique sprawled on the other side of his bed.

"Are you there? What's the matter?"

"No, I'm . . . I'm fine. Spilled a bit of paint on my shoes."

"This is very serious. I assure you that if you are hiding something from me I will have no choice but to pass on this information to my friend."

"I've told you everything I know. I promise." Lying would not have come so easily to Oscar if he had been given a chance to think it over, but faced with a sleeping or possibly dead Veronique in direct contact with him, it took all of his concentration merely to speak. "To tell you the truth I'm not even sure how *I* got home last night. She'll turn up. She's probably having a restorative drink at the Floride by now."

"Well, if she is the gendarmes will find her. They are on full alert. I thank you for telling me what you know, but *do* try to be more responsible in future, won't you, dear boy?"

Oscar signed off and asked Elizabeth to replace the receiver for him because he was incapacitated by Veronique's arm and his own considerable paralysis. He felt Veronique's pulse and diagnosed hangover, nothing worse.

This was what revelry and wild abandon begot, thought Oscar: a cartoonist soaking wet, naked, and half paralyzed, in bed with the object of an Interpol dragnet.

III

"THERE WILL BE AN ABORTION," BRIAN FABLE SAID, BEFORE SPEEDING away with ample excuses about fleeting time and its general dearth.

Oscar was left in the Domino bar to order coffee and mentally cross one obligation off his list, having conveyed Gail's depressing message to Fable. He flipped through his remaining duties until a harried-looking Philippe, the pseudo-French Domino employee in whom Oscar had entrusted Elizabeth's care for the evening, rushed into the bar.

"Mister Lemoine," said Philippe, who in his excitement had abandoned his French accent.

"Hmm?"

"Come quick, man. It's your dog."

The chilling statement had Oscar out of his chair and across the lobby and into the elevator before he could begin to ask Philippe what was the matter.

"*Onze, onze!*" they shouted in unison into the elevator's ceiling.

"*Merci, messieurs,*" came the calm canned voice.

"She doesn't look good," said Philippe. "I checked her every half hour as you said, I promise."

"Don't worry," said Oscar, who had always striven to be magnanimous in a crisis. "Whatever it is, it isn't your fault. You did the right thing to get me at once."

"I only gave her a bit of chocolate," said Philippe.

"Fine. Don't worry. Indigestion, maybe."

"I don't think so," said Philippe, as the elevator doors parted on the eleventh floor.

Oscar streaked down the ersatz Hall of Mirrors with Philippe on his heels and used the domino-colored pass card to open his door.

"By the window behind the bed," said Philippe.

Oscar found it difficult to walk all the way across Room 1107 and look behind the bed, partly because his knees had gone weak, and partly because he didn't want to see what Philippe had told him was there. Halfway across the room he turned and instructed Philippe to go down and call a doctor, and to search the guest list for vets.

When Philippe had raced away Oscar stole across the carpet and forced himself to look behind the bed, next to the window: Elizabeth lay on the floor with her muzzle halfway out the six-inch opening Oscar had left in the window to give her air; her eyes were wildly white and her ears were drawn back against her head like a terrified horse; her rib cage heaved and her gums flapped against her teeth as she sucked filthy New York air through the crack in the window.

As Oscar gently lifted Elizabeth into his arms her legs flailed in space and her dry tongue fell limply between her teeth. He tore a blanket from the bed, wrapped her in it, sat down in his drawing chair, and held her in his lap. Philippe rushed back into the room a few minutes later to say that a doctor had been summoned. Oscar acknowledged this news with a nod but made it clear that he preferred to wait alone. After Philippe retreated, Oscar tried to soothe Elizabeth with a few words of comfort, but found himself straying into an apology for having brought her back to New York in the first place. He did so because he knew, deep down, that whatever a doctor might say about her condition, this was no natural deterioration, no illness associated with age, no indigestion or heart palpitation or stroke: this was an attempted suicide. As far as Oscar was concerned Elizabeth had tried to throw herself out of the window on the eleventh floor of the Domino Hotel.

"I should never have brought you back," Oscar said. He rocked Elizabeth as he spoke. Her breathing seemed to slow somewhat, but her eyes remained wild. "It's all my fault. You always did hate it here." Oscar knew that his decision to move away had been based in part on his concern for Elizabeth's welfare. The thought of his labrador living out her twilight days in the inhuman—not to say uncanine—atmosphere of New York had been intolerable to contemplate. Being a poor dog artist in New York was no way to live. Squalid digs and vicious streets combined with the insecurities and health hazards inherent in the life of the creative artist: Elizabeth had needed a break.

"And now this," Oscar was saying, as a young doctor in hospital whites entered with the still-frazzled Philippe in tow.

When Oscar asked him if he were a human doctor, the young man said "Very funny," and Oscar didn't understand this remark because he had forgotten for the moment how to joke. The doctor worked briskly, lowered Elizabeth onto the bed, looked into her eyes, took her pulse, and felt her chest. Without asking Oscar's permission he gave Elizabeth an injection in her thigh, and began to pack up his equipment without explanation.

"A week's rest," he said. "Shipshape, for such an old dog."

Oscar felt the usual embarrassment of having taken up as much as five minutes of a real doctor's time for the sake of an animal, so he did not pry. He thought he knew what the problem was: Elizabeth had suffered a nervous breakdown; she had tried to end it all.

It was not long before Elizabeth showed signs that the drug was taking effect. Her eyelids drooped and her legs stopped shivering. Oscar covered her with the blanket and left her on the bed. Before she fell asleep Oscar swore to her that after her recovery he would have her back in Val d'Argent before she could say "Arf."

IV

DARKNESS FELL IN VAL D'ARGENT LONG BEFORE OSCAR AND VERONIQUE awoke. It took some time for Oscar to remember his conversation with Neville Hacking-Cough, and even longer to explain it to a very puzzled Veronique as they lay in bed recuperating.

"This is very, *very* bad," she said, after swallowing four aspirin. "Hansie will be so cross."

"I was a little more worried about the *gendarmes*, frankly. They could burst in at any moment."

"I think that's just Neville exaggerating as usual. He loves to get his teeth into a crisis. I will make some telephone calls soon and straighten everything out, don't you worry. We will organize an alibi."

Oscar was dying to ask Veronique how much she remembered of the previous night.

"I've been piecing things together," he said, broaching the subject as gingerly as he knew how. "I have a feeling there was a certain amount of drinking going on."

"You were so funny in that scuba gear," said Veronique.

"Oh, yes," said Oscar. He remembered nothing about scuba gear. "Silly me. Whose yacht was that?"

"It belongs to Alain's father and mother."

"Alain?"

"You remember, the tall one with the red hair who made you put clothes on before we went back to shore."

"Of course. Alain."

"You insisted on wearing one of his mother's frocks."

"How did I look?"

"Ravishing. Better than Alain's mother, I assure you."

"Ah. And speaking of ravishing . . . " But Oscar could not bring himself to ask. Instead he asked her how she thought he ended up in his driveway, and she in his bed.

Veronique giggled and winced and held her aching head. "If you don't remember *that* . . . "

"I honestly don't," Oscar admitted.

"You weren't exactly well, on the boat."

"Oh?"

"Then you got your second wind and wanted to drive Alain's car."

"I wasn't being nice to Alain."

"I'm sure he thought you were very amusing."

"And?"

"Alain's car is fast. You said you had never been in such a car, and wanted to 'test your skills.'"

"And?"

"And you tested your skills all the way to the roundabout past the Floride, where you went round and round and round until you had to stop to be sick again."

"I hate myself."

"Then Alain started to drive us home, stopping at your house first. You were being gallant again. You told Alain to 'bugger off,' I think it was, and you took me inside. Then suddenly you said you had to walk your dog before joining me. I was feeling very tired anyway. You said you were going to be right back after 'interviewing the nuns.' What does this mean?"

"Research."

"Interviewing the nuns?"

"Trust me."

"You have a funny job. Last time you were researching was in the Honclours Caves."

"That I remember."

"You poor boy," said Veronique, rolling onto one elbow and looking down at the ravaged cartoonist. "You never came back and I fell asleep. They shouldn't have made you drink all the Coeur de Lyon."

"It was my fault." Oscar felt a genuine confession coming on. "I ordered some when I saw you enter Le Village. I was so glad to see you, and I wanted to appear to be having fun. You and your friends seemed to be in a very good mood. My alcohol tolerance isn't what it should be—but I'm practicing."

Veronique smiled down at Oscar and said that if she didn't feel as if she'd been in a serious car accident she would want to make love to him.

"There'll be time for that," Oscar said, and went on to admit that as things stood any attempt at lovemaking could only end in disappointment. "By the way," he asked her, "we *weren't* in a car crash, were we?"

"No. You thought you were going very fast, but we were hardly moving."

"Typical."

"Now I have to organize my alibi."

"Elizabeth," said Oscar. The dog's nails were heard ticking

along the floor in the hall outside Oscar's bedroom. "Do us a favor and bring us the telephone, if you would. Telephone."

Veronique was duly impressed as Elizabeth dragged the telephone across the floor by its cord and left it within Oscar's reach.

"Good girl," said Oscar. "Hop up here."

He patted the comforter and Elizabeth climbed arthritically onto the foot of the bed. She curled up at their feet and rested her chin on her paws.

"If I do this right," said Veronique, starting to dial, "I can spend the night."

V

AS ELIZABETH RECOVERED FROM HER BREAKDOWN OSCAR THREW himself into his work as he had not done in some months. He set aside the Jesus sketches and addressed himself to the half-finished nude of a future *Lowdown* cover, which constituted something of a departure for the magazine because it depicted two people—a European politician and a woman-not-his-wife. What this picture lacked in imagination it compensated for with garish colors and an almost nauseating sense of motion as the puffy, puffing old man chased the bouncy, raddled woman through a field of poppies.

When he wasn't working, Oscar ventured out into the city to touch base with people he had kept up with during his absence. There was Mrs. Killarney, now seventy-five years old, who had tutored Oscar in pen-and-ink drawing for two years during his early twenties. In many ways she was his favorite New Yorker, and in her company he had enjoyed his closest approximation to a salon social life. She remained an energetic woman; Oscar could not understand how she had put up with half a century of living alone in one cluttered room three flights up in a neighborhood that had been transformed during that period into a battle zone so terrifying that newspapers dispatched only seasoned war correspondents to cover its frequent eruptions of violence. She talked about Paris as if she still intended to move there, and as if the two months she had spent in that city just after the war had been the dominating influence in her long life.

A few days later Oscar gathered up his courage and ventured out again to visit Brendt Zenner, a fellow draftsman who had worked briefly and unsuccessfully in advertising, and who lived in similar circumstances to Mrs. Killarney's. Brendt said none of this would last long, that things were looking up, and that as soon as he amassed ten or twenty million dollars he would take steps to erect the necessary barricades around his life. It would mean getting a new job, he knew, but he thought he was finally up to the challenge.

Oscar next dropped by his artistically inclined former girlfriend Hope Vincent, née Kilburn, who had quite sensibly married a man who was not only employed, but owned a small apartment to boot. Hope claimed to be getting child-rearing out of the way before striking out on the glittering career she thought was her due; she was unsure of what field she would enter, but she knew it was out there somewhere, ready to be tapped, like an oil well. She had three children, and Oscar told her he had to admit that the first part of her plan had gone off without a hitch.

On another of his daring excursions into the city, Oscar tracked down Freddy Budge, the only other member of Oscar's boarding-school class to leave in disgrace. They drank instant coffee together in a studio full of moving boxes: Freddy was going uptown. His new and powerful job paid him enough to live in an apartment with reliable water and nearly all the windowpanes intact.

There were others Oscar saw, mostly unchanged, uniformly optimistic. They shared with most young New Yorkers of Oscar's acquaintance a tendency to list endless complaints about their city, to note their general revulsion with its danger and decay, to suggest that only a billionaire could afford the insulation that would make life tolerable, and then to conclude that New York was the greatest city in the world and that they would not leave it for anything.

In a sober but generous mood after the last of these rendezvous, Oscar decided to give a dollar to every mendicant he encountered on his short walk back to the Domino Hotel; he reached his destination sixty dollars poorer, wiping phlegm from his blazer.

Waiting for him in the lobby, under the suspicious eye of the assistant manager, was young Rachel, daughter of Oscar's presumed sister-in-law-to-be. She wore the same little black outfit and booties and feather earrings she had sported at their first meeting on George's balcony. She hopped out of her armchair, threw down the magazine she had been reading (not the *Lowdown*, which even the newly tacky Domino Hotel would have considered in bad taste), and rushed over to greet the spit-spattered Oscar.

"Sorry I didn't tell you I was coming," she said. "We just *have* to talk."

"My office, then?" said Oscar, gesturing toward the bar.

"Maybe your room," said Rachel. "I'm, like, underage."

"So you are. Happy birthday, by the way."

Once installed in Oscar's room—where Elizabeth still lay recovering amid satin pillows courtesy of the chagrined Philippe, seeming to relish the pampering of her lengthy convalescence—Rachel sipped an illegal beer and began to confide her worries to Oscar.

"It isn't that I think the marriage is a bad idea," she said, after a rambling prelude Oscar could hardly understand, so chock-full of likes and kind-ofs was her syntax. "I think it might be totally like the right thing to do, kind of. It's just that my mother—"

"I see," said Oscar, not seeing.

"My mother's at a vulnerable place right now."

"Oh?"

"If she could get her therapy thing together she could deal with it."

"Place? Thing? It?" Oscar asked. He could see that Rachel was trying to be communicative, but her educational system had failed her.

"I was kind of hoping it could all be, like, slowed down."

"Are you saying you don't want the marriage to take place just yet?" Yes-or-no questions were probably the best tack, Oscar thought.

"Kind of," said Rachel. "Maybe if you talked to him? He's your brother, right?"

Oscar thought his absence must have imbued him with an aura of considerable dependability for so many people to entrust him with their most personal negotiations.

"I don't like being a go-between," he said, hoping Rachel would comprehend the correct usage of the word "like." "Yes, he's my brother, and yes, I'm interested in his welfare. But surely *you* could just as easily raise the issue. After all it's your—"

"Right," said Rachel, frowning. "It's my mother."

They continued to talk circles around each other in this way for ten more minutes, separated by Oscar's social myopia and Rachel's grammar. When at last Oscar realized what was going on it was only because Rachel coincidentally spat out three fully coherent sentences containing all the ingredients necessary for his comprehension: "If George marries my mother right now, I think he's only doing it because he's desperate. He isn't thinking of her, and she's liable to go along with it just because she's a nice lady. They're both alcoholics, and I think George is a bit in love with me, too."

VI

THE OPENING NIGHT OF ELIZABETH'S EXHIBITION IN VAL D'ARGENT WAS a particularly balmy one: palm trees rustled in a warm breeze; the seaside cafés were clogged with thirsty tourists; African curio salesmen competed with fire-breathers for spare change. Dressed in the flashy white suit and dark glasses he had thought appropriate to his role as artistic impresario, Oscar strolled casually along the harbor with Elizabeth sauntering beside him wearing a pink bow tie. The sun melted into the hazy horizon as the pair slowly made their way to the exhibition.

All had been arranged well in advance at a recently bankrupted seafood restaurant owned by a relative of Monsieur Berlinger: the briny decor had been stripped from the stucco walls and replaced by Elizabeth's tastefully framed paintings; the restaurant's kitchen, which remained in working order, was used to provide hors d'oeuvres for the sixty invited guests; a striking and provocative Lemoine nude caricature of the artist hung outside the restaurant; arc lights and a red carpet had been leased from a minor convention center in the city.

Oscar and Elizabeth paused for a few minutes to sit on a

bench and look at boats; they did not want to be early. Elizabeth needed no further coaching, and it was Oscar who suffered most from butterflies. Since Veronique's successful alibi after their night of overdoing it, Oscar had decided that his dog's art exhibition might not be such a bad milieu to announce his intentions to Herr Dohrmann, or at least to make it as plain as possible by his behavior that he and Veronique were more than good friends.

When he judged the time to be right, Oscar hailed a taxi; it was only a short distance to their destination, but Elizabeth and her handler wanted to arrive in some semblance of style. When they rolled up outside the restaurant, they found the entrance surrounded by a crowd attracted by the lights and the velvet ropes that cordoned off the red carpet. Monsieur Berlinger had spared no expense on external appearances, giving the tiny restaurant the look of a Broadway opening in miniature.

Monsieur Berlinger himself, in evening dress and blue-rimmed spectacles, was on hand to open the taxi door and present the artist to the crowd, whose applause was enthusiastic. Oscar followed behind and did his impression of a bodyguard, walking backward, scanning the palm trees for snipers, glaring from behind his dark glasses at individuals who leaned too far over the ropes.

Inside the restaurant awaited the shining faces of the invited guests: some had been coerced by Monsieur Berlinger into attending, and into feigning deep interest; some were Oscar's friends; and some were genuine believers in Elizabeth's retrospective as one of the premier artistic and social events of the season. These last far outnumbered the other categories, so that the atmosphere was one of hushed expectation as Elizabeth was led around for introductions. Wine and food were in plentiful supply, and Elizabeth was provided with a little china bowl of wine-spiked water and a plate of canapés.

Monsieur Berlinger had done a beautiful job with the

paintings. Elizabeth's exuberant early works caught the setting sun that glanced off the walls near the doorway; her brooding middle works, executed over a period of perhaps three weeks during her first winter in Val d'Argent, glowered in the back near the kitchen; her masterful late works, including *High Dive*, took pride of place along the broadest wall under track lights that brought out their mystical suggestion of suffering and alienation.

Oscar deliberately left Elizabeth alone to roam the converted gallery, to be petted, to have her paw shaken, generally to be idolized by her fans. He had warned her in advance not to let all the attention go to her head, to be gracious to envious fellow painters, and not to bite anyone because one never knew who the critics were.

An excited Monsieur Berlinger gave Oscar a glass of wine and drew him to one side, toward the kitchen door.

"Fantastic!" cried Monsieur Berlinger in French. "Incredible!"

He used these two words within earshot of the milling crowd, and reverted to his natural, conservative personality only in the privacy of the kitchen.

"It's okay," he said. "Something very interesting is happening. There are those out there who think Elizabeth's art is wonderful for its own sake. There are those who think it is wonderful because it was painted by a dog. And then there is a growing number who believe that *you* painted everything and are only pretending that it was your dog. They know about your—how should I put it—artistic shenanigans."

"We must prove it to them then," said Oscar, who could not believe anyone would doubt his word.

"No no no," said Berlinger, putting a calming hand on Oscar's forearm. "I don't think you understand, my friend. This is *good* that they think you are the artist"—here Berlinger lowered his face and smiled shyly—"from a commercial point of view."

"How so?" This interested Oscar, who often felt that he did not have enough money.

"This is it: they believe—and some of these people are good friends of mine—that regardless of the quality of the paintings, which is considered by almost everyone out there to be quite high, the artistic significance of these works lies in the unusual fact that the artist claims they were painted by a dog. They find this terribly affecting. One man was telling me it represented the humility of an artist whose gift was divine . . . well, and so on. The argument is not important. What is important is that you win either way. If they like the paintings and believe they are valuable because they are the first important works created by a household pet, fine. If on the other hand they believe that this is a hoax on your part, but an artistically significant one, even better. The key is for you to be slightly ambiguous. That is what I wanted to tell you. Behave as if you are not letting on. Okay?"

"I read you."

"The point is, my friend," said Berlinger, whom Oscar had never seen so exercised, "that out there are wealthy members of your community drinking wine and looking at your—at *Elizabeth*'s paintings. This is an opportunity not to be missed."

"Let's get at them," said Oscar.

Oscar and Monsieur Berlinger emerged into the gallery in time to observe the glamorous entrance of Herr Dohrmann and Veronique, with a particularly dashing Neville in tow. Veronique walked down the red carpet under the lights between the two men with her hands through the crooks of their elbows, acknowledging the swelling crowd outside with winning nods of her glorious head. Photographers' flashes captured the arrival.

Oscar was no longer jealous of Neville the Aged, not after the spectacular night with Veronique once her hangover alibi had been successfully established. The old man might be able to execute a perfectly genteel swan dive, and he might be able to arrive at an art opening wearing immaculate evening clothes, but Oscar was sure he could not have sustained the night of noteworthy erotic activity that Veronique had admitted might have changed her entire life view. Oscar stood to one side and merely nodded hello to the trio as they swept past, without so much as a wink for Veronique. She wore black, as befitted a labrador's art opening; Oscar could see how pleased Monsieur Berlinger was that such a woman would lend the weight of her glamour to the occasion.

Next to arrive, to the oohs and aahs of the *cognoscenti*, was Cristobal Koch (pronounced throat-clearingly), the region's most hotly celebrated modern artist. In his early forties, dressed flamboyantly in earth-tone leathers, peering dubiously at the crowd over the rims of his yellow-tinted granny glasses, Koch escorted not one but two young protégés.

Koch was an artist of indisputable standing—so much so that even the out-of-touch Oscar had heard of him. The man was so hip he limped. As a young man he had splashed onto the canvas of artistic celebrity with five years of paintings perpetrated entirely in his mother's menstrual blood, and had gone on from there to do things that were frankly distasteful. He continued to work wholeheartedly and exclusively in body fluids, which meant his creations sometimes constituted public-health hazards, but there was nary a breath of disapproval from the critical world. Cristobal Koch was known in English-speaking circles as "Crystal Ball," because he always stood one step ahead of the critics. His nationality was not widely publicized but he was thought, rather disappointingly, to be Canadian.

Now Monsieur Berlinger was beside himself: what a coup it was to have Koch himself grace Elizabeth's showing. The idea that a master had appeared to keep an eye on the competition sent a shiver through the crowd. Koch and his protégés made straight for the first painting on the left, *D'Artagnan*, which was Elizabeth's most representational work: a blood-soaked épée in two brushstrokes, a feather-hatted figure in two more. (Oscar had been trying to train Elizabeth to paint straight lines, but never mind.) There was noticeable quiet as the crowd gauged the Koch reaction. Koch lowered his granny glasses on his nose, stepped forward, stepped back, spent on the whole quite a long time with *D'Artagnan*. It was quite possible that he found this painting derivative of his own bloody masterpieces.

The fans and critics did their best to appear uninterested as Koch moved onto the next work, *Tangier*, described in Oscar and Berlinger's accompanying literature as "A circular work of ominous political undertones." By "circular" Oscar had simply meant "a circle"; circles were hard for dogs to paint, especially on purpose. But Elizabeth had achieved the nearly round splotch after two-dozen haphazard attempts. There was no denying that "circular" meant different things to different people. Koch, by the look of him, appeared to take the word to mean "regenerative," as in nature's cycles, or perhaps "never-ending," as in a circular argument or an oscillating universe. As for the political undertones, well, Elizabeth would never escape the social and political responsibilities of any black artist.

Oscar joined the crowd in scrutinizing Koch's progress and reactions. Those who had already inspected Elizabeth's paintings divided into conversational cells to exchange their views and interpretations. Monsieur Berlinger threw himself into more handshaking and wine pouring. There was one predominant murmur from the invited guests, which Oscar pieced together from snippets in several languages: "Are they for sale?" Oscar had discussed this question in advance with Monsieur Berlinger, and they had agreed that the answer should be a theatrically reluctant "Yes."

The first person to ask the question directly of Oscar was one of Koch's protégés, presumably dispatched by the master for this purpose. The youth, who introduced himself in English as "François," wore the required artist's uniform of black on black, and had done something strange with his plentiful dyed-blond hair so that a shellacked triangular lid protruded from his brow like a visor.

"So amusing," said François. "Do you know, I think that Cristobal is highly amused?"

This was Oscar's first artistic conversation, so he had to be careful. "I don't believe the artist was trying to amuse. She is not a frivolous dog."

"*Merveilleux!*" said François with a laugh, tossing his hair-lid; he added "Marvelous!" just in case Oscar needed the translation.

"I'm not kidding," said Oscar. "Her paintings are sincere."

François loved that one. "Oh-you-are-so-funny," he said. "What I want to know is, are any of these paintings for sale?"

Others standing nearby overheard the question; ears were cocked in Oscar's direction.

"I would have to consult with the artist," said Oscar demurely.

This remark resulted unintentionally in laughter.

"You ask your dog, then," sniffed François. "We await the answer."

Oscar found Elizabeth nosing through the jungle of legs, her bow tie slightly askew. He knelt down and said "Sit." Elizabeth sat. The crowd formed a circle around dog and master. Elizabeth smacked her chops, arched her eyebrows sweetly, and focused on Oscar. He leaned over and whispered. "They want to know if your beautiful paintings are for sale. Nod yes, girl. Good girl. Nod." With only the slightest physical prompting from Oscar, Elizabeth nodded.

Monsieur Berlinger clapped with gusto. Cristobal Koch squinted incredulously. Neville stepped forward to have a closer look at the animal. Oscar stood up and opened his palms to the crowd, as if to say that despite the better judgment of her handlers, Elizabeth, Bête Noire, had opened her show to auction. Herr Dohrmann made straight for the middle works near the kitchen, his experience perhaps having taught him that for investment purposes an artist's early and late periods are least likely to stand the test of time. Other eager collectors followed suit. Rich husbands were pushed to the fore; rich wives were asked for permission to join any bidding that might ensue. Monsieur Berlinger called for more wine. Elizabeth trotted up to Veronique to say hello.

Cristobal Koch came over to introduce himself to Oscar, which for a man of his status meant simply to extend a lazy hand and listen insouciantly for a name to be uttered.

"Oscar Lemoine," said Oscar truthfully.

"Koch," said the artist. He made his name sound like an expression of arrogant disbelief.

"It was nice of you to come."

"I am pleased that I did. All the right people are here, eh?" Koch spoke conspiratorially now, artist to artist.

"Sure."

"You have many of them believing that the dog paints, you know that?"

"The dog *does* paint."

"Wonderful," said Koch. "Genius."

"She'll be pleased to know you think so," said Oscar.

"Oh, come on, man," said Koch, losing a layer or two of his mid-Atlantic accent. "You can push a good idea too far."

Oscar did his best impression of a man who was about to say "I haven't the slightest idea what you are talking about," then asked Koch if he planned to buy any of Elizabeth's works.

"I have my eye on that one," said Koch, pointing over Oscar's shoulder at *High Dive*.

"It's my favorite too," said Oscar. "I might try to convince

Elizabeth not to part with it for the time being. But thank you for admiring it."

Koch melted back into the crowd, leaving Oscar face-to-face with Hansie and Veronique, who had returned from studying the pictures near the kitchen.

"So very nice to see you again, my young friend," said Hansie, whose dinner jacket was sumptuous but appropriately worn at the edges, as if he attended such an event every night. "Last time, if I am not mistaken, you wore no clothes. My friends have not forgotten your performance. You made such an impression—you are an Impressionist, yes? Ha ha ha, good chap. What is this funny thing with your dog? She not only swims, she paints, you say?"

"These are her paintings, yes, sir."

"Veronique and I have been discussing them. She keeps up with young people, and she tells me you are very famous in New York. True?"

"My work is widely seen, I suppose." Oscar could see Veronique's mischievous look out of the corner of his eye. She was setting Hansie up for a purchase.

"And it is your intention to sell these works as if they were painted by a dog? Is this what artists do nowadays, they play these games? I admit it is very funny, but . . ." Herr Dohrmann lost the track of his sentence as he fumbled in his jacket pockets for cigarettes.

"Elizabeth painted them, sir," said Oscar. "I promise."

"What is her price for that one, then," Herr Dohrmann wanted to know, inhaling smoke with a bronchial click, "that one behind you." Like Koch, Hansie seemed drawn to *High Dive*.

"I think you had better talk to Monsieur Berlinger about specifics," Oscar said. "We'll let people have a look around for a while longer, and then if you wish to discuss this sort of business with him, I think that's fine, sir. Elizabeth has given her approval."

"Oh, this is wonderful," said Herr Dohrmann. "It reminds me of those Dada fellows, or something. Very exciting, what young people get up to."

Oscar took a step nearer to Veronique, the first phase of his plan to clarify his intentions toward Herr Dohrmann's daughter. He kissed her on both cheeks, and said, "I never actually said hello in all the excitement." Oscar noticed that she gave a worried glance at Hansie, but the German still beamed with goodwill at the American cartoonist. Far from being upset by this show of intimacy, he clapped Oscar on the back and said, "You two have a little chat. I am going to put on my glasses and get a closer look. A dog. Wonderful!" Hansie pivoted on his heel and limped off toward *High Dive!*

"Now, you see," said Oscar, slipping a hand around Veronique's waist, "that wasn't so bad. I think he likes me, even."

"You're right, he does," said Veronique. "He likes young people and artists."

"Of course he does."

"And I told him you were homosexual."

VII

RACHEL'S DISTURBING ANALYSIS OF GEORGE'S LIFE-STYLE AND MARITAL plans prompted the cartoonist to give his brother a call to suggest that during their earlier telephone conversation he might not have been so supportive or helpful as a younger brother ought. He reached George's secretary at his office, where the background noise sounded like a train station at rush hour, and was told that George would call him as soon as he had a minute. Four hours later the telephone rang. George said he couldn't talk right away, but that he would pop by Oscar's hotel after work. It was already seven o'clock.

At ten o'clock Oscar's telephone rang again. George's voice hissed over the line, informing his brother that he was in fourth gear on Third Avenue, that he'd be right there. Fifteen minutes later another call came through.

"I'm right outside, little brother. What have they done to the Domino? It's *awful.* Come on down, there's no place to park. I want you to see my new car. We'll drive around."

Oscar tucked Elizabeth into bed and left the television remote control within her reach. He emerged from beneath the Domino's ghastly new awning to find his brother sitting behind the wheel of a car that made the cartoonist gag with disapproval. The passenger door unlatched itself electronically, and Oscar settled into the psychiatrist's couch of a seat. He waited for George to finish another telephone call, this one apparently to an all-night dry cleaner, then said good evening.

"Gaw," said George. He accelerated at such a rate that Oscar was crunched astronautlike into his couch.

"What's the matter? Slow down. Why does everyone drive this way?"

"I'm sorry. Just the usual. Fifteen hours screaming into my telephone, and things fall apart."

George continued to drive at high speed, when traffic lights allowed, and because his right foot was still encased in a plaster cast he had great difficulty slowing down or, on the rare occasions he stooped to defeatism, braking. He pointed out a few buildings and landmarks as they sped aimlessly along, as if Oscar had not lived most of his life in Manhattan. Where Oscar saw ruin, George described his own personal triumph in having risen above the degrading morass. One would have thought from George's self-congratulatory monologue that he had not been provided with every conceivable advantage along the way; it was as if he had started a hundred-yard dash leaning against the tape, only to boast after the race about his record time.

George told Oscar that they were taking the same route he used every morning to drive to work. It occurred to Oscar as he heard this that George probably spent weeks at a time moving about the city without once soiling his soles on pavement. He left from a subterranean garage in his apartment building in his space capsule of a car; he muttered instructions into his telephone as soon as he reached street level; he fought traffic downtown, cooled or warmed by his vehicle depending on the season; he drove into another garage in the basement of his office building and stepped into his second elevator of the day without once having been spat at, vomited upon, cuffed about the face, shrieked at, pissed upon, called a Prince of Death. This was protection.

Oscar blocked out most of what George was saying and mulled over the scant intelligence he had winkled out of the inarticulate Rachel. The girl had expressed a worry that George and Diana had sunk to the level where they eschewed other people's company; that George came home late and the couple got drunk together (although Rachel's word for "drunk" was a scatological hyphenated phrase); that George was selfish and increasingly obsessed with his work; that Diana was making a terrible mistake because she thought George might be her last chance; and most disturbing of all, that George's affection for Rachel was rather more than stepfatherly. Oscar was aware that it was his fraternal duty to look out for George's welfare at the expense of Diana Burke's, but for the moment he could not imagine that it was his place to interfere.

"I know she's a little old," said George suddenly, as if reading his brother's thoughts. "And there's Rachel."

"True."

"But Diana looks great, no?" George could have been talking about a car. "There's so little time anymore. No time to look around. How *do* you look around? Do you know how many new women I meet on my schedule? Young girls, they want to dance and talk all night, and they want *me* to make *them* happy. Diana, she devotes herself to *me*."

"True."

"I'm beat. I give up. I need her."

"Do it, then." Oscar believed in, and relied upon, divorce. At least Diana Burke was experienced in this increasingly common loophole.

In the darkened cockpit of George's car, Oscar turned to look at his brother's puffy profile. It wasn't so strange, when Oscar considered the situation carefully, that a man willing to exchange most people's idea of happiness and comfort for larger and larger amounts of money, would long ago have abandoned the notion of romantic love in favor of a cost-benefit analysis of his emotional needs. George's eyes peered nervously into the near future of his vehicle's progress, checked the rearview mirror for pursuit, glared at red lights as if willing them to turn green.

"Ah," said George, braking clumsily with his injured foot. "Here we are. The Mecca."

Oscar's window glided down.

"Take a look up there," George said. "Go on, take a look. That's where old George plies his trade. Welcome to the salt mines."

Oscar leaned out of his window and looked up.

"Count the floors," said George. "Number twenty-two, that's me. Can you see it?"

"I can see it," said Oscar, though all he could really see was the flickering orange halo of a diseased streetlight.

VIII

"SEVEN THOUSAND," MONSIEUR BERLINGER WAS SAYING. "SEVEN thousand it is. All done? Eight thousand, there, thank you."

Standing in the back next to Veronique, Oscar wondered what currency the Frenchman was quoting to his bidders; it didn't matter, things were going very well indeed.

"Thank you," said Monsieur Berlinger. "All done?"

D'Artagnan was on the block, and while Monsieur Berlinger did not lack for offers, most of the heavyweight bidders seemed to be holding back for Elizabeth's later works.

Elizabeth was in good form, posing on a low table near the auctioneer's elbow. Her stare moved from bidder to bidder, a practice unheard of at art auctions, but no less adorable for that. Oscar knew her sweetest expressions to be coincidental, but she created quite a stir among animal lovers when she seemed to look expectantly at an undecided potential buyer, let her pink tongue dangle, cocked her head like an irresistible child begging for crusts on a street corner. Neville waited for the other bidders to show signs of nerves, then stepped in to snap up *D'Artagnan* on his first bid: Monsieur Berlinger bowed to Neville and moved on to the next painting.

Any conversation Oscar attempted with Veronique had to be conducted in whispers, yet there was so much he wanted to ask her.

"Say again? Homosexual?" Oscar liked to think this was not believable.

Veronique found it all frightfully humorous. "Neville was able to report seeing you in a lady's dress the other night," she said. "And pearls."

"Ah."

"To someone of Hansie's generation that means something."

"Call me old-fashioned," said Oscar, "but it means something to me, too."

"Sold!" cried Monsieur Berlinger. A happy buyer was hugged by his wife. Elizabeth was patted on the shoulder, her second sale a matter of history.

"Don't worry," Veronique said. "Think how much more we can see of each other this way."

Nice as that thought was, Oscar was more determined than ever to have his man-to-man talk with the disagreeable German.

The auction moved informally from one picture to the next, the perspiring Monsieur Berlinger barely able to suppress his glee as each work was snapped up at prices something in the order of one hundred times the values he had predicted to Oscar.

"I'm rich," said Oscar. "Isn't this fun?"

Knowing very well how it felt, Veronique agreed that being rich was fun.

"Does your dog have many more paintings to sell?"

"Yes, but still you can rest assured that she'll be hard at work again on Monday morning. Assembly line. Monsieur Berlinger wants to take a show to Paris."

"How long will people be fooled?"

"Ask our friend Monsieur Koch. He'll tell you."

"I'm sure Hansie will buy *High Dive*. He likes to talk about your dive to his friends, and this will be a conversation piece. 'Painted by the chap's *dog*,' he will tell them."

"*High Dive* is my favorite, but I can be convinced to part with it, the way things are going."

"You should tell Hansie that," said Veronique. "It will make him stubborn and he will pay a fortune."

Oscar looked at Veronique in profile, felt a wave of pleasure at what he saw, and, of course, became queasy with lust.

"You aren't planning to go away anytime soon, are you?" he asked her. "Do you go away in the winter?"

"Every year, yes."

"I think I'm going to have to come with you."

Oscar meant this very sincerely and was somewhat taken aback when Veronique laughed at him, as if he had said he intended to buy Herr Dohrmann's mansion and pay for it in cash. It was even worse when she said "You know that will be impossible."

Oscar didn't know anything of the kind, and was unable to imagine that he would be deterred. Only the necessity of allowing the impromptu auction to continue prevented Oscar from striding across the room and challenging old Hansie to a duel.

Monsieur Berlinger, mopping sweat from his brow with a waiter's checked towel, gulped from a glass of wine between sales. Cristobal Koch suffered the indignity of having to climb down from the furious bidding on *Tangier*. Herr Dohrmann stood to one side perusing the accompanying literature and biding his time. Neville had cornered a pair of very young girls near the makeshift bar, who paid rapt attention to the anecdote he was relating with his characteristic flair. Departing guests came over to Oscar to offer their congratulations; he said he would pass them on to the artist.

By the time the auction reached *High Dive*, a waiter had been dispatched to purchase a crate of champagne. Elizabeth had dipped her tongue a few times too often into her bowl of diluted wine, and had begun to make passes at Koch's pouting protégés. Oscar was on the giddy side himself and stood unashamedly with his arm around Veronique's slender waist. He had gauged

Herr Dohrmann's expression, and indicated with a nod to Monsieur Berlinger that *High Dive* was definitely for sale. An exhausted and rather drunk Monsieur Berlinger stood to one side of *High Dive*, bowed his head, folded his hands before him in a graveside pose, and waited for silence.

"The artist's most recent work," he said in French, implying that it might very well be her last. "Entitled *High Dive*, and completed only in the last few weeks, the painting is a summation, a defiant stab at the innards of mercurial valuation. . . ." In French all of this sounded very convincing and poetic.

Monsieur Berlinger drew his critique to a close, paused for effect, and quoted an astronomical price.

Oscar gulped and had to remind himself that for most of those in the room this sum meant only a glance into the old wallet to see if one's assistants had remembered to fill it up that morning. Elizabeth too seemed shocked at the success of her own exhibition, and stopped sniffing amorously at François' trouser leg when she heard the bidding begin. Neville had brought his two girls over to Hansie's side for a closer look at the action.

In a matter of minutes it had become clear that Herr Dohrmann would not be denied this painting. He calmly blurted out his bids in English without looking at the artwork or the bidding competition, making it perfectly clear that *High Dive* already belonged to him no matter how long he had to repeat meaningless numbers. Cristobal Koch had wisely purchased another painting earlier in the progression of Elizabeth's retrospective and was able to drop out of the bidding with his dignity intact. Herr Dohrmann's main competition came from one of Monsieur Berlinger's plants. The trembling bidder waited for a sign from Berlinger to drop out, but performed his job with admirable outward confidence. It was up to Monsieur Berlinger to judge when the German's temper might snap, but fortified as he was by brisk sales and countless glasses of wine, the Frenchman did not call off his accomplice until the tension in the room had reached an excruciating level.

"Sold," said Monsieur Berlinger, with transparent relief, just as the doors burst open and the champagne arrived.

Veronique rushed from Oscar's side to congratulate Hansie and to admire the painting that would soon take its place on a minor wall in their mansion overlooking the cliffs. Monsieur Berlinger picked Elizabeth up and kissed her forehead. Elizabeth was smashed out of her mind; she liked being a successful modern artist. When Berlinger put her back on the floor she stumbled around in search of drink and fornication.

Monsieur Berlinger, wearing the shameful drunken smirk of a successful con man, came over to Oscar and kissed him five times on each cheek.

"Monsieur Lemoine," he said tearfully, no doubt already having totted up his fifteen percent, "you are my best friend. I love you. I love your beautiful dog."

IX

THE NEWS IN THE NEW YORK PAPERS WAS NOT AT ALL GOOD THAT autumn. Propped up against his pillows with Elizabeth curled heraldically at his feet, Oscar scanned stories of riot, rape, arson, murder—murder by handgun, murder by knife, murder by crossbow, murder by garrote, murder by shotgun, murder by Uzi, murder by jackboot, murder by *sex*. Interspersed with these stories were items concerning city corruption, Wall Street corruption, medical, religious, sporting, industrial, judicial corruption, corruption big and small, corruption far and wide.

"Have you been reading the papers, Elizabeth?" Oscar asked his dog. "No wonder you tried to off yourself." Two weeks after her collapse, during which time Oscar had only rarely risked the streets, Elizabeth had returned to something like her previous form. She slept more than usual, but had regained her sense of humor.

The television screen beamed images of firefighters, body bags, policemen, hitmen, ambulances, junkies, car crashes, burst water mains, and court appearances by various stool pigeons in diverse fields of white- and blue-collar criminality. There was little room for national or international news—not when the city's local horrors registered almost seismographically on their own. News broadcasts ended with human-interest dramas about Good Samaritans rescuing child prostitutes from the streets; young police officers undergoing physical therapy after paralyzing gunshot wounds to the spinal column; unwed multiple-mothers who had graduated from law school with high honors; terminally ill children whose last wishes were granted by publicity seeking property developers; eccentric millionaires who wasted their money in hilarious ways; and the obligatory lottery winner who said he would keep his job manning the smelter despite a huge guaranteed annual income for the rest of his life.

Wedged in among the gore and greed lurked the unfolding Bunny Fenton story. As yet the television personality had not come forward with her tragic tale, and the Domino Hotel switchboard had been good enough to screen telephone calls from reporters; it was left to the papers to speculate as to why she had wept in the "callous caricaturist's" hotel room. With fantastic intuition, the newspapers knew there was more to the leaked episode than mere displeasure on Bunny Fenton's part. They reasoned that wealthy celebrities did not sneak into the hotel rooms of relative nobodies for routine displays of emotion; people in the limelight grew rhinoceros hides, and Bunny Fenton would never risk exacerbating the situation in the absence of unusual circumstances. One newspaper speculated rather obviously about romance between the callous caricaturist and the single star. Another asked if Bunny Fenton might have been caught weeping with joy at the publicity Oscar's nude caricature had provided for her sagging ratings—including the unavoidable joke about the things that were most definitely *not* sagging in Oscar's caricature.

The Bunny Fenton story was lost like a bay leaf in the stinking stew of New York news. Oscar need not have worried that the saga would hold the papers' interest for long, even if Bunny Fenton decided to go public with her medical history. Oscar could hear Fable's advice: "Great for her, great for us. The important thing is toughness. Can't back down. That's the key. Don't let her see you sweat. You did your job. It's her fault if she makes a production out of things. You are one hundred percent in the clear. I guarantee it. You are the man they called Indomitable. . . ."

Oscar knew this advice to be correct. A professional in the business of insensitivity and irreverence should be encased in emotional armor-plating, just as someone in Bunny Fenton's position must be prepared to face the inevitable indignities of life in the public eye. Any attempt at apology would undermine his motives and jeopardize his livelihood. Fable would surely have counseled further frontal assault if Bunny Fenton ever decided to take the distasteful step of revealing the real reason for her anguish. Take no prisoners, would be Fable's advice.

And yet Oscar Lemoine could not think this way. His embarrassment was monumental, his pity overwhelming. He watched every appearance of Bunny Fenton on television and pulled at his hair with remorse. He pounded his pillow with his fists, he gritted his teeth, and berated himself in the expressive colloquial French he had polished in Val d'Argent. His occupation was suddenly exposed to him: irrelevant, not irreverent; gratuitous, not amusing; hurtful, not clever. It sickened him to think that he had added further suffering to a perfect stranger who had already had to cope with such a ghastly combination of disease and disfigurement.

In his state of acute self-loathing, Oscar decided that there was nothing to do but search out Bunny Fenton and apologize. Nothing would alleviate his guilt but forgiveness from the source. The problem was to make his regrets credible: who in New York would believe that someone actually felt sorry for successful self-promotion at another's expense?

X

IN AN EXULTANT MOOD AFTER HIS AVANT-GARDE PURCHASE, HERR Dohrmann invited Oscar and Elizabeth to return to his clifftop mansion for a celebratory drink. This suited Oscar's plans for a manly tête-à-tête, so after further embraces with Monsieur Berlinger, High Dive was packed up and he departed with Hansie and Veronique. Neville had been invited along as well, but the Englishman indicated that his hands would be full entertaining the two young art lovers he had befriended earlier in the evening.

Oscar held his drunk and wealthy labrador in the cramped backseat of Hansie's black convertible; Veronique took the wheel; Hansie sat in the passenger seat with his new painting. The German handled the conversation. He spoke excitedly in

English about having met Cristobal Koch, and told Veronique to remind him to invite the artist to their next party. "His paintings sound simply disgusting," said the German. "I *have* to own one." Veronique chided Hansie for going through his annual patron-of-the-arts phase; the excitement would fade by morning and he would not remember Monsieur Koch. Hansie dismissed Veronique's remark and returned to fondling and kissing the frame of Elizabeth's most recent painting.

They drove along the harbor in Val D'Argent beneath carbon-stained palms, then twisted uphill past Oscar's own address and beyond it to the site of the cliff-diving party. Oscar should not have been surprised to find that what he had taken for Veronique's magnificent house was merely an overblown beach cottage close to the cliffs and mini-fjord, and that their main residence was an isolated mansion half a mile farther up the winding driveway.

So this is the citadel, thought Oscar: Veronique's prison tower. Closed-circuit video cameras and dog-handling guards watched the front gate. A separate inner fence enclosed the mansion's immediate grounds. Oscar had seen this house before, from above, and had assumed it was a health spa for film stars or a hotel for European royalty. Oscar pressed his face against the car's side window and took in what parts he could see of the rambling residence, which he supposed Hansie referred to as his "summer cottage." Veronique guided the sports car into a subterranean bunker that garaged half a dozen other cars and limousines.

"Here we are!" said Oscar cheerfully from the backseat.

Herr Dohrmann turned round and looked at him as if he had forgotten that Oscar had come along. Veronique gave him a reassuring wink, and they piled out of the car. Male minions in blue blazers appeared from three directions to disencumber their master. Hansie handed his painting to one of them, then raised his arms and stretched his aged frame.

"Go along then," he said, reverting to French. "Find us a place for the painting. How nice to hang it in the presence of the artist."

The minions automatically looked at Oscar.

"Not the man," scolded Hansie. "The dog."

The three minions nodded politely at Elizabeth as if nothing had ever made more sense. They rushed off while Hansie put his arm around Oscar's shoulders and played host.

"This way," he said. "Veronique can change and we will walk around the front. We will see you in a few minutes, my dear."

"Come, Elizabeth," Oscar said.

They left the bunker from the direction they had entered, and walked to the perimeter fence under starlight. It seemed a shame to Oscar that a high-altitude 300-degree view of the Mediterranean should be masked by a security fence, but there you had it. He looked instead at the sky and tried to control his excitement that Herr Dohrmann had finally seen fit to have a reasonable, fatherly talk. There was the small matter of Veronique's little joke about homosexuality to be cleared up before Oscar could state his intentions, but the cartoonist felt up to the task.

"You must be very pleased, young man," said the German. "Your dog is a star. Do you see the Dog Star, there?" He pointed overhead. "I am making a little pun."

"Yes, sir. She's a Sirius dog." Elizabeth sat to one side, nose in the night air.

Herr Dohrmann took a deep breath. "What a nice evening we had. I so enjoy mixing with young people."

"I've had a good time in Val d'Argent. So has Elizabeth."

"It is a wonderful place. I came here first as a boy, before the war. That is when I first met Neville. What a funny little chap he was. We both decided we would live here one day if we possibly could."

"It worked out for you, I see."

A chuckle from Hansie. His damaged eye shone like an oyster in its orbit. "Neville overdoes the social side, I fear. It is not enough for him merely to fraternize with the younger set, he feels it is necessary to . . . you know?"

"Yes."

"But we should not gossip. Actually there was something I wished to say to you, in private."

This was the moment Oscar had been waiting for—a chance to seek fatherly approval. They had reached a corner of the grounds, next to the security fence, overlooking a steep hillside and the satiny sheet of calm sea below. They stopped walking and faced each other in the starlight.

"I wanted to tell you—Oscar, is it?"

"Yes, sir."

"I wanted to say how pleased I am that you have befriended Veronique. I realize she must have friends her age here, but most of her crowd, I must say, have failed to meet my approval. Perhaps this is unfair of me, but I must be candid about my feelings. When you are my age, you see, you look back at youth and say, 'We were never like that. We were never so frivolous.' The truth is I suppose we were worse, but there were . . . extenuating circumstances."

Oscar did not want to know about the extenuating circumstances of Herr Dohrmann's youth.

"Friends of my generation tell me I am overprotective of Veronique, especially Neville. He says I should relax and enjoy the time I have with her and not be angry when she seeks the company of her contemporaries. I simply wanted to tell you I am grateful that she has found you. And your little black dog, of course. Veronique is so precious to me. You, too, can help to protect her."

What further endorsement did Oscar need? He had forgotten for the moment that Hansie lived under a misapprehension of his own—namely an erroneous understanding of Oscar's sexual orientation.

"I'm so happy you feel that way, sir."

"What is it with your 'sir'? You are not my servant. Were you in the army?"

"No, sir. I was brought up that way. I can't help it."

"I think you are a wonderful chap. Let's go now and have a drink. Veronique will have changed by now."

"I'm with you, sir. Come along, Elizabeth."

Oscar strolled beside Herr Dohrmann with his hands deep in his pockets and his head lowered in self-conscious thought, the way he imagined plutocrats walked when no amount of conversation could convey their feeling of egotistical satisfaction. The spongy lawn, the screeching crickets, the buzzing security fence, the distant surf—all was as it should be. Veronique awaited them atop the steps to a semienclosed veranda: white ankle-length skirt and cable-knit jumper against the chill—yes, all was in place. What a wonderful moment, thought Oscar, as the two men approached her: aged father, veteran of unthinkable evil; bright young suitor, untainted and untried; a gap of eons between their outlooks and experiences, conspiring on this starlit night to usher pure Veronique into a more benign age.

Veronique extended her hands, one to Oscar and one to Hansie. The men turned and stood with Veronique between them, holding her hands. They held this pose on the veranda for some time in contemplative silence, watching the sea.

Each had a different view, as it were. Hansie was no doubt lost in thought about the business of the morrow, experiencing perhaps a minute amount of pleasure taken in the presence of such a nice and conveniently deviant young man and his talented dog. Veronique was certainly the most anxious of the three, the only gap in her knowledge being Oscar's blissful ignorance of reality. And Oscar, his heart full of love, gazed out blankly at the ancient waters, standing in the dark, in the dark.

"Look there," said Oscar, raising his free hand to point out to sea. "Tristan and Isolde. The islands. What a nice day we had. Remember . . . ?" He was cut off by a tight squeeze on his other hand. "It's okay," he said, turning to Veronique. "Everything's okay now. We've had a nice chat, your f—"

The crucial word Oscar had been on the verge of uttering was cut off when he was startled by the appearance of one of Hansie's blazered minions, who had crept out of the darkness behind them bearing a tray of drinks and a cordless telephone.

"Take your drinks," said Herr Dohrmann. "I won't be a moment." He took the telephone and moved along the veranda out of earshot.

Oscar raised his glass for what he hoped would be a romantic toast, only to be met by the emerald ice of Veronique's angry stare.

"I really wonder about you, Oscar," spat a livid Veronique. *"Really."*

"Eh?"

"Do you enjoy this? Do you enjoy danger, pushing this to the limit? Perhaps you have been waiting all along to be alone with us together this way, in order only to humiliate me. I promise you, you will regret it. He will feed you to his dogs."

"I beg your pardon?" Oscar still held his glass in the air, having intended to say something more along the lines of "To the most beautiful girl on the shores of the Med."

"You know what I am saying."

"I assure you, Veronique, that I do not."

"Arrogant, that is what you are."

"Pff," said Oscar. When he heard this noise, which was supposed to convey ridicule at her suggestion, he heard the aural epitome of arrogance. "What I mean is, please *clarify*."

Veronique reverted to French, so that she could criticize Oscar in a higher gear. She sped off into her vilification of the

cartoonist, accelerated through whole categories of traduce-
ment, all the while keeping her voice so low that Oscar had to
lean forward and place his left ear directly in the stream of her
staccato railing. He understood almost everything she said,
losing only the occasional aspirated argot insult.

"Now let me get this straight," said Oscar, when Veronique
had spluttered to a stop (". . . *imbecile, merde!*"). "You would
appear to be accusing me of reckless openness. As I tried to
explain a moment ago there isn't a problem anymore." Hansie
had finished his telephone conversation and his limping foot-
falls could be heard on the tiled veranda as he approached
through the shadows. Oscar hurried to finish his thought:
"There isn't a problem because I believe he and I have come to
an agreement. Your father told me himself." Oscar looked up
and smiled as Hansie returned, expecting Veronique to drop
the conversation and do the same. He had observed her expert
social adaptability in the past, after all. Instead, Veronique
continued to stare at Oscar with ever-widening eyes.

"My *what?*" she exclaimed, in English.

"You are having a little argument?" Hansie wanted to know.
Still Veronique did not turn to greet Hansie, but gaped instead
at Oscar.

Oscar beamed at the German. "Not at all, sir. I'm just teasing
her."

Hansie put an arm around Veronique's shoulders. "My little
darling," he said. "You are letting him tease you?"

"My *what?*" Veronique said again, her stare still fixed on the
mortified Oscar.

"Now, now," said Hansie, whose telephone call must have
related good news. His long teeth glinted in the starlight.
"What a display. This is so unlike her, you know. Please, my
dear."

It was only beginning to dawn on Oscar what was the matter;
he tried not to let this creeping realization seep into his facial

expression, which at the moment had fixed itself into one of complete goodwill. He set his jaw and looked from Veronique to Hansie and back again, engaged in the difficult physical maneuver of separating his emotions from his expression.

Chaotic as they were, his thoughts managed to sort through the various possibilities offered up by Veronique's angry remarks, and to isolate a single disturbing solution: Hansie was not her father. So far so good, thought Oscar, grinning like hell. If not her father, then—and here his mind wrestled the possibilities to the ground and pounded on them until only the sturdiest one survived—if not her father, then her husband? His smile automatically broadened, aided this time by such a triumph of deduction. It was only when his conclusion passed through the proper channels and reached understanding that the smile faded from his face. He turned away from Veronique and Hansie and looked down, ashamed and confused. There, as if she had been awaiting his discovery, was Elizabeth. The sea breeze ruffled her coat. It might have been a shiver from the chill, or a reorientation of her noble head in the breeze, but when Oscar focused on Elizabeth she seemed to shake her head in disgust.

FIVE

I

OSCAR'S NECK ACHED FROM TALKING ON THE TELEPHONE ALL morning in Room 1107 of the Domino Hotel. Several calls to parents and stepparents had confirmed his brother George's statement that all was in its accustomed disorder, and that if he could pencil in a weekend three months hence he might even be able to meet one or two of them in person. (This state of affairs was only faintly nagging for Oscar. Those who heard of it secondhand urged him to probe the recesses of his psyche, to root out and expel his resentment. Oscar's more placid view was that his parents had far more problems than he, self-inflicted or not, and that if forced into their position he would want to be left alone to sort things out in peace.)

Brian Fable made a string of telephone calls from all over town, as he did most mornings. Each call came closer to telling Oscar that a change of tone, leaning toward the pornographic, might not do circulation any harm. Like George Lemoine, Fable frequently repeated himself and often forgot previous telephone conversations. He criticized Oscar for rarely leaving the Domino—correctly diagnosing Oscar's difficulty in readjusting to urban life—and urged him to pay a morale-boosting visit to the Hoyt Tower headquarters. Elizabeth felt up to the journey, so cartoonist and dog walked downtown together to the Fable Enterprises offices.

Not a believer in leash laws, Oscar had trained Elizabeth to walk close to his trouser leg, like a guide-dog, and he kept one arm stiff at his side as if his hand clutched the handle of her lead. In this way, and by wearing dark glasses and holding his head stock-still, he hoped to deceive the authorities. If it would not have compounded his offenses to impersonate a blind person by carrying a white cane, Oscar would have done so.

They strolled on in this manner through the midtown lunchtime rush, and were therefore jostled and accosted with regularity. Mighty Manhattan looked terrifically good, though—crisp and clean, windswept and electrically charged. Oscar relaxed as sights and sounds revived old memories: car horns and pretzels, steam and smoke, cascades of diamonds in bulletproof displays. Elizabeth too seemed rejuvenated by the walk, as no doubt her gray nose flooded her canine imagination with olfactory reminiscences. Oscar even dared to make eye contact with passersby, and detected ample good cheer among his fellow New Yorkers. Self-consciously pretty girls lugged modeling portfolios, taut-skinned Diana Burke's toted heavy shopping bags, businessmen and businesswomen slowed their pace to a mere trot to savor unfamiliar fresh air, and tourists risked back injury and shoe-soiling in their craning awe of skyscrapers.

It was in a cheerful and nostalgic mood that Oscar and Elizabeth swung through the revolving doors of the Hoyt Tower. They shared an elevator with messengers and secretaries who looked as young and fresh as the day. On the forty-second floor the elevator doors opened onto a receptionist's lobby decorated with framed reproductions of Oscar's celebrity nude-caricature *Lowdown* covers. The receptionist, new since Oscar's day, quickly changed her lackadaisical demeanor when she learned his identity. While she was friendly to him, Oscar thought he detected a tinge of annoyance in her voice, as if she had been waiting months to meet the person responsible for her having to spend eight hours a day in a gallery festooned with sexually explicit artwork. She escorted Oscar and his dog into the open-plan editorial offices where the anniversary party had been held. There she left him in the hands of copy-editor Travis Hall and Fable's three inseparable intellectuals.

"She's racked," said Travis Hall, employing slang Oscar had never heard for putting a publication to bed. Travis provided Oscar with a master dummy of the latest issue. Fable's intellectuals stood by nervously as the cartoonist perused its pages.

"Beautiful," said Oscar. "As ever. Do you mind if I sit down and read it? You guys can play with Elizabeth."

Oscar was given a private room and a cup of coffee. He inspected his own caricature first, which he hardly remembered drawing. The *Lowdown's* editor sometimes sat on seasonal work for several months before publishing—in this case the nude caricature was of Myles Standish, wearing only a peaked and buckled pilgrim's hat, looking down despairingly at a fistful of withered corn that mirrored the state of his private parts.

Oscar sighed. The young man had grave doubts about his job. Since the Bunny Fenton fiasco he had found few positive aspects to his work and for the first time a cover failed to bring the slightest trace of a smile to his lips. He felt like a cabaret singer forced to perform the same torch-song encore every night for twenty years in smoky rooms, watching his audience grow fat and weepy. He sighed again and turned the page.

The first twelve pages of the *Lowdown* contained advertisements for products Oscar could not afford. This was a marked improvement on the old days, when not even escort services deigned to buy space. Now jewelers and fashion houses and car manufacturers and luxury hotels vied for full pages. Oscar could not imagine why Brian Fable worried when his organ had traveled so far upmarket. Oscar sighed again, and turned the page.

Here began Marcus Barnard's feature article, headlined on the cover beneath Oscar's nude, entitled "Sure I Beat My Wife—The Jason Lundquist Odyssey." Oscar tried to read the convoluted article, but Marcus Barnard employed the trademark jargon of urban trendiness that relied for its comprehension on allusions to and within a field of almost instantaneous turnover: had he read the previous issue of the *Lowdown*, Oscar might have recognized some of the names of the people who in one month's time had become legends of pop antiquity. As matters stood, Oscar found it difficult enough to dissect individual sentences, much less to latch on to what must have been the formidable personality of Jason Lundquist—who claimed, at twenty-two, to have published a volume of ghost-written memories of his life in the performing arts, or perhaps Performance Art. Uninitiated Oscar could not be certain.

Oscar tried to write off this article as satire, and turned the page. On the left-hand side was an erotic photograph of more than two people, naked men or women or both, perspiring heavily in a setting of exotic opulence, their limbs wound together like a tangle of serpents. On closer inspection this photograph proved to be an advertisement for high-fiber breakfast cereal. On the right-hand side was a similar photograph, in soft-focus sepia, which turned out to be not an advertisement but the first in a sequence of nude or partially clad photographs of an Anglo-Hungarian actress who would—if the biographical information accompanying the pictorial was correct—be ineligible to purchase a bottle of wine in New York

City for some three years more. Oscar began to see how the *Lowdown* might have blurred the line between trendiness and vulgarity, not to say obscenity, but tried to assure himself that this was also satire. In his heightened state of awareness in the wake of the Bunny Fenton episode, Oscar found that he could not approve of the young actress's admittedly succulent flesh being displayed on the pages of his magazine. He had seen the books: the *Lowdown* paid high modeling fees and fame-factor bonuses that no innocent young person—especially one managed by handlers and agents with alimony to pay—could afford to turn down. This was known, Oscar believed, as coercion. The cartoonist lingered for a few minutes more on these photographs, thinking they were skillfully executed and about as arousing as a two-dimensional reproduction of reality could possibly be. He sighed, for different reasons, and turned the page.

Here was an article by Harold Hampsten on the joys of a sexual act it had never been Oscar's privilege to experience. Harold Hampsten's piece read like a safety manual for a radioactive waste-disposal technician. Clearly written and morbidly humorous, the article taught the reader how to equip himself for entering the hazardous zone, and how to enjoy an endeavor that was on the one hand perfectly acceptable to the writer, and on the other hand potentially lethal. Harold Hampsten's concluding advice was to live for today and pay the price.

Oscar looked up from the *Lowdown* and through the glass partition that separated him from the open-plan cubicles. Harold Hampsten had hefted Elizabeth onto a desk and was forcing her to shake his hand, over and over again. On the far side of the room stood Gail Gardener, staring straight back at Oscar. Oscar pretended not to have seen her, and looked back into the pages of the *Lowdown*. He found it difficult to focus on the next article, which had to do with indispensable fashion accessories for New York's clubhoppers, knowing that a chat with poor Gail Gardener was inevitable. Besides, his own magazine's humid content had plunged him into reminiscence.

II

"YOU CAN'T POSSIBLY EXPECT ME TO BELIEVE YOU," SAID VERONIQUE, once Oscar had protested for the fifth time that he had lived under such a substantial misapprehension for so many weeks. Hansie had limped upstairs to bed half an hour ago after a ceremonial drink, as Elizabeth's painting was hung on a wall next to the sliding windows that overlooked the sea. Oscar and Veronique sat close together on a love seat in one of the sparsely furnished downstairs drawing rooms. Elizabeth snored softly in an armchair across the room.

Oscar reached out and took Veronique's hand. "I will say it one more time: I promise. I promise you I had absolutely no idea. Reconstruct it in your mind. How would I have known? I can see now that Neville tried to warn me, tried to tell me the truth, but he simply never *spelled it out*. I am a very literal-minded person. I need people to be straightforward with me. Innuendo and conversational undercurrents escape me entirely."

Veronique finally appeared to soften. The anger had evaporated from her eyes. She rubbed Oscar's forearm with her left hand.

"And this?" she asked, wiggling the finger that bore, Oscar had to admit, a wedding ring.

"You wear a lot of different rings. It simply never crossed my mind."

"It is true that I don't always wear the ring." She smiled now, giving Oscar some hope that she saw the humorous side of his blindness.

Oscar began to think that his misunderstanding might have been all to the good. It was important that Veronique should be exposed to his social blind spot before things went any further. She could serve as his guide.

It was not lost on Oscar that, however retroactively, he was involved in an adulterous affair. Neville's previous warnings returned to him with the full weight of their true meaning, as did Veronique's recent assertion that Hansie would feed him to his dogs if he found out. He wondered if danger was supposed to add spice to their affair.

"I am relieved," said Oscar. "Just think. At any moment I might have blurted out something. . . ."

"Don't think about it," said Veronique.

Oscar allowed a minute of silence while he thought about how to proceed. He did not subscribe to spoken dissection of romance. One of the more troublesome aspects of his love life back home had been the tendency of young women to talk, endlessly, of "relationships" and "sharing" of experiences and "building" of lives, which for Oscar were concepts so spontaneous and ineffable that to think them through, even when alone and in private, was to risk destroying them. He supposed that these women knew other men who responded positively to their deconstruction of love or lust, and it saddened him to think of such couples, trapped in cramped quarters, hashing out their emotional affairs like chess players replaying a game for analysis. During his minute of silence Oscar resolved not to raise the subject of his future with Veronique. He would simply have to seduce her all over again in the usual unspoken manner, preferably outdoors and far from the Dobermans' range of scent.

"Care for a walk?"

"I think that would be wise," said Veronique. "We can walk to the cottage."

When they rose to go, Elizabeth woke from her sleep with a snapping yawn.

"Come along, girl," said Oscar. "The air will do your hangover good."

Oscar and Veronique walked away from the mansion without touching, until they could be certain none of the household's servants or guards would see them. Once they had descended an asphalt path, passed through a gate in the security fence, and left the mansion dark against the hillside behind them, they held hands. Elizabeth trotted close to heel, no doubt terrified of the murderous canine scents in the air.

Neither human spoke. Oscar tried his best to enjoy the nocturnal ambience, and not to ponder the interesting paradox that he had experienced his first adulterous affair without knowing it. Less amusing was the worry, which he forced from his mind each time it popped into his clouded awareness, that Veronique must be some kind of freak to marry so elderly a man. Oscar had heard of such arrangements, of course, but had always assumed that the young women involved in those transactions were strictly high-profile and unabashed prostitutes. He squeezed Veronique's warm hand almost involuntarily as this ungentlemanly thought crossed his mind. He would find out, soon enough, what had motivated such a sweet girl to devote herself to the ancient German. Perhaps Herr Dohrmann suffered from ill-health of some kind, and saintly Veronique had stepped in to nurse him. No one could blame Veronique for granting the dying wish of a old man who merely wanted to pass on his vast wealth to the one person brave and true enough to stay by his side. Oscar felt that this was a reasonable and likely scenario. Above all, it was comforting.

The asphalt path turned to gravel as it steepened toward the back garden of Hansie and Veronique's "cottage." All was dark on the unguarded premises. They circled around the house to the front lawn, the site of Oscar's high-dive. Veronique slipped off her sandals, led Oscar along the cushiony lawn to the edge of the cliff, and showed an admirable reluctance to speak.

The washing of the sea was now audible from the dark depths of the mini-fjord. Because it was precisely what made Oscar feel good, he put his arm around Veronique's waist and placed his hand on her skirted hip; she did likewise on his trousered one. Elizabeth cautiously patrolled the edge of the precipice, then settled on the high-divers' cement launching pad. Oscar shivered in the chilly air, and Veronique rubbed the small of his back to warm him. It wasn't long before Oscar's mind went satisfyingly blank and he was able to live through his physical senses, through the touch of Veronique's hand and hip. He would allow Veronique to break the silence, in her adorable accent. He would wait until dawn in this pose, if necessary, for her to be the first to speak. He imagined what she would say: words of comfort, words of desire, words of love—words of apology, even, for having lost her temper. Oscar waited for Veronique to speak, deciding that she was most likely to say, perhaps in French, which would be nice, "Make love to me, Oscar."

After a minute or two in his sensual trance, Oscar was so certain that this was what Veronique would say, and had heard these words so many times in his aroused imagination, that he had to ask her to repeat what she actually did say, when she finally said it.

"I said," repeated Veronique, in English, "I want to see you dive at night."

III

BY THE TIME GAIL GARDENER KNOCKED ON THE DOOR OF THE OFFICE
Oscar occupied at the *Lowdown* headquarters, the cartoonist
had nearly reached the conclusion that he was morally obliged
to firebomb the Hoyt Tower and all it contained. He simply
could not understand how it had escaped his notice that his
own creations adorned the cover of a high-gloss smut
magazine—that, in fact, his cartoons were merely the first of
many layers of obscenity. For all these months Oscar had
labored, in absentia, under the false belief that his nude
caricatures amounted to nothing more than mildly amusing and
sometimes provocative political and cultural commentary, and
that the *Lowdown* was a satirical magazine. Satire was no longer
a possibility—the *Lowdown* had left all of that behind. Now
Oscar's caricatures were exposed to him as the standard—the
calling card—of an organ devoted to exploitation and vulgarity.

"Come in," said Oscar, responding to Gail Gardener's knock.
She entered the office shyly, dressed in a casual, masculine
manner. She sat down across from Oscar at the room's only
table. She looked thoroughly unhappy.

"They're being mean to Elizabeth," said Gail.

Oscar glanced into the outer offices, where all three of Fable's
intellectuals had gathered around to experiment with the dog's
abilities.

"It's all right," he said. "It is actually Elizabeth who is being
entertained. She's older and wiser than they are. How are you,

Gail?" Oscar was eager to clear the air. His first night in the city, spent for the most part in Gail Gardener's company, had set an unfortunate tone for his visit.

"Oh, terrific," said Gail, confirming that she had meant this sarcastically by bursting into tears. She was already equipped with tissues, so Oscar remained seated.

"Has Brian spoken to you?" Oscar wanted to know.

Gail sniffled and nodded.

Much as he felt sorry for Gail, his priority for the moment was to clear his own name in the matter, to make it plain that whatever atrocious things Fable might have said to her were none of Oscar's doing.

"Did Brian tell you I spoke to him?"

Gail nodded again, and recovered her voice: "Thank you, Oscar," she said.

A satisfying reply.

"Good news, then?" Oscar thought it was now possible that he had performed one good deed, that he might have shown Fable the gentlemanly path, that he was solely responsible for Gail Gardener's future happiness. But Gail's renewed and even more prolonged sobbing made him think this was unlikely, unless, once again, he had mistaken the tenor of an emotional woman's words.

"What was that you said?" asked Oscar, his voice full of concern and uncertainty, for Gail had said something through her tissue. "What was that you said?"

"I said," sniffled Gail, "I said, you *bastard*."

"Ah," said Oscar, nodding his comprehension.

Reminded of his altercation with Bunny Fenton, Oscar knew enough to gird his loins for further abuse. He was not disappointed. Gail spared no expletive as she compared Oscar to human waste; to those who actively pursued Oedipal urges; even, surprisingly, to the substance a fisherman might clean from his creel after stepping too deeply in stagnant water. Oscar concentrated disapprovingly on her words, words he would never have dreamed of uttering himself, and decided that Gail Gardener was angry at him out of all proportion to what he could possibly have done to her, even accidentally.

When Gail ran out of ways to defame Oscar's character, she glared at him while fishing in her Third World handbag for more tissues and a hairbrush.

"Now," said Oscar, sitting forward in his chair, resting his elbows on the open copy of the *Lowdown*. "That's over with. Try, if you would, to spell it out for me."

"F-first," spluttered Gail Gardener, "f-first you try to . . . try to . . . you *bastard*, you tried to . . ."

There were no words in Gail Gardener's vocabulary to describe what it was Oscar had tried to do, but after a quarter of an hour of intense interrogation the cartoonist was able to discern that she wished to accuse him of attempted, or perhaps even successful rape. This was only the first in a long list of serious charges Gail wished to bring. She accused Oscar of telling Brian Fable that she was psychologically unstable and unfit for marriage or motherhood; she accused Oscar of advising unequivocal insistence on abortion; she accused Oscar of monumental conspiracy and betrayal in his dealings with Fable.

"I trusted you," said Gail, who two years ago would probably not have spoken to Oscar without witnesses, "and you do *this*."

Oscar appraised Gail Gardener: blue-gray circles hung beneath her tearful eyes; a scaly red rash marred her forehead; a collection of dirty blond strands of hair had adhered to her damp face; her flushed skin hugged her cheekbones. Oscar wished he knew what to say to her. He had seen where she lived, he knew how much she earned, he was well aware of how intolerable life could be for a woman in her neighborhood unprotected by wealth. Her day probably began trying to prevent lead-impregnated ceiling plaster from falling into her coffee mug. He imagined Gail Gardener returning home from the office every day, often late at night, praying silently to herself, clutching her can of tear gas, slamming her door behind her and setting a dozen bolts, checking the closets for madmen before pouring herself a drink. He pitied her and all lone women in the city, and thought that under the circumstances she could be forgiven her false accusations of rape.

Oscar also remembered how he had once admired Gail Gardener—fantasized about her, actually—and how he had thought she epitomized independence and *joie de vivre*. Even as a recent arrival in Oscar's native city from a safe but bland outpost of Manifest Destiny, Gail Gardener had seemed to know exactly how best to cope with both the dangers and delights of Manhattan. But the city had defeated her. Gail's supposedly gentrified neighborhood, bursting with comforts and conveniences for the rich, remained scarcely livable for a woman of Gail's modest means; it was filthy, threatening, and insecure. Oscar remembered that Gail had boasted to him on the night of his return to New York that three other single women in her building had fled the city for more tranquil lives beyond the river. Two others had married men they despised in exchange for shelter. Her one source of pride lay in having surmounted the city's ceaseless onslaught of degradation.

Thinking these things, Oscar vowed that he would help Gail Gardener if he could.

"I just want to tell you I understand," he said. This heartfelt statement was met with a searing look. Gail had finished crying and had gone back on the attack.

"Never mind that," she said. "I'm just glad I have you alone. This is the first time I've wanted to kill someone."

"I assume you are referring to that night. . . ."

"I am not. That sort of thing I can handle." Oscar could see that he had not dispelled the false notion that he had tried to have his way with Gail. "I'm talking about your kind advice to Brian. I really thought I could trust you."

You can, you can, Oscar wanted to say, but was unable to do so through a stream of random epithets. He only wanted to help, but it took all of his concentration to follow her sentences when her inbuilt sarcasm reversed the meaning of most adjectives. It was as confusing, but in a different way, as talking to Rachel.

"I just want to say, Gail," said Oscar, staring earnestly into her streaming eyes, "that I never, never advised Brian to ask you to terminate your pregnancy." Oscar's words were as quick and clear as they were euphemistic. "I never brought up the matter. I merely did what you asked me to do, to explain the situation to Brian. No more. If you heard otherwise from him, either you misunderstood, or he misspoke. Listen to me, Gail." Oscar leaned forward. He felt saintly. "You mustn't do *anything* you don't want to do. Understood?" Oscar leaned back in his chair like a prosecutor satisfied with his summing up, and waited for Gail Gardener to respond.

She too leaned back. Sarcasm drew itself onto her pale features.

"Didn't you notice?" said Gail. "I already have."

IV

OSCAR LEMOINE STOOD NAKED AT THE EDGE OF THE CLIFF. HE TOOK A quick look at the mini-fjord beneath his feet and saw its surface glinting in the starlight.

This is all a game, he thought. This is what Veronique looks for in a man: recklessness. Who was Oscar to say that this was an unfair criterion in weeding out suitors, especially for the woman who had everything? The more Oscar thought about it (and his thoughts were moving along at quite a rate just now), the more he thought Veronique's request was downright adorable.

He looked out to sea, where the lights of tankers and fishing boats glowed like embers in the darkness. The humid night air blew warmly over his naked body. He decided that on the whole things had worked out admirably, given his uncontrollable infatuation with Veronique. Why would she have gone to the effort of lying to her husband—her *husband*—if she expected anything less than a prolonged and possibly *quite* prolonged covert relationship?

Oscar looked over his shoulder at beautiful Veronique. She stood nearby, with Elizabeth at her heel, clutching Oscar's cast-off clothing. He blew a kiss to her and saw her smile light up the night; his knees trembled at the sight. Was she not the perfect woman, shivering there in anticipation of Oscar's dive?

Oscar turned to face the sea. He paused for a moment to wonder if Veronique had done this before to another lover, and to run through the short list of things he liked about being alive. This done, he emulated Neville Hacking-Cough by expanding his chest and raising his arms. He launched himself from the cliff in a swan dive of the utmost grace.

Something happened to Oscar in the air. His willingness to dive for Veronique's late-night amusement derived in part from his past experience of leaping from Hansie's cliff: he had expected a blind, unconscious few moments before being consumed in the frothy sea. But here he was, alert and aware, falling through space over a foreign body of water. The thought that struck him during free-fall was that poor Veronique, living under the strict rule of the elderly German, probably required the sensation of power gained by telling a man to jump off a cliff. Psychological spelunking was not Oscar's forte, but this explanation pleased him and made him feel that under the circumstances his dive would be worth the risk if it made Veronique feel better. With eyes tightly shut he accelerated toward the water. He clenched his fists and pointed his toes and tried to relax. There was no way of telling, of course, at what attitude he would strike the Mediterranean. His last thought before impact was that Veronique's challenge must amount to the most sophisticated form of foreplay he had yet encountered, and that the payoff was likely to be ever so memorable. •

It came as something more than merely a physical shock when Oscar felt the water crash not into his hands and head, but into his back. How silly I would have looked in broad daylight, he was able to think, before losing consciousness: perfect form, daintily pointed toes, slamming into the water upside down and backward. His last thought before blacking out was that he simply *hated* to appear ridiculous.

The cartoonist was next aware of existence when he opened his eyes to a confusing sight: he seemed to be trapped in a gigantic spider web in outer space; all he could see were the steely strands of webbing, and stars. He felt himself twisting weightlessly beneath this otherworldly panorama—rolling and pitching and yawing. Outer space nauseated him, and Oscar desired a return to coma.

"I say," said an alien voice. "Like an iguana he blinks."

If Oscar had not recognized the voice as Neville Hacking-Cough's, he would have made an attempt to decrypt the unlikely language for deeper meaning. He squinted through the spider web and felt his eyes focus, so that it was exposed as nothing more than the stays and halyards of Neville's yacht.

Into his line of sight came the angelic face of Veronique, all worry.

"You silly man," was what she chose to say. "I didn't mean really . . ."

Oscar heard a sound and recognized it as his own groan.

". . . that you should do that," concluded Veronique. "You silly man."

So I have been plucked from the brine, thought Oscar, tasting salt, and once more I have taken someone too literally. He found that he was naked, covered by a navy blanket. He turned his head to one side and took in the sight of the two art-lover girlfriends Neville had been cultivating since earlier in the evening. They held champagne glasses to their lips and were dressed in the uniforms of Neville's crew.

"I'm terribly sorry," Oscar said. "I really am."

"We heard a splash," came Neville's voice. "We thought it was an asteroid."

"I'm so sorry."

"Veronique was down here in a flash, as was your talented bitch."

Elizabeth was near at hand, available for comforting her master if absolutely necessary; part of her expression suggested that he deserved everything he got.

Oscar soon felt better, if seasick and achy. He was able to sit up and see that more people populated Neville's wife's giant yacht, some drinking, some sleeping, some playing backgammon and two, rather noisily and above decks for all to see, making love. Veronique went below to get Oscar a mug of hot chocolate (the numerous crew had been sent ashore with pockets full of cash), leaving the cartoonist sitting on the cabin roof with the blanket around his shoulders, trying unsuccessfully to avert his gaze from the act of copulation going on near the stern. The sight did much to revive him.

"Now, Mr. Lemoine," said Neville, who had separated himself from his girlfriends and approached Oscar from behind. "Mustn't let them distract you. Americans, you know. Something to do with 'marriage counseling,' if the husband is to be believed. Exhibitionism was prescribed—used to be *pro*scribed, when I was their age and went in for much the same thing. Now tell me—"(Neville sat down next to Oscar, obscuring his view of the maritally recuperating couple)"—tell me, was this a *voluntary* plummeting from the heights, or was the master of the house somehow involved? He may be an old cripple, Hansie, but he could carry you over his shoulder and toss you like a sack of rags."

"Voluntary," said Oscar.

"It's true, you know, about his strength," Neville said, as if Oscar's answer made no difference to his line of argument. "A veritable ox, in his day, Hansie was."

"I don't know if I should. . . ."

"People—men, that is—of your generation, have absolutely no conception of what it means to possess courage. Don't think it is a simple matter of hurling yourself off a cliff every now and again. My son's idea of valor is shattering jade figurines in friends' houses and writing checks for the damage."

"I'm sure I don't. . . ."

"Half a century ago," continued Neville, "think of that: half a century ago."

"I'm thinking." Oscar could not imagine why he was being lectured to in this way.

"Do you know what old Hansie was up to?"

"No."

"His arse in snow and blood," said Neville, rather unexpectedly, "that's what. Most unpleasant, but you could not possibly grasp this."

"I'm sure that's right, sir. I . . ."

"How old are you, Lemoine? Thirty?"

"Not yet, sir."

"Of course. Marvelous time. Just a few years ago Hansie would have been three times your age."

Oscar made a few quick calculations. "I'm catching up," he said.

"Don't be clever," scolded Neville, trying to cross his thin brown legs and missing on the first two attempts. "When he was your age he'd been through years of the most appalling battle, two wives, four children. And he had almost single-handedly rebuilt an entire industry from ruins."

"Amazing."

"Don't be sarcastic, young man."

Oscar had not meant to be sarcastic. He thought these facts of Herr Dohrmann's youth were amazing, and he had said so. He wished Veronique would come back.

"A great leader of men, that's what he was. Never mind the propaganda. This is what I try to tell my son, who keeps muttering 'Nazi' under his breath even when staying on as a guest at Hansie's house. War is war, young man, is what I tell my son. All this righteousness, from children who think it is heroic to spend a night in jail for wrecking their parents' cars. I could go into specifics about our Hansie, but I doubt they would mean a thing to an American of your generation. Even my own son wouldn't know Arnhem from Ascot."

Oscar knew of both places, but did not say so.

"My point is this," said Neville, as Veronique made her way along the deck with one hand on the rail. "If Hansie did throw you from the cliff, you most certainly deserved it. You would not be the first man he'd killed. You have got to learn respect."

"Thank you, sir."

"Ah, my dear," said Neville, changing his tone. "A little something for me too, I hope?"

"Of course," said Veronique. "Now Neville, you are in your lecturing pose again. You are not being mean to poor Oscar, I hope, after what he has been through?"

"A little history lesson, dear. History! I do hate it when your husband is misunderstood or underestimated. A bloody good soldier is a bloody good soldier."

"I've taken it all in," said Oscar cheerfully, sipping his hot chocolate, thinking with certainty that Hansie was a war criminal and Neville an Axis spy.

Neville's girlfriends called out for him. The American couple in the stern, following doctor's orders, reached a shrieking climax and rolled overboard. Elizabeth patrolled the gunwales. Neville grunted and returned to his girls. Veronique installed herself next to Oscar, beneath the blanket.

"Nobody reads Virgil anymore," Neville could be heard to say to the girls.

Oscar's seasickness dissipated somewhat when he felt Veronique's arm around his back. They huddled together and listened to the splashing American couple, who congratulated each other in loud voices on the intensity of their on-deck experience. The roll of dice and click of backgammon pieces were the only other sounds to be heard, except for Neville's droning voice and the plinking of ice cubes in his drink.

"Sobering," said Oscar.

"Your jump?"

"No, Neville's speech. He seems to hate his son, and anyone who reminds him of his son."

"Don't listen to him."

"He idolizes your . . . your *husband.*" Oscar furled a nostril.

"Don't let's talk about that. Let's talk about what a wonderful night we've had. And how nice it was you were not killed. Silly man."

Oscar would have taken offense at this third reminder that he had flown from the cliffs unnecessarily, but Veronique added the endearing gesture of stroking his inner thigh with her beringed left hand.

"You're right. A wonderful, endless night. I can hardly remember when it began. Elizabeth's artistic coup, I suppose."

"Where has she gone?"

"No doubt she's spying on the Americans. You've seen what a Peeping Tom she is."

"I don't know if your dog trusts me," said Veronique. "She looks at me sideways."

"She probably smells Dobermans," Oscar replied. "I wouldn't take it personally."

"Listen to Neville," she said, for Neville's laughing voice carried easily from the bow to where Oscar and Veronique sat: "That Cristobal," said the Englishman. "His art would make a cat laugh."

Veronique reverted to French to say that the Englishman was the heaviest drinker she had ever known, and at the same time the most energetic seducer of tender young flesh.

"Does he really . . . I mean does he . . ." Oscar did not wish to be vulgar.

"You saw him in the caves. You know very well that he does."

"And his wife?"

"Perhaps you will meet her one day. She comes to Val d'Argent every now and then to inspect her boat." Veronique rapped the deck of the yacht between Oscar's legs with her knuckles, then raised her hand to collect Oscar's vulnerables in her palm.

Oscar thought this was just fine, that he had cleared a considerable hurdle, that from now on his association with Veronique could be conducted on the basis of mutual disclosure. What else was there to learn?

"I have to tell you something, Oscar," said Veronique, once again in English.

"What's that?" Her sharp tone of voice worried him, enough so that he felt a momentary panic because she held him in the way she did.

"I'm going away in two weeks."

"Do you mean *for* two weeks?" asked Oscar, hopefully suspecting a rare lapse in Veronique's linguistic skills.

"*In* two weeks. To our home in Germany. And then . . ." Veronique went on to list an itinerary covering five or six months of frequent travel. ". . . It has been this way every year since we were married."

"When was that?"

"Four years ago. I should probably explain. . . ."

"Not if you don't want to."

"At the time I felt it was either that,"—she pointed up the cliffs to the right, at Hansie's mansion—"or *that*." She pointed to the left, where the convent loomed against the black sky.

"It can't have been that simple."

"Oh, no?"

"You wanted to be a *nun*?" Veronique was doing some very unnunlike things at the moment, which accounted for Oscar's almost impolite tone of disbelief.

"It seems like a very long time ago. I was not serious, but yes, it was fairly common in my family and I thought I might want to. Still, I fell in with the summer people—you met some of them at Le Village—and through them Hansie. He has aged so much in four years. When I met him he was more like . . . well, I suppose you could say he was more like Neville. Full of life and quite glamorous."

Oscar found this tale awfully sad, but then his was a narrow range of experience. Conveniently, it was time to stop talking. He forgot about nuns, he forgot about Neville, he forgot about Hansie. He slid down onto the deck with Veronique, sheltered by the cabin wall, and forgot.

V

OSCAR REVOLVED THROUGH THE DOORS OF THE HOYT TOWER AND lurched down the avenue. He wanted to run, but because Elizabeth was with him, leashless, he was forced to pose as a fleet-footed and expert blind man. He had fled the *Lowdown* offices without excuse, without apology. Enough already, he had growled to himself: next flight out. He did his blind-man's jog all the way to the Domino Hotel, glared at the innocent tourists naive enough to make eye contact with a stranger, snarled at the beggars who saw through his ruse and proffered their receptacles, elbowed aside in true New Yorker fashion the feeble pedestrians who slowed him down, slouched along crosstown streets ignoring the solicitations of drug dealers, stepped deliberately in gobs of phlegm, kicked aside spent hypodermic needles, and generally pressed on.

He barked his floor number into the elevator ceiling and scowled at the mirror. He flung open the door of Room 1107 and hurled his suitcase onto the bed and tore his clothes from the closet and drawers.

"Enough already," he repeated, liking the sound of the phrase.

Elizabeth kept her distance as Oscar violently packed. His art supplies he left where they were, because he had a plan. He called reception and demanded telephone silence and a steady stream of coffee and snacks. He positioned himself at his desk, swept aside his misguided Jesus sketches, rolled up his sleeves, and attacked his new subject from memory.

As always he started with the head, which he knew very well because he looked at it in the mirror sometimes several times a day. He drew his own head looking over one shoulder at the observer, with much the same expression he had drawn in Christ's face to represent horror and disbelief. It was also a face, he wanted to think, of abject contrition. As the hours passed, as tired old Elizabeth slept, Oscar added every nuance of remorse he could muster: a pleading quality in the corners of his desperate eyes; a ragged look to his hair as if he had pulled it from its roots in nightmare sleep; eyebrows raised into deep furrows on his forehead; lips seeming to form the beginning of the word *please*.

Oscar rested for an hour, stared into space, and as darkness fell outside he turned on the desk lamp and started the caricature of his own body. He drew the shoulders hunched, like those of a man expecting the lash of a whip. He drew supplicating, meshed-fingered hands in the shadow of his wretched torso. He drew crooked legs and gnarly feet and long, dirty toenails. He sighed, looking at the pathetic, pigeon-toed self-portrait, and pushed on to the obligatory genital representation. He drew a dark and diseased-looking scrotum hanging well below his knees by nothing more than a thread of scarlet tissue; he drew an elephant trunk of a penis, emerging from behind one of his legs and dragging disgracefully between his feet in the dust. He gave his member a mouth, and an expression very much like the one on his lips: *"Please."*

He drew a rocky trail underfoot leading toward a dismal desert horizon with the words "Sorry, Bunny Fenton" encoded in the whiskers of a forlorn cactus. He drew Elizabeth in the foreground, frowning at her unworthy master, not following him. With his usual blend of ink, colored pens and watercolors, Oscar finished his darkest work as dawn broke and the creeping sun reflected off the face of the neighboring skyscraper into Room 1107. He sat still and watched his painting dry.

He stood up and found that both of his legs were asleep, so that a springing semi-cartwheel was required to deliver him bouncing onto his bed.

"Sorry, girl," he said, because he had awakened Elizabeth. "Don't be frightened. Go back to sleep. I have a plan."

VI

CONFRONTED WITH ONLY TWO WEEKS LEFT IN VERONIQUE'S COMPANY, but determined to make the best of what little time he had, Oscar threw himself blindly into the cloak-and-dagger romantic liaison he had been enjoying for some time without being aware of the fact. These maneuvers were made simpler by Herr Dohrmann's constant jetting here and there, driving hither and yon, preparing for his annual worldwide business-and-pleasure pilgrimage. As before, except this time believing he knew at least the bulk of the facts, he allowed Veronique to lead in their surreptitious dance. She telephoned, they met. Oscar's only requirement, out of which he refused to be talked, was that each rendezvous be accompanied by a diverting activity of the outdoor variety: swimming, sailing, dining in an inland village; strolling, chatting, driving to a scenic view. In this way he hoped to make their alliance as much like it might have been had Hansie not existed—or had the German really been Veronique's father.

By exposing himself to so much of Veronique's company,

Oscar learned a powerfully attractive quirk of her personality, which was her enormous and intrepidly deployed English vocabulary. She taught Oscar words in his own native language. When she used the word *impercipience* correctly, he wanted to crush her in his arms.

"This is a trick, right?" he asked her, watching the moon from the reclining passenger seat of one of her convertibles. "You consult the dictionary before meeting me, you bide your time, you wait for an opening, and you deliver: 'Your impercipience amazed me,'" Oscar mimicked. "You are toying with me, Veronique."

In the back of Oscar's mind was the idea that Veronique should put her verbal skills to some practical use. When he raised this thought his remark was met with guttural Francophone sound effects of dismissal.

"Don't be silly," she added.

"I wish you wouldn't call me silly. Most people like working. I like working. Do something you enjoy—you have a lot of advantages. You could do many useful things."

From what Oscar could gather from Veronique's multilingual response, he had missed the point of being fantastically wealthy. Being fantastically wealthy, besides bestowing unimaginably heavy responsibilities upon the individual, meant being intrinsically useful. She sounded like Oscar's brother when she described the duties of her position, or rather Hansie's, as those of a reluctant and harried *volunteer*.

"You're quite right," Oscar found himself admitting. "You could have been a nun, after all."

That Oscar knew he was in love with Veronique was now beyond argument. Their two weeks together were spent, at least on Oscar's part, in a state of frantic pleasure and virtually no productivity. A rare telephone call from Fable Enterprises reminded Oscar that he had a job to do, that people relied on him. "You in love, or what?" asked a personal telex from Fable.

"Whom, me?" giddy Oscar telexed back, adding, "Nude's in the mail; male's in the nude." In public, Oscar affected stereotypical homosexual characteristics. This was part of the deal. He did this only at Veronique's explicit urging, and, he imagined, poorly. Val d'Argent homosexuals were not persuaded by his act, but then they were not the audience; they, at least, could keep a secret.

Despite the enforced outings, the vocabulary lessons, the homosexual posing—despite these amusing diversions—Oscar would remember those two weeks mainly for the midnight-to-dawn shifts, when Hansie was out of town, in the open-window sea breeze of Oscar's rented cottage bedroom, experiencing a physical pleasure so intense that it brought into question all other human pursuits.

Elizabeth was the most patient and supportive of labradors, throughout. She accompanied the pair on most of their outings, and did not appear to be too afflicted with jealousy. When her master was happy, she was happy. She executed a brilliant new acrylic painting in Veronique's presence, putting to rest any doubts the woman might have held about the authenticity of Canine Expressionism. When the human couple wished to be alone, Elizabeth tick-tick-ticked down the stairs and out into the starlit garden and sniffed the perimeter of Oscar's rented property. In the morning she nuzzled open Oscar's bedroom door and woke the couple with her eager little face.

Oscar dreaded Veronique's departure like a date of execution. He could not imagine what he would do without her during the chilly months ahead. He had been putting off a return to New York, and thought Veronique's prolonged absence might provide him with an excuse to make the unappetizing voyage. As the date approached he slept less and less, forestalling the inevitable and prolonging his enjoyment, so that by the eve of Veronique's departure he was a wan, exhausted young cartoonist. Hansie was already at home in Germany, awaiting his wife, so Oscar had her to himself. He drew up plans for a celebration. He purchased gifts. He bought Elizabeth a new bow tie. He said to himself, "I am going to be one of those people who knows how to have fun."

VII

OSCAR HAD DECIDED, EARLY IN HIS TEENS, THAT HE WOULD MEET THE affronts of New York City with nothing but stoical politeness. Graciousness and courtesy would be his only weapons of defense. Sooner or later, he had believed, his deference and humility would be repaid. This posture spanned the whole range of social contacts, from the everyday (apologizing to people who were not only rude but clearly in the wrong), to the fairly rare (thanking muggers). Oscar had been physically attacked only eight times in his many years in the city, and just once had his body required hospitalization. On this last occasion he did not have an opportunity to thank his assailant or bid him Godspeed, for the attack came from behind, out of the night, and Oscar's next view on the world was the ceiling of a hospital room through the gauze of a head bandage. When he was interviewed by the police he apologized for not remembering more details of the assault. He agreed with the policemen that it was a particularly ruthless individual who cracked the skulls of skinny teenagers with a tire iron to get at their loose nickels, but hastened to add that one must never underestimate the dehumanizing effects of poverty and despair.

The policemen criticized him for straying into the darkness unaccompanied; he apologized yet again. Oscar still intended to stick to his moral guns, to continue to say please and thank you to people who either literally or figuratively spat in his face.

In the Domino Hotel he lay back admiring his self-portrait, with Elizabeth snoring at the foot of the bed. The Bunny Fenton episode had put it most starkly: he should continue to be polite to everyone, because he could never be sure that they were not privately suffering. He realized that it was his very own brother who had tried to teach him this lesson years ago: "Treat people as if they have just been told of their parents' death" was George's only prep-school advice. George had later remarked that Oscar seemed to be taking this advice too literally, that he ought to speak up for himself a bit more, but it was too late: Oscar was a pacifist; thanks and apology poured from his lips. This might have gone some way toward explaining the content of his drawings, into which he funneled all of his accumulated rudeness.

"Ah, but no more," Oscar said aloud. "My last nude sits before me, and it is I."

With his thoughts collected he showered and shaved and packed up his belongings. He called reception and announced his imminent departure. When he realized how many nights he had spent at the Domino, he instructed them to add a large gratuity for Philippe, to send the bill along to Fable Enterprises, Inc., and not to take any guff. "Sue them if necessary," he ordered.

He jotted down the messages that had piled up during his telephone silence, including an "urgent" one from his older brother that asked Oscar to call him at home.

"Gah," said George, who answered on the first ring. "Disaster."

"What is it?"

"Dee-double-you-eye," said George.

"I don't understand."

"Driving while intoxicated," George explained.

"I'm sorry. What will this mean?"

"It will mean lawyers, that's what it will mean."

"How did they catch you?"

George seemed to find this question amusing.

"*Catch* me? It was actually more a matter of pulling my limp body out of a flaming wreck, if you must know the truth. The car is a write-off, thank you for asking. Did you know how much that car cost me? It cost me—"

George told Oscar how much the car cost.

"That's revolting," said Oscar. "But a shame to smash it, I suppose. And you?"

"Black eyes. My broken leg is more so."

"I'm sorry. Why aren't you in the hospital?"

"I was, until an hour ago. I called you from there, but that little prick at the Domino wouldn't let me through this time, no matter what I threatened."

"I'm sorry," said Oscar. "I was trying to be firm with the people downstairs. I actually told them not to believe any excuses."

"No great harm. Diana is taking good care of me, aren't you, babe?" Oscar could hear Diana in the background. "I'm on the most amazing pills."

"What can I do for you?"

"Not a thing. I'll get my people to work on the case. Rest up for a few days. Maybe I'll have time to see a bit more of you now."

"Actually," said Oscar, "I was thinking of getting out of town."

"Back to your woman, is it?"

"Absolutely. I'm afraid New York is wearing me down. I feel ill and claustrophobic. I made a fool of myself and it got into the papers."

"Yes, so I read. What's the scoop?"

"I'd rather not say. It may all come out. I made a mistake. Then I think Elizabeth tried to kill herself. And a woman at work has accused me of raping her. And Brian Fable is using me. And the *Lowdown* is pornographic. Things just aren't working out very well at all, you see."

"Gah, what a volatile little brother I have."

At least, thought Oscar, forgetting the fairly recent past, I do not drink and drive.

VIII

UNLICENSED, UNREGISTERED, UNINSURED AND DRUNK, OSCAR NEGOTI- ated the corners of the Val d'Argent corniche behind the wheel of one of Hansie's sports cars. From the passenger seat, trying to pour champagne, Veronique urged him on to excessive speeds. Elizabeth stood on her hind legs in the backseat with her front paws on the windowsill and her head in the wind. Wild thunderheads growled out to sea, while Oscar drove through the warm light of a scarlet sunset.

Hunched over the steering wheel, Oscar added his own sound effects to the ones provided by the car's engine as he clumsily shifted through its gears, for no particular reason. Up and down, right and left they drove, to the first stop on Oscar's itinerary, a hilltop war memorial that was most suitable for sunset watching and the consumption of wine. Oscar brought the frisky vehicle to a jolting stop half on, half off the first step leading to a monolith covered with the names of dead and deported.

"Hurry, hurry!" he cried, for the sun had nearly set. "Veronique! The picnic basket! Elizabeth! My camera!"

They rushed up the steps to the monument. They spread out their picnic on a grassy slope overlooking the sea. Oscar raised his glass and toasted the water, the sunset, the hills, the harbor, the dead, the deported, Elizabeth—and Veronique a dozen times. They drank, they ate, they photographed each other.

"Onward!" Oscar cried, for the sun had set and it was time to move. Veronique would be gone in twelve hours; there was not a second to waste.

He flung the sports car down the switchbacks to the main road that led to the motorway and the port city beyond. He drove at a terrific speed, yet was not terrified. He nosed into the city, taking a route he had memorized in a taxi in preparation for his last night with Veronique. He drove through areas unaccustomed to the sight of such a car, ducked down increasingly narrow cobblestone streets, and jerked to a halt outside a pastel-blue dwelling. The clientele of a two-table café across the street clucked first at the car, then at Veronique as she slid her legs out of the passenger seat.

The broad oak door of the house was ajar. Oscar conducted Veronique and Elizabeth through it, into a cobbled, torch-lit courtyard. A table laid for four awaited them. Oscar ushered Veronique to a chair, poured her a glass of wine from the chilled and opened bottle that had been placed to one side in advance, and told her to wait there for him.

When he returned he bore a vase of flowers, a lighter for the candles, and a flat gift-wrapped box.

"Our hosts will be here shortly. In the meantime, I thought you looked a little chilly, even here, out of the wind. Please open it."

Veronique tugged at the ribbon, opened the box, and

extracted a knitted turquoise shawl. While she admired it, Oscar moved behind her to assist in draping it over her bare brown shoulders.

"Our hostess made it. You may thank her when she arrives. I hope you don't mind company for dinner—Monsieur Berlinger and his wife are very nice people. You met him at Elizabeth's auction. This is their house."

Veronique seemed not to remember.

"Do you smell where we are? Right near the water. But so still, in the courtyard. I hope you're having a good time."

Veronique did not reply, but the way Oscar judged her smile and the situation in general, she was speechless with pleasure. His intention had been to remove her from the social battlefield of Val d'Argent, to expose her to simpler pleasures and humbler folk.

"Ah, here they are now," said Oscar.

Monsieur Berlinger and his wife, Marla, emerged from a passageway into the courtyard. Slim Berlinger wore a smart tweed jacket and a red tie. Madame Berlinger, very dark and much larger than her husband, wore a white caftan beneath a shawl similar to the one she had made for Veronique.

Introductions and reintroductions were made; Veronique politely thanked Madame while fingering her shawl. Soon a young man appeared with plates of olives and hot peppers and a basket of bread. He served these dishes, then paused while Berlinger introduced him as his very own son.

"Pascal is a musician," said Berlinger with pride. "As you will see. Also a talented waiter." Pascal had inherited his father's slimness and his mother's Mediterranean smile. He fended off Oscar's suggestion that he should join them at the table, and rushed off at his father's command to fetch more wine from the cellar.

The moon rose into view over the eaves of the courtyard.

"My mother is cooking," said Monsieur Berlinger, as Pascal

returned with wine and assorted plates of pâté, artichoke hearts, garlic meatballs, creamed cauliflower, and fried squid. "A little of everything, so that everyone is happy. Yes?"

"Yes," said Oscar.

"Where is Elizabeth?" asked Veronique.

"In the kitchen," said Monsieur Berlinger. "She is good friends with my mother. She has been here before and was served tasty scraps."

Only Monsieur Berlinger could possibly have understood so quickly what it was Oscar had required by way of celebration. The whole plan had been arranged in a three-minute telephone call, without much explanation on Oscar's part. "Be here at nine," was all Monsieur Berlinger had said. "You will have a wonderful time with your young lady. It will be a cool night. My wife will knit something that you may present to her."

When Pascal had served the main course—a grilled sole, which he dispensed from a platter with oversized fork and spoon—he informed the group that they would have to pour their own wine from now on. He returned five minutes later in his singer's costume, guitar slung round his neck, stood at a polite distance, and sang ballads of love and kindness.

Monsieur Berlinger looked proud; Madame looked anxious, but dignified. Berlinger's mother brought coffee and brandy, so that her grandson could continue strumming and singing without interruption. The group discussed Elizabeth's art, and the prospects for a Paris exhibition and auction. Veronique volunteered to invite her Paris circle, a comment that caused much eye-widening on Berlinger's part.

"That's it, then," said the Frenchman. "Paris, in the springtime."

As if on cue, Elizabeth trotted into the courtyard, looking pleased with herself in her new tie.

"Elizabeth says it's time to go," said Oscar. "You have made this a wonderful evening."

Veronique concurred, and after heartfelt embraces and promises to reciprocate, the couple departed.

"What a nice surprise," said Veronique, once Oscar was behind the wheel. "I haven't had such a relaxing dinner in ages."

"They're very nice people."

"I think I could get Pascal a job singing at Le Village. Do you think that would be all right?"

"What a good idea. Let's do that. Let's get Pascal Berlinger on stage. Anything would be better than old Antoine. But now—onward!"

"Not the caves again?"

"I had thought," said Oscar, "that under the circumstances you might wish to say good-bye to André at the Floride. He has a table waiting for us. And later, a swim in my pool?"

This suited Veronique, so they sped down the highway toward Val d'Argent. On the way, Oscar remarked innocently that he had never been so exhilarated behind the wheel of a car.

"You like my little car, do you?" Veronique asked.

"Very much."

"You will keep it, then."

At this suggestion Oscar's immediate instinct was to launch into an I-wouldn't-dream-of-it-not-in-a-million-years speech, but he stopped himself in time.

"How very nice of you," he said, with a forced nonchalance that he hoped would not betray his embarrassment at having been offered a car he was not only unqualified to operate, but could probably not afford to keep on the road. He told himself that for Veronique this gesture was the financial equivalent of his buying her a glass of wine, and that she probably only meant it as a loan during her absence. "How very nice of you," he said again. "I accept."

IX

IN A GREAT HURRY, BECAUSE HE HAD A PLANE TO CATCH, AND LACKING the packing materials necessary to protect his work, Oscar Lemoine found himself striding down Fifth Avenue during rush hour carrying a two-foot by three-foot nude caricature of himself. It was impossible to conceal the painting by pressing it against his body, for it had not yet fully dried. In fact he wished to dry it on the way to the Hoyt Tower, which meant waving it in the air overhead and calling attention to what was, in broad daylight, a shockingly explicit article of draftsmanship.

The guard in the Hoyt Tower foyer tried to pretend he hadn't noticed the caricature. The three people who shared Oscar's elevator, and therefore had quite a long time to inspect the painting, were openly interested. Oscar considered this mild humiliation a mere prelude to his ultimate act of contrition, the mass circulation of this, his last caricature.

Fable Enterprises were headquartered one floor above the *Lowdown* offices. While maintaining his composure, and making sure to say please and thank you to the Fable Enterprises receptionist, Oscar made a show of striding purposefully and unannounced into Brian Fable's office. Young Fable sat behind his gigantic desk, talking on the telephone, and reacted to Oscar's dramatic entrance with an index finger pressed to his lips and a working of eyebrows meant to suggest that his telephone call was several orders of magnitude more important than anything Oscar could conceivably have to say, no matter how out of character it was for the cartoonist to barge into his office.

"Brian!" shouted Oscar, emboldened by a new commitment to recklessness and, more important, a lack of sleep. "Hang up!"

"Look, ah, Monty," said Fable into the telephone, glaring at Oscar, "a terrorist has just burst into my office. If I don't get back to you in fifteen, call the police." He cradled the receiver. "Ah," he said. "The man they called Impetuous. Have a seat, Oscar. This looks serious. You've never come upstairs before."

"I only have a few minutes," said Oscar. "I have a plane to catch. I have brought you the Christmas cover. And my apologies."

"What for?"

"For leaving you in the lurch. I'm sorry, but I'm afraid I won't be doing any more of these." Oscar handed over the caricature of himself.

Fable looked at the drawing.

"Actually," he said, in so offhand a way that Oscar could only imagine his words were heartfelt, "I was about to suggest the same thing. It's a tired joke. Time to be rid of you, my friend. We'll run this one—but only as a favor to you, you understand. I think a parting of the ways is long overdue. Okay?"

"What do you mean, 'okay'?" Oscar was not nearly so adept at games of intimidation.

"I mean," said Fable, "*off . . . you . . . go.* I mean— *adios, au revoire,* bye-bye. Got me? I mean get *lost,* is what I mean."

For once, thought Oscar, Fable had made himself clear.

"I'm sorry," said Oscar, "that you felt you had to use that tone of voice. I had a good time working for you. I thank you for all your help and encouragement."

Oscar bowed cordially, turned on his heel, and walked across Fable's office toward the door. Behind him, Fable dialed.

Before leaving the building Oscar took the elevator one floor down to the *Lowdown* offices. He deposited an envelope with the receptionist. "It's for Gail Gardener," he explained. "I've written her name on the front. Would you be nice enough to see that she gets it, please?"

The envelope contained a letter which used clear language to protest that Oscar had not raped Gail Gardener, but that he was sorry if she still thought otherwise. It went on to reiterate his promise that he had never counseled abortion. Without using the vulgar language that came most readily to mind, Oscar's letter explained to Gail that Fable was a coarse and brutal man; that a wise woman would avoid him; and that the threat of a sexual harassment charge might go some way toward chastening him. Oscar left the building telling himself to feel cleansed.

"Taxi!" shouted Oscar. "Taxi!"

This was an almost impossible demand, for although there were cabs available, Oscar could not bring himself to hire one when there were so many fellow humans nearby with the same intention. Elderly couples, fragile young women, tormented businessmen, encumbered shoppers—all these people vied with Oscar for the yellow cars, and he ushered them one by one into taxis that by all rights should have belonged to him. At last the immediate vicinity was clear of more deserving passengers, and Oscar was able to climb aboard and issue instructions: "Airport," he said. "Via the Domino. Please get me out of here."

Philippe awaited him beneath the awning of the Domino Hotel with Elizabeth and luggage close at hand.

"A million thanks," said Oscar. "You're a nice guy, Philippe."

"My pleasure," said Philippe, who had long since dropped his French accent in Oscar's presence. He began to help Oscar load his bags into the trunk of the cab, then remembered something: "Listen, you had a visitor just now."

"Oh?"

"It's a little embarrassing, We had to call the police, actually."

Oscar thumbed through his mental list of people who might have dropped by to make a scene. It said something about his stay in New York that several candidates sprang to mind.

"Name?" Oscar asked.

"Elkin," said Philippe.

"The Eliminator?" asked Oscar, remembering his hate mail.

"That's correct. Combat fatigues. Took a swipe at your dog. The hotel can press charges. . . ."

"No, no. Elkin's a friend of mine. A fan. Set him free."

"Whatever you say."

Oscar shook Philippe's hand and said good-bye.

"I hope she'll be okay," said Philippe, as Oscar got into the taxi.

"She'll be fine. The city doesn't agree with her. I'm taking her back to France—but don't tell Elkin."

Philippe saluted a last farewell and jogged back into the hotel.

"Onward!" said Oscar. "Please get us out of here."

X

AFTER A NIGHT OF EMPHATIC WAKEFULNESS, OSCAR AND ELIZABETH drove Veronique to Val d'Argent's private airport. Their good-byes were subdued, owing to exhaustion and a general feeling of having said it all shortly before dawn. Veronique flew away over a calm sea in her husband's alarmingly large plane. Oscar and Elizabeth stood on the tarmac, waving good-bye. On the way home in his slick new car, Oscar experienced a rare elation: a clear mind, a sated body, a near future of uninterrupted work in a quiet, off-season Val d'Argent. It was still possible that he could gather the energy to make a quick probe back to New York, just to pass the time until his great, illicit love returned.

The next weeks saw daily meals at the Floride; philosophical chats with Neville, whom Oscar increasingly admired for his entertaining conversation and his wife's yacht, but rarely met after dark for fear of drunken lectures; assembling his "Nun of the Above" serial about a beautiful girl saved from life in a French convent by a dashing American cartoonist; making anonymous telephone calls to the French authorities to determine exactly how severe his punishment might be were he arrested behind the wheel of his sports car; teaching Elizabeth to shed her artistic inhibitions and fill every nook of canvas.

When the time came to plan his trip to New York, Oscar's expenses were considerably reduced by the discovery of a working telephone beneath the dashboard of Veronique's car. Since he dared not drive unnecessarily, and because Anton seemed to be waiting for a school to accept him, many was the time Oscar's pyromaniac neighbor caught the cartoonist sitting in the stationary vehicle in the driveway, furiously dialing far-flung numbers. For all practical purposes, Oscar's car amounted to nothing more than a preposterously luxurious telephone booth. Whatever guilt he felt over this unethical use of another's telephone was alleviated by the belief that whatever charges he managed to incur would be lost in the Amazonian rain forest of Herr Dohrmann's mammoth outlays—like stealing a matchbook from an international hotel chain. So he dialed on, revved the engine to maintain current, and talked through time zones to friends and colleagues.

Having made his plans, Oscar and Elizabeth took a last swim in the pool, ate breakfast at the Floride, and took a taxi to the airport to leave for what he hoped would be a brief, friendly, exploratory probe of New York City.

SIX

I

D*RUNK AND DISCOMBOBULATED, OSCAR LEMOINE BOUNCED ON TO* the windswept tarmac of Val d'Argent's private airport in the middle of a November night, protected from physical injury by an airplane. Elizabeth lay curled in a seat next to him. His drunkenness was due to having sat on a Paris runway drinking gin for three hours—after assisting a desperate fellow traveler in convincing a sympathetic crew member to bend the rules— while the authorities held their collective finger in the air to gauge the winds on the southern coast. Oscar imbibed an even larger amount while airborne because the flight attendants had all gone pale and were hugging each other as if for the last time. On landing, while Oscar held hands with his drunken seatmate and petted Elizabeth's brow, the smallish and disreputable-looking airplane skidded ninety degrees in a unexpected inch of slush, while trying to turn toward the terminal. The craft tipped one of its wheels off the ground, and made most of the passengers scream. The captain quickly apologized; the flight attendants swore and made hand gestures suggesting that the pilot was a boozing-soaked incompetent.

Both heavily tranquilized, Oscar and Elizabeth descended the gangway into a meteorological crisis: sleet fell insultingly into the palm trees that lined the airport road, only to be blown horizontally like gravel by a violent wind. There were no taxis to be found, and most of the other passengers were quickly swept away by limousine. Oscar consigned his luggage to the authorities, who were at their most cordial because they had not expected anyone to survive the landing. Elizabeth looked alarmingly unwell—more so than a generous dosage of tranquilizers could account for—so Oscar carried her in his arms and tried to solicit a ride into town from one of the forlorn-looking people who had also alighted at this place, at this time. Oscar played shamelessly on mankind's love of dogs, until an elderly mink-stoled woman agreed to give the pair a lift to town. It did not hurt his cause when Oscar told the woman he thought his dog might be dying.

During the car ride, in the spacious passenger compartment of the limousine, Oscar gave his white lie some thought: Elizabeth's signs of mental instability and ill health in New York did not seem to bode well for the aged artist's future. Oscar told himself that once they were installed again in Val d'Argent, and the refreshing Veronique reappeared, Elizabeth would regain her thirst for life and all would once again be well.

The owner of the car, who proved to be English, chatted in a loud voice with her French driver, whom she apparently had not seen since the previous summer. She wore a broad-rimmed black hat and enough diamonds to read by. Short and plump and heavily wrinkled, she spoke correct French to the driver in a gravelly smoker's voice and a lazy accent, and insisted on pronouncing all interchangeable words in English. When she had finished interrogating her driver about local gossip, she lit a cigarette with a slim gold lighter and reclined in her seat. Oscar thought it only polite to strike up a conversation.

"I'm very grateful to you," he said. "I had no idea the weather would be so bad. My name is Oscar Lemoine."

"How do you do," said the woman, carelessly blowing smoke into Elizabeth's face.

"I live in Val d'Argent."

"Oh, do you?"

"Yes. I like it here. Especially in the off-season."

"Oh, do you?"

"Oh, yes. I am unemployed, you see." This was Oscar's attempt to make himself sound immensely wealthy, so that the woman would not hate him out of hand.

"How nice for you," said the woman.

"Yes," said Oscar dreamily.

"I loathe France," added the woman unexpectedly, through an exhalation of smoke. "I loathe it."

"Well," said Oscar, the diplomat, "on a night like this . . ."

"I despise the French," the woman interrupted. Oscar thought he could hear the French driver sighing. "But the country is still so clearly rife with them, isn't it? Petty, arrogant hateful . . ." (the woman paused to inhale more smoke) ". . . cowardly, selfish, *loathsome*."

Ah, thought Oscar, remembering his meeting with Brian Fable only a few hours ago: the woman they called Intolerant. Oscar felt he should stick up for his adopted country, the land where he had fallen in love, the nation where they never maligned England (because they never thought of England, in any sense of the phrase).

"I am French," said Oscar, in a mild French accent. The driver glanced warily at Oscar in his rearview mirror. "And I resent your remarks."

By Oscar's standards this was a stinging slap, but the woman was not only unfazed, she merely compounded her abuse: "Thank *God*," she said. "I thought for a moment you might be *American*." A little ball of two-hour-old smoke popped from her mouth as she made a noise of hatred.

It was only now that Oscar realized the woman on the seat next to him was not only profoundly full of smoke, but absolutely pickled with drink. That was not an exotic perfume he smelled, that was an elderly skinful of scotch.

"That was quite a flight we had," said Oscar, retaining for the moment a French accent. "I find I have to drink quite a lot to stave off fear. In bad weather, that is."

The woman's head lolled in Oscar's direction and her nearly crossed eyes looked up at him beneath the brim of her hat.

"Excuse me," she said.

"Why?" Oscar wanted to know.

The distinguished lady allowed a certain amount of wind to escape from her mouth before replying: "That's why."

"Quite all right," said Oscar. "Your car, after all."

The woman emitted a profound sigh, unrelated to her eructation. "My *Christ* this is unpleasant," she said. "Has to be done, has to be done."

"What has to be done?"

"Terrible chore," wheezed the woman, searching her hand-bag for her cigarette case.

"I don't understand."

The woman suddenly leaned back in her corner of the car and gave Oscar an alarmed, eye-popping look, as if discovering an intruder in her bedroom.

"Who *are* you?" she cried. "Who *are* you?"

"I thought I introduced myself. Oscar Lemoine." He let his French accent slip away, for the woman was clearly not capable of noticing the difference. She still seemed frightened, so Oscar continued in more soothing tones. "I recently quit my job. Now I manage my dog full time. She paints." Oscar felt a bit wicked saying this, expecting that it would confuse the woman still further, in her defenseless state.

"Oh, that," said the woman, not at all confused. "Oh, yes, that I know all about."

"You've heard of her?"

"I'm not so out of touch as that," she said. "I keep abreast. My husband told me about the dog who paints. Victoria, isn't it?"

"Elizabeth."

"Quite."

"Do you hear that, girl?" Oscar said to the dog. "International fame. You're *huge*."

"Rot," said the woman. "Excuse me"—another escape of gas—"rot. Animals who paint. And she looks frightfully unhappy, your dog."

"She hates flying."

"No, I mean ill. Too thin."

"Do you think so?"

"Certainly. Oh, yes, I remember now. I've heard about her tricks. The dog swims, paints, drinks martinis, wears a tie. My husband wrote to me."

"You're not . . ." Oscar felt himself leaping to conclusions. "Are you Neville's wife?" He realized too late that it might be impolite to use his elder's Christian name.

"Neville Hacking-Cough, yes," said the woman. Oddly enough her inebriated slur made the name sound just as it had with Neville's mouth full of ice cubes. "You know him, do you?"

"I used to see him frequently, yes. Is he here in deepest winter?"

"Neville has stayed here more or less constantly for nearly thirty years. He feels unwelcome in England, quite justifiably." The woman paused for a moment and stroked her wrinkled chin in thought. "I have an idea," she said at last. "Paul, the cabinet!"

Oscar tried to work out the meaning of this command, until a drink cabinet opened and slid along the floor from beneath the front passenger seat.

"Make us a drink," said the woman to Oscar. "Mine is scotch with three ice cubes."

Oscar obliged. When they had their drinks, Neville's wife became conspiratorial, leaning well over toward her traveling companion and actually touching his leg with her gnarled and bejeweled fingers.

"You are going to do me a favor, Mr. Lemon," said Mrs. Hacking-Cough. She giggled and covered her mouth.

No, I'm not, Oscar wanted to say, having so recently botched all the other favors asked of him.

"I don't know if that is possible."

"Very simple, young man," she said, patting his leg. "Neville is not exactly . . . *expecting* me, if I may put it that way. Not so soon or in this weather, at any rate. I simply want you—and your little dog—to be there when I see him, which will be for the first time in some months. Just to witness the occasion, don't you see? So that when he explains what he has been up to, it will be in front of someone who knows the *truth*!" Old Mrs. Hacking-Cough fairly punched the air with satisfaction at the devious plot she had concocted. "And you will do this little favor for me," she said, "because I saved you and your little dog from the elements."

"Right," said Oscar. "I'm your man." Much as he hated to be plunged into further intrigue so soon after his return to Val d'Argent, Oscar thought he had learned a few things in New York, and that he was prepared to meet the challenge of subterfuge on his own terms: he owed Neville a favor or two as well, after all, for not betraying his association with Veronique to Herr Dohrmann. "When do I go into action?"

"Immediately!" Mrs. Hacking-Cough was flushed with anticipation.

II

AFTER TWENTY MINUTES IN THE LIMOUSINE WITH MRS. HACKING-
Cough, Oscar had gleaned that her worst fears concerned little
more than the presence of "riff-raff" in Neville's life, a term that
presumably applied to Oscar as much as anyone else. She
complained that in his effort to enjoy himself Neville had
lowered his social standards. He seemed to think that anyone
off the street might be capable of showing him a good time. She
also candidly, or rather drunkenly, expressed the belief that
Neville might be something of a philanderer. How easy it would
have been for Oscar merely to list for her the times he had
personally seen Neville keeping disreputable, even underage,
company. Instead Oscar feigned shock and disbelief, he protested Neville's innocence, he vowed his personal revenge if
the Englishman had so much as glanced at another woman, and
his retaliation against those who spread such vile rumors. He
crossed his legs and shunted Elizabeth onto the floor of the
passenger compartment; he sipped his drink; and, as Brian
Fable might have put it, he "anecdoted." Oscar told stories of
debauchery, and noted Neville's absence; he told stories of
rectitude and athleticism, and noted Neville's participation.
Oscar went so far as to describe Neville as his mentor and moral
conscience. "Pure as the driven snow," he concluded.

Mrs. Hacking-Cough listened skeptically between sips of
scotch and sucks of smoke. It did not occur to Oscar that a
woman married to Neville for several decades might have

accumulated damaging evidence of the Englishman's misbehavior all on her own, so pleased was the former caricaturist with his newfound ability to dissemble in behalf of a friend and ally. In addition he was revived and excited by the prospect of bursting in on Neville, who could be counted on to have designed an interesting way of coping with the freakish stormy night on the coast. Mentally he practiced the words he would use to explain to Mrs. Hacking-Cough why they had found her supposedly loyal husband dangling naked from a chandelier by his knees, alternately trying to drink champagne upside down and pouring the beverage from a great height into the gaping mouths of half a dozen prostrate nymphets.

Mrs. Hacking-Cough's driver crept cautiously along the icy and deserted main street of Val d'Argent, past shuttered cafés, slush-covered benches, cringing palms, sleet-lashed windows. The marina's sailboats huddled together against the cold. Amber streetlights illuminated the desolate town center.

"Siberian," said Mrs. Hacking-Cough. "South of France, indeed."

They climbed the hill past the roundabout, site of Oscar's drag-racing, past Oscar's own house—Elizabeth's ears perked up at this—and along the corniche near the convent.

"Here we are," said Neville's wife, who was as excited as Oscar was, as they rounded a sharp bend and reached the gates of a mansion Oscar had seen many times before but had not realized belonged to Neville (or his wife). "The lights are on."

"Naturally," said a delighted Oscar. "Your husband is a voracious reader." The car nosed through the gates and crunched along the icy drive. "And music lover," Oscar was forced to add, for even in the confines of the probably bulletproof limousine, a suggestively pounding music was audible. "My, he owns a lot of cars." There were dozens of cars parked randomly about—on the verge of the drive, on the lawn to the side of the house, on the patio near the pool.

Paul the driver pulled up to the front steps, leaped out of the car with an umbrella, opened Mrs. Hacking-Cough's door, and escorted her to the landing. He returned for Oscar and Elizabeth with a humorless pucker to his lips, which might have had to do either with Oscar's phony accent or with his being a mere hitchhiker suddenly invited to the big bash.

"How nice of Neville," said the ever-cheerful Oscar, "to throw a little party for his friends on a night as bad as this."

Elizabeth shook herself and tried to get her bearings. She sensed that she was near her home, but not quite near enough.

Mrs. Hacking-Cough did not hesitate. She hunched her shoulders and lowered her head and made for the half-open door. The sounds from inside were unmistakably those of revelry. Oscar adjusted his rumpled clothing, cleared his throat, and followed behind her like an anxious public-relations agent.

It was apparent to Oscar that he was going to experience some difficulty in convincing Mrs. Hacking-Cough that her husband lived the life of a home-loving bookworm: the marble-floored front hall was occupied mainly by debris—crates of champagne, boxes of glasses, trays of uncovered and half-eaten food, cast-off winter coats and gloves and shoes. A roaring central heating system made for a nearly tropical atmosphere. Only one person stood, or rather tottered, in the hall—a young woman half wearing a silvery ball gown who was either looking for a lost earring or about to be sick.

"Let's not jump to conclusions," said Oscar, helping to clear a path to the staircase, bowing to the silver-gowned woman.

Up the stairs they climbed, toward the source of a rousing polka. On the landing they discovered opened trunks overflowing with costume clothing and party paraphernalia. Here a tall man in a green leotard and sequin-stitched shift appraised himself in a mirror. The unmistakable odor of sweaty bodies wafted down the hall.

On they marched, Oscar and Mrs. Hacking-Cough with

Elizabeth close behind. Mrs. Hacking-Cough paused at a tall double-door, as if to catch her breath, then pushed the doors open and pressed into the crowded room. As if in response to her entrance the music abruptly ceased and the crowd went quiet, but she remained unobserved behind the throng. This provided her and Oscar with time to analyze the confusing tableau before them.

The crowd formed a circle around the perimeter of the room, decked out in robes and tiaras and random articles of antiquated costume. In the center of the room, all eyes upon him, stood Neville, dressed dashingly as a musketeer. (Oscar noticed with pride that behind Neville, on the wall, hung Elizabeth's beautiful painting of D'Artagnan.) Neville stood erect, right hand on the hilt of his épée, the other outstretched at shoulder level. In his left hand, pinched between dainty fingertips, he held aloft a white lace handkerchief. Neville evidently intended to start a race or duel of some kind, the contestants in which were presumably the four naked young women lined up before him. Their object remained unclear to Oscar until he observed the four large canvases propped against the far wall. These women were going to paint; art was to be perpetrated.

At the drop of Neville's handkerchief the music resumed—an accordion and brass arrangement of the "Minute Waltz"—and the four women raced across the room to their respective canvases. Not surprisingly, because they wore no clothes, they intended to use their bodies to apply paint. The crowd converged to witness their work. The women, perhaps because this is what they thought was expected of them, concentrated on employing their chests. In a frenzy of slopping and pressing, dipping and smudging, the women created their paintings in a race against the music. The most enterprising one among them gathered a great brush of her long brown hair, soaked it in orange paint, and whipped it energetically at the canvas. The guests cheered this maneuver and the contestants' efforts in general as their paintings took shape. When the music reached its conclusion the winded women stood back from their creations to an ovation of clapping and catcalls. Neville strode musketeer-style to the paintings, raised his épée over each work, and judged a winner based on the volume of his guests' applause. The painting by the woman with the long hair and the most spectacular bosom was deemed victorious, and was hung directly on the wall above the others, there to begin its inexorable increase in value.

Throughout this exercise Elizabeth had tried without success to poke her way between people's legs to get a look at the action. She knew a thing or two about painting, after all. It was as the orange nudist's painting was finally hung on the wall that Elizabeth managed to squeeze through the guests' legs and into the clearing around Neville. When Neville spotted her he threw out his arms, one of which still held a sword, and demanded total silence: "An apparition!" he cried. "A canine visitation! A true artist among us at last!" He bowed low to Elizabeth, then searched the room for the dog's master. In finding Oscar, of course, he also found his wife.

III

"MY DA-HAH-LING!" GASPED NEVILLE. "EVERYONE! LOOK! IT'S my . . . my wa-hife!"

Neville advanced toward his wife as the crowd parted. He still held his épée outstretched, and Oscar thought for a moment he would try to run the lady through in front of fifty witnesses in an attempt to make uxoricide seem like a drunken accident. Instead he sheathed his weapon as he crossed the room, hugged and kissed his immobile wife, and shook Oscar's hand.

"Everyone!" he shouted once again. "Now this is truly cause for celebration! Music!"

The gaudily dressed crowd swirled into motion. Someone lifted Elizabeth onto a table so that she had a better view of the costumes and the dancing. The accordionist launched into an oomphy waltz, and the revelers were back in business. The four nude artists joined in, colorful and sticky with paint.

"My goodness, wha-*hut* a surprise," said a flushed and nervously laughing Neville Hacking-Cough. "What a trip you must have had on a night like this. You were jolly lucky to *survive*."

"Oh, do shut up," said Mrs. Hacking-Cough, "and get me a drink."

Oscar knew it would have been polite to leave the couple alone at this juncture, but he was still keen on the idea of defending Neville, high as the odds against this project had become. Neville also seemed to want Oscar around for support: he took both the cartoonist and his wife by the elbow and frog-marched them down the hall and into a library equipped with a bar. To prevent the onslaught of his wife's accusations, Neville sustained an inane monologue about the weather, about air travel, about the availability of good scotch in Val d'Argent. Without his tan, Neville looked both older and more dissipated. Tiny and round, Mrs. Hacking-Cough looked more fearsome and determined than ever once she held a drink in her hand. Oscar too remained determined: he wished to seize the initiative, lie through his teeth, repay Neville for past services rendered.

"Cheers," said Neville, and all three drank. Then to his wife he said, formally, "I am pleased beyond measure to have you here."

Oscar could see that Neville had reached the end of his ability to forestall his wife's attack. The cartoonist cleared his throat and stepped into the breach.

"I can't tell you how impressed I am with the party, Neville," Oscar began. He raised his voice to prevent interruption, and assumed a demeanor he hoped amounted to a great smiling embodiment of American earnestness: "I've been to, what, four or five of your charity extravaganzas? You must be making a fortune out of this one, sir. All my congratulations. The nuns will weep with gratitude. Not to mention the orphans, of course. They must think of you as a foster-parent, with all you do."

Oscar beamed at Neville, who returned an expression first of bewilderment, then of horror. For her part, Mrs. Hacking-Cough seemed intrigued by Oscar's revelation.

"I thought you said you were French," she said to him.

"No," said Oscar, enjoying a new facility for untruthfulness. "I never said that."

"I could have sworn . . ."

"Now, Neville," said Oscar seriously. "Where do I send my check this time? The usual?"

"Er," said Neville. It was particularly satisfying for Oscar to see Neville at a loss for words.

"You are telling me that all of this . . . foolishness," said Mrs. Hacking-Cough, turning in mid-sentence to look at her husband, "is for *charity*?"

"Er," said Neville.

Oscar imagined that the Englishman had probably begun to feel somewhat idiotic and out of place in his musketeer outfit.

"That's right," said Oscar. "Just repaying the community for all the wonderful years of hospitality. Eh, Neville?"

Neville could still only grunt.

"Now if you will excuse me," said Oscar, "I will leave the two of you alone. I must make sure my dog doesn't overdo—and perhaps I can convince her to donate a painting to the orphans."

His good deed done, his white lie told, Oscar took his leave, issuing to each Hacking-Cough a series of utterly inappropriate winks and waves. Back down the hall he marched, pausing on the landing to pick up a cape and feathered Tyrolian hat, then into the ballroom, where recorded music had replaced the accordionist and nudity prevailed. Oscar danced and drank, drank and danced, and tossed girls into the air. He told the naked artists that as a professional he considered their works to be masterpieces. He shouted for more drink. Round and round the room he danced. Happy to be home, he conversed recklessly with anyone who would listen, until, dizzy and breathless, he found the party had thinned to a small number of those semiconscious stragglers who would sleep where they dropped.

"Come, Elizabeth," he said to his dog, who had fallen asleep on a pile of discarded costumes. "We can walk home from here."

Knowing Elizabeth's personality as he did, Oscar thought the labrador would be particularly proud of his behavior on this night. She had always looked at him sideways when he let people get the better of him, seeming to deplore his diffidence. She had never liked it when people got the better of Oscar, and he thought that if she could have heard his intervention in Neville's affairs she would have been mightily impressed with her master's decision to join the ranks of white-lying meddlers.

Oscar replaced his cape and hat in the trunk on the landing and began to descend the staircase.

"Psst," came a sibilant from behind. "Oscar."

Oscar turned to see Neville Hacking-Cough, now robed in silk and bare-headed, standing at the top of the stairs with a forefinger to his lips. He tiptoed down the stairs behind Oscar and led him by the wrist to a drawing room on the first floor.

"My wife is asleep at last," he said, "now that the music has stopped. She explained how you met."

"Yes?"

"And well, I . . ." Neville was having difficulty expressing himself again. Oscar assumed this was due to the Englishman's not being used to owing enormous debts of gratitude. "I simply wanted to say to you, Oscar, that . . ." Neville shuffled his feet and bowed his head like a guilty schoolboy.

"She bought it?" asked Oscar, hoping to expedite Neville's thank you.

"Oh, that, oh goodness me. Well, that was terribly nice of you to make the effort, dear boy. Jolly nice, but I'm afraid it was probably quite pointless. She won't remember a thing. The drink, you know. If she remembers anything it will be you. She thought you were charming."

"Charming?"

"Listen, Oscar. I really must say something to you. I'm glad I caught you before you left."

Oscar had difficulty understanding Neville's next few sentences. The Englishman appeared to be quite embarrassed about something, but what it was Oscar could not yet tell.

". . . not sure of what *magnitude* an error in judgment this might have been, if you follow."

"I'm sorry, you'll have to repeat that, sir."

"Oh, *Christ*, I wish you wouldn't call me sir. I haven't yet been knighted."

"I'm sorry."

"Now look. What I'm talking about could be rather serious. I'm afraid I may have been somewhat indiscreet."

"When, tonight?"

"No, no, it was three weeks ago. I was in Bermuda, having

a wretched time of course, not even any sunshine, but feeling I owed it to old Hansie to pay him a visit there."

"Oh, no."

"Yes, well. The thing is I *believe*, but cannot, due, shall we say, to overindulgence on my second or third night there, be absolutely positive that I did not commit an indiscretion."

Oscar furrowed his brow in concentration: "Would it be unfair of me to infer," he said, "that whatever it was you did could be called a gaffe of some not inconsiderable proportions?"

Neville too was concentrating on the cul-de-sac of double negatives they had stumbled into. "No," said Neville. "It would not be unfair. I really and truly put my foot in. Out of Veronique's earshot, of course, and really, not to put too fine a point on it, I can admit it, stupid with drink, I told Hansie all I knew of your . . . *alliance* with his young wife. With some sordid embellishments, I assume, but cannot remember."

This is the thanks I get, thought Oscar.

"I do appreciate your telling me, Neville," he said, beckoning Elizabeth and moving toward the door.

Neville clutched his robe around his throat and followed them onto the landing outside. "I suppose that will put a bit of *zest* into the spring, eh wot?" he called after them.

Pip pip, you old bastard, Oscar thought, but could not say, waving his hand and thanking Neville once more for a wonderful party.

At last Oscar Lemoine's long-held and deeply ingrained fear of being pursued by a murderous Nazi had become reality. He thought it queer and cruel of life to select his one pure terror, one he had thought was remote beyond all possibility, and to tease and torture him with it. He trudged through the slush toward his cottage, carrying his sleepy and shivering dog, and joined the ranks of countless souls who had walked at night and asked themselves tricky questions about the meaning of it all.

Oscar arrived at his cottage thinking of Anton, his pyromaniac neighbor, who would soon be on a skiing holiday, setting fire to chairlifts and chalets, dreaming of winter battles. Oscar's flashy car remained safely in the drive under an inch of slush. As he approached his car, with Elizabeth still in his arms, Oscar heard the telephone ringing inside. He patted his pockets and found the keys, unlocked and opened the door, placed his soggy dog on the passenger seat. He sat behind the wheel and answered the telephone, assuming the distracted and impatient tone of a man interrupted at work: "Yeah, hello."

"Little brother," said George Lemoine. "Welcome back to our native France. I tried the car when you didn't answer at home."

"Yes, I'm not exactly home yet," said Oscar. "I keep getting waylaid. But thank you for calling. Where are you?"

"Just where you left me. The women are pampering the master of the house. Bouillon. Sponge baths. I'm going to marry the older one, did I tell you?"

"I think so. Congratulations."

"Don't worry about having to come back for a wedding. Diana's family is even more shamefully disorganized than ours. We'll swing by on our honeymoon, no doubt."

"Wonderful."

"It's very, very good to be alive. No more high life for this Boy Scout. Hired drivers only, dead sober. Speaking of which, I think whatever drugs I'm on are mixing well with the wine: I'm going to patent the mixture and make a fortune on the streets of our fair city—are you still there?"

"Yes, I'm here. You really have to be careful, George."

"Aw, get you. The jobless wonder. I suggest you find gainful employment, O. Get a life. People have been calling me to get this number, because you don't answer in the house. Avenues are open to you."

"Sure."

"Listen, gotta run, so to speak. I'm experiencing visions."

"Fine. Good-bye, George."

Oscar hung up the telephone. It was dark and cold inside his car. His body felt limp and heavy. He picked up his dog and struggled out of the car, back into the elements. He walked around the back of his house, past the covered swimming pool, to the screen door where he had hidden a spare house key behind an unhappy rose bush. Once inside he carried Elizabeth upstairs and tucked her under a blanket on a bed in the guest room. He clumped down the hall to his own bedroom, home at last, and undressed. He crawled beneath the covers and exhaled mightily as he felt his body press into the mattress. He plummeted, rather than drifted, into sleep. He dreamed anthropomorphically of New York as a diseased human heart beating erratically in the body of a drug addict undergoing withdrawal.

IV

OSCAR AWOKE EARLY IN THE MORNING, DONNED HIS ROBE, AND WALKED out to his upstairs balcony to find that the storm had passed and left a diamond-blue day behind. The air smelled of wet rocks. The red-tile roofs and chimney pots of the town center glinted in slanting sunlight. Oscar breathed deeply and rattled his head to test his skull for symptoms of hangover. A pair of nuns in navy coats climbed the switchbacks from town toward the convent, pulling shopping trolleys with loaves of bread protruding from their checked-canvas bags. They noticed Oscar and waved; he returned their greeting and added a shake of his hand meant to indicate that nasty nature had behaved irresponsibly. They nodded both their comprehension and their agreement, and it struck Oscar how simple communication could sometimes be, and yet how often he seemed to misconstrue remarks and intentions even when abundantly supplied with verbal cues and pertinent information. Having fled New York in part for this reason, Oscar had still stubbed his social toe immediately upon his return to Val d'Argent. He took heart only in the likelihood that Neville's supposed betrayal stood every chance of being as exaggerated as most of the Englishman's stories had been in the past. It was likely that Veronique had quashed the domestic crisis effectively enough, and that Oscar's fear of rampaging Nazis would prove unfounded.

Any misgivings Oscar might have had about the state of his affair with Veronique were more than outweighed by the increasing heft of a more primordial concern, namely the requirement of close body contact with another human being; he doubted his ability to survive until Veronique's return, but resolved to be strong. He took several more deep, grateful breaths, and congratulated himself on having left behind his nightmare city of filth. He glanced at his watch, intending to set it forward to local time, and discovered to his dismay that he had slept not for four or five hours, but for twenty-eight. He had slept a night and a day, and another night. The missing of a day ranked high on Oscar's scale of immoral behavior, and he swooned with the effort of recalibrating his circadian rhythm. Then he wondered what had happened to Elizabeth.

He hurried back through his bedroom and down the hall to the guest room to find only a rumpled nest in the center of the bed. Wherever Elizabeth had gone, she had taken her blanket with her. Down the stairs he ran, into the kitchen, the living room, his study—no sign of Elizabeth. To his relief he saw that he had left the back door unlatched, so that Elizabeth could have left the house of her own accord (in her youth she had been quite handy with even the slipperiest doorknob, but no more). Barefoot, he walked across the cold wet lawn to the swimming pool and looked for a telltale lump beneath the plastic cover. Ever since Elizabeth's possible suicide bid in New York Oscar had feared for the canine artist's sanity. Perhaps it had been more than an overreaction to the degradation of the city—Elizabeth might have begun to feel that her creative powers had deserted her, that she had no more to offer, that without her art she could not go on. Oscar had to curse aloud to stop himself from thinking this way. He had begun to believe his own fabrications. Elizabeth was an old dog, possibly senile, possibly racked with disease, nothing more.

Clutching the skirts of his robe around his legs, Oscar made a tour of his grounds, calling Elizabeth's name. In the drive, between pools of melted slush, he searched for tracks, and found them. They led to the gate, through the bars of which Elizabeth must have squeezed her still-girlish figure. He un-latched the gate and continued. The tracks led uphill, then disappeared as they crossed the drying asphalt. Oscar tripped his barefoot way uphill, hoping Elizabeth had not chosen the dramatic exit sometimes favored by frustrated artists. Desperate final cliff-dives looked good in biographies, and the individuals might believe at the time that hostile society would take note at last, but where did this leave their loved ones? Oscar pressed on with that peculiar mixture of worry and anger that possesses the panicked.

He caught up with the pair of nuns, who turned and started, thinking the mad-eyed man in the bathrobe had seen them from his balcony and given chase. Oscar fired off a succinct and believable explanation of his presence, in French: "My dog has gone missing." He charged ahead, modestly cinching his robe.

At the first switchback, one level beneath the gloomy brick convent, Oscar departed from the road along a clifftop trail. He searched blindly now, like a parent, acting on instinct and desperation. He ceased calling the dog's name out of superstition, for he had dreamed a scene eerily like this one, in which he saw himself screaming "Elizabeth!" in a dripping forest while standing almost on top of her decomposing body. In silence, then, he plodded along the path, breathing hard and wincing from the pain of his tender unshod feet. The path was known in town as the *Chemin des Preservatifs*, but in December the lovemaking debris had been swept away and nothing slopped underfoot but salty sand and soggy leaves.

Oscar decided to continue along this path until he reached the grassy rise below the convent's main parapet and clock tower, if only because he would have a calming view of the sea. He slowed his pace as he neared, because along the ground he once again detected paw prints. He rounded a gentle bend between a clump of trees, came within view of the grassy clifftop, and stopped dead. There, on the grass, sitting erect on her blanket, staring out to sea, was Elizabeth. The tufts of hair on her ears blew in the breeze. Her thin body shivered. Her tongue hung straight from her mouth with a graceful upward curve at the tip. Her eyes were wide open and stared expectantly at the horizon. This was Elizabeth's widow's-walk pose. Oscar found it hard at first to believe she had not sensed her master's presence, until he realized she knew perfectly well he was there but had chosen not to look at him. He leaned against one of the trees and watched his meditating dog until, at last, she turned her head and looked directly at him without retracting her bobbing tongue.

There is a facial expression dogs make that breaks humans' hearts, and Elizabeth made it now: a slight lateral tilting of the head; eyebrows raised pleadingly upward and to the center; corners of the mouth drawn almost imperceptibly downward. In younger and less worldly dogs this is an expression of vacuous curiosity; in humans it is the expression that precedes tears; in

Elizabeth's case, as Oscar interpreted it, the expression signified farewell.

Master and dog looked at each other for some minutes. Oscar thought of Elizabeth, the artist as a young dog, in the days before she discovered Canine Expressionism, when she devoted her skills solely to city survival. She had learned to fetch coffee and doughnuts from the corner store; she could operate any elevator in the city. She had learned to dial the police and start a prerecorded tape giving Oscar's address at the slightest sign of fire or break-in. She had learned to dance rather erotically. She had adopted Oscar's pacifist stance and nonconfrontational attitude when faced with metropolitan indignities. While always a stoical and uncomplaining dog, she never for a moment lost the dignity of her undeniable superiority complex. As far as Oscar could ever judge, her politics were liberal but faintly aristocratic. Her late-blooming artistic career had conveniently avoided the live-hard-die-young rut to which the greatly talented are often prone. Always eager to meet new people, Elizabeth nevertheless had cultivated no close friendships other than Oscar's—and here the feeling was more or less mutual. She never asked more from life than to be spoken to politely, and Oscar could not remember a single instance of teeth-baring in her long and active life.

Oscar climbed the last few feet to the grassy patch and sat down on half of Elizabeth's blanket. He put his arm around her shoulders, and they stared out to sea together. He stroked her coat and felt her ribs close to its surface. Her gray muzzle sniffed at the air. Her head panned slowly from side to side as she took in clouds, ships, treetops, cliffs, as if ticking them off a list of sights she wanted to see for the last time. Oscar looked too, but mostly he looked at Elizabeth. He moved closer to her and put his face down so that his nose touched the back of her neck. He smelled the damp odor of her coat and felt the hurried rate of her shallow breathing. With his other hand he encircled her neck and held her tightly without obscuring her view of the sea.

Oscar spoke soothingly to Elizabeth, his voice muffled by her black coat. He told her what a good dog she was, what a good friend, what a good painter. He asked her if it would be out of the question if she did not die just yet. In a half-scolding voice he told her he would be lonely in her absence and would lose a fortune without her art to trade. He said Monsieur Berlinger would be devastated. He spoke to her in this way, by turns joking and pleading, until he felt tears running from his face into her fur. Her body relaxed, and he let her lie down on the blanket with black eyes and gray muzzle pointing past Oscar's face toward the sky. She closed her mouth but still a tip of pink tongue protruded, like a rose petal. Oscar lay down next to her and pulled a corner of the blanket over her shivering shoulders. At the last moment her eyes seemed to focus on Oscar's and to flash the gamut of her canine expressions: Elizabeth at her best and bravest; Elizabeth condescending when Oscar misbehaved; Elizabeth scornful of a world unfit for dogs; Elizabeth delighted with artistic achievement; Elizabeth giddy with small pleasures; Elizabeth loving Oscar. Elizabeth died with a smile and a sigh.

V

HAVING SUBCONSCIOUSLY PREPARED HIS PSYCHE FOR THIS MOMENT, Oscar surprised himself by his rather violent reaction to Elizabeth's death. He had hoped to remain phlegmatic—much as Elizabeth almost certainly would have, had their roles been reversed: she would have nuzzled Oscar's body to be sure of its

demise, then alerted the authorities and gone into the mourning for which she was perpetually dressed. But not Oscar. Oscar
clutched Elizabeth's limp, cooling body for a quarter of an hour,
feeling rage and anguish build inside him. Then he covered her
body in the blanket and found himself rising to his feet in his
mud-stained bathrobe, raising his arms, clenching his fists, and
keening skyward in a supernaturally loud voice which was
entirely beyond his will to modulate. He shrieked and howled
and wept and dug his toes into the grass. A part of him felt
removed from this experience, watching himself as he reached
a pitch of misery that he feared might result in loss of bowel and
bladder control, so fierce were his sobs and lung-wrenching his
cries.

Punching at the sky, tearing at his hair, Oscar stumbled
about the grassy clifftop knoll. Unwittingly flirting with the
edge, Oscar stomped and wheeled, leaped and pirouetted. He
fell to his knees and clutched at soil and grass. He rolled onto
his back and covered his face. He regained his feet, he jumped
and twisted, he ran in place, all the while emitting the savage
groans and wails of a possessed participant in a primitive ritual
dance. The part of him that watched this display from afar
knew that it could only end when exhaustion made further
exertion impossible. Because he was still in good physical
condition, it took a quarter of an hour or more for Oscar's
hysteria to dissolve into less gymnastic stompings, his cries into
muffled sobs. Dizzied by hyperventilation, covered in mud, he
stood with his back to the sea and his bathrobe undone, and
looked once more toward the sky. As he raised his head his eye
was caught by an arresting sight: a line of nuns' habited heads
peering over the parapet of the convent, their hands gripping
the wall, each nun justifiably agog.

"Pardon me, sisters!" cried Oscar in French, polite even *in
extremis.* "My bitch has died!" His voice echoed off the mossy
stone wall. Under his breath, in the direction of the blanket, he

added an aside to his late dog: "I'm glad you can't see me, girl. Not this way."

He covered himself and retied his robe. He made further gestures of apology to the nuns, who seemed satisfied by his explanation but disappointed that his seminude dance of despair had come to an end. Their blue-and-white heads dropped behind the parapet one by one like ducks in a shooting gallery.

Weakened by his energetic mourning, sickened by the dead weight of his inanimate labrador, Oscar folded the edges of the blanket around Elizabeth's corpse and carried her down the path to the road. He reached his cottage and deposited the tragic bundle on a sliver of unmelted slush in the shade of his porch.

Oscar showered. He moped about collecting Elizabeth's personal effects and packing them in one of the moving boxes he had planned to use if things had gone well in New York. He telephoned Monsieur Berlinger to break the news, which the Frenchman took badly. Between sobs and fond memories they agreed to meet for lunch at the Floride, one of the few Val d'Argent establishments that remained open in winter. Oscar removed a dark suit and black tie from mothballs and started the lonely walk to town. Berlinger arrived in his commercial van shortly after Oscar did on foot. They fell into each others' arms and were rewarded with a free bottle of pastis from loyal André, who had immediately remarked upon Elizabeth's absence and had nearly collapsed with emotion when he heard the sorry news of her recent death.

The two men drank in silence for a few minutes, then beckoned for André to join them. André draped his towel over a chair, pocketed his bottle opener, spat an invective or two at the sea, seated himself, then freely imbibed. More ice and water were called for, supplied by one of André's teenaged apprentices. The men were drunk in a matter of minutes. Silently they toasted each other. They grumbled darkly, they drank glumly.

In winter the village of Val d'Argent reverted to an unglamorous routine, waiting for the return of carelessly spent currency. Housewives hobbled along the seafront lugging groceries. Spotty youths revved souped-up mopeds and dragraced along the quay. Solid citizens buttoned up against the cold and strolled proudly along boulevards foreigners had made famous, returning to houses that had not yet fallen under the scythe of profitable development. Lonely young women braved inclement weather wearing inappropriate clothing, cheered on the racing bikers, bit their lips, waited for the rich employment of spring.

Monsieur Berlinger was the first to break the silence, with an overemotional and therefore incomprehensible toast to Elizabeth. Smart as ever, Monsieur Berlinger wore a black flannel suit and a black tie. The more he drank, the lower his dangling cigarette angled from his lips. André bowed his head and waved a limp hand in the air without comment; every few minutes he spat grotesquely onto the pavement and wiped his mustache with a handkerchief. As the center of their bereaved attention, Oscar kept quiet and drank as he had not done since the humiliating night at Le Village.

Soon the men had begun to sing in the empty café. Monsieur Berlinger and André each slung an arm around Oscar's shoulders. Hunched over, they swayed back and forth and sang lugubriously into the tablecloth. They sang a favorite love song, the native anthem of year-round Val d'Argentians, a tortured sailor's threnody of alienation called "*Les Rochers et la Mer*," penned a decade ago by a local-boy-made-good:

> *Les rochers et la mer de Val d'Argent,*
> *Où je vous ai vue il y a si longtemps;*
> *Je me promène sur les rochers au bord de la mer,*
> *Tout . . . seul . . . main . . . te-nant.*

Les rochers et la mer de Val d'Argent,
Aveugle aux orages et aux saisons passantes,
Je monte sur les rochers au bord de la mer,
Tout . . . seul . . . main . . . te-nant.

(CHORUS:)

Ooooooh! Que je suis angoissé!
Aaaaaah! Je regrette mon passé!
Meeerde! Que votre coeur est glacé!

(SEVENTEEN FURTHER VERSES AND CHORUSES, UNTIL:)

Les rochers et la mer de Val d'Argent
Où je vous ai vue il y a si longtemps;
Je me jette des rochers et meurs dans la mer,
Tout . . . seul . . . main . . . te-nant.

On the whole it was not a happy song. The men sang it until they were hoarse and choked with emotion. They killed the first bottle and ordered food to help them through the second.

"To think," drooled Monsieur Berlinger, whose commercial interest in Elizabeth had not gone entirely forgotten in the pathos of the moment, "that our dear Bête Noire will never paint again."

His two companions nodded sadly—especially André, who had heard of Elizabeth's artistic calling and did not doubt her talent for a moment.

"Wait a minute!" said Oscar, pushing back from the table and attempting to stand so that he could announce his brainstorm—and falling backward into the arms of a ready apprentice waiter. Oscar was helped back into his chair, unhurt. "Wait a minute!" he repeated, remaining seated this time. "I have the answer. You, my friends, will tell no one."

"Of course," said the two Frenchmen in unison, raising fists signifying their oath of honor. "What are we not to tell?"

Oscar told them.

"We will help you!" cried Monsieur Berlinger.

"At once!" agreed André.

"Bring the bottle!" said Oscar.

They helped each other to their feet and made for Monsieur Berlinger's van.

VI

GIDDY FROM TEARS AND AWFULLY DRUNK, THE THREE MEN PILED INTO the front seat. Monsieur Berlinger drove, or rather swerved rapidly from side to side so that forward progress was still achieved, until they reached his art-supply store. Along the way Oscar and André shouted encouragement to Monsieur Berlinger and congratulated him on every successful turning, every legal signal, every juddering stop.

Like bank robbers they rushed into the store and started their work. Every piece of canvas Monsieur Berlinger could lay hands on was cut and stacked, every drawing pin sorted and packed; all of these supplies they dragged to the van and loaded, pausing only to toast their mission with some of the wine Monsieur Berlinger kept on hand at all times. With a great mutual sense of purpose, and under the disbelieving gaze of Monsieur Berlinger's shop assistant, they completed this first phase of Oscar's plan. With Oscar's cry of "Onward!" they jumped into the front of the van for another haphazard journey along the coastline back to Val d'Argent.

The men grew solemn and silent as the next phase drew near and its true meaning dawned on them. They arrived at Oscar's cottage and rushed inside to drink and steel their nerves.

"She would want it this way," Oscar assured his partners. "She would get a laugh out of it."

"Right, then," said Monsieur Berlinger. "All for one and one for all."

They ferried the art supplies into Oscar's study and set to work stretching and tacking canvases. They were sufficiently equipped to construct two dozen of these, and sufficiently adept at this skill from years of practice that despite their inebriation the whole job was completed in under two hours.

"Now," said Oscar, "a quick drink and I will fetch the artist."

Oscar would not have been able to accomplish this phase of his mission without such a staggering quantity of alcohol occupying his bloodstream. He walked outside through the back door to discover that darkness had fallen. He tiptoed over to his porch, but stopped short to allow his eyes to grow accustomed to the dark. Soon he could make out the outline of the blanket that covered Elizabeth's body. He took two steps closer but had to stop again. Remembering that his fellow musketeers relied upon him to follow through, he set his jaw, blocked his nostrils, and advanced. He believed his mission could be accomplished to everyone's satisfaction without actually having to look at Elizabeth's dead face and eyes. He reached down and picked up the heavy bundle, cradled it unnecessarily gently in his arms, and returned through the back door to his study, where Monsieur Berlinger and André awaited him with downcast faces.

"Cheer up, men," said Oscar. "Soon we will be finished."

Oscar placed Elizabeth's covered body on the floor, knelt

down beside it, and with half-closed eyes reached beneath the blanket to expose one of her stiffened front legs. André approached with a tray of black acrylic paint; Monsieur Berlinger handled the canvases. In a systematic, assembly-line fashion, Oscar applied a posthumous paw print to each canvas in turn. Monsieur Berlinger arranged the canvases along the walls of the study where the prints could dry. The operation was carried out in reverential silence. When they were finished Oscar tucked Elizabeth's leg back beneath the blanket and crawled across the floor to an empty spot on the wall where he could lean and compose himself.

"I thank you, my friends," he said. His colleagues nodded. "But we are not yet done. To the tool shed, then?"

Pick and shovel were retrieved, canine corpse was transported through the chilly darkness to the back garden, sweat was expended on the digging of a little grave. Elizabeth was buried, blanket and all, along with a few mementos: her favorite bow tie and beret and a tooth-marked paintbrush. André, the strongest of the three, filled in the grave, tamped down the wet soil, replaced the grass they had cut.

"Hard work for a good friend," said Oscar.

After a few moments' silence the threesome returned to Oscar's house for what they thought would be further drinking, but what turned out to be mutual collapse. When Oscar awoke the following morning he stumbled downstairs in some confusion, and was reminded of his absent friends only by a study lined with canvases, each bearing a black paw mark.

VII

THE NEXT FEW MONTHS PASSED SWIFTLY FOR OSCAR, MARKED BY FOUL weather, continuous mourning, and few events of note. He worked sporadically at forging Elizabeth's presigned paintings, finding to his surprise that her effect was difficult to imitate even for so skilled a draftsman: in her random way Elizabeth had never repeated herself, and Oscar was therefore left to his own devices in predicting where her Canine Expressionism might have led had the artist lived longer.

Oscar continued to use Veronique's car as a telephone booth. When it wasn't raining he left the car window open so he could hear the telephone ringing from inside his house. He dialed freely here and there around the world, making the telecommunications equivalent of pen pals. It was as he sat behind the wheel one night, speaking to some chatty night owl in Sri Lanka, that Oscar was frightened almost out of his skin by a face pressed against the car window.

Anton, Oscar's pyromaniac neighbor, had returned. When Oscar rolled down his window and asked the boy if he shouldn't be in school, Anton—armed with a six-gun and holster— replied that he was no longer welcome at his new school, or what was left of his school after he had experimented with great lakes of siphoned diesel fuel in combination with open flame. Oscar told Anton to get in the car on the passenger side for a little man-to-man talk. He told Anton in a fatherly way that he too had known the humiliation of expulsion from school—

although only once and not at quite so young an age, and for not nearly so destructive an offense—and that the world had not necessarily come to an end. If Anton could learn to put his talents to practical and preferably peaceful use, he might yet lead a fulfilling life. Anton was disappointingly unaffected by Oscar's consoling advice, and continued to speak in a hateful way about his superiors at home and at the several schools he had attended. He said his parents had sent him to their summer villa in the company of a nurse and a psychiatrist who spent most of their time locked in his parents' bedroom, leaving their dangerous charge free to roam the neighborhood as he pleased.

Oscar was about to try again to help Anton adjust to his new life, when the car telephone rang. He lifted the receiver and heard Veronique's whispering voice on the line. Oscar covered the mouthpiece and told ungrateful Anton to scram. Anton climbed down from the car, slammed the door, and ran off firing volleys of gunfire into the night.

This was not the first time Veronique had called since Oscar's return and Elizabeth's death, but it was the first time she had reached him in her car. During their previous conversations Oscar had not dared broach the subject of Neville's supposed indiscretion, and judged by Veronique's tone that Neville had invented it. She could not have sounded more loving or natural.

"Where are you, Oscar—you are driving?"

"Out for a little spin, yes," lied Oscar, revving the engine for effect. "Missing you."

"I miss you, too. I am in the most awful hotel. I have always hated Buenos Aires."

"Hmm, me too," said Oscar. "Theoretically."

"Where are you driving?"

"Up to the monument. Remember our evening there? I have photographs of you in the sunset. I have one here with me in the car." Oscar switched on the interior light so that he could inspect the photograph.

"How do I look?"

"Veronique, you could not look more beautiful."

"Tell me how I look."

"You're posing a bit, my dear. One hand behind your head and the other on a slender brown knee. Your eyes are shining at me in quite an erotic way, if you'll forgive my saying so. I am aroused as we speak."

"What else?"

"Elizabeth is in the background."

"Oh. Tell me more about me."

Oscar went on to detail more examples of her glorious beauty, but he had been distracted by an eerie aspect of the photograph he held in his free hand: Elizabeth, sitting a few yards behind and to the right of Veronique in the shadow of the war memorial monument, had fixed an unmistakable expression of disdain on her face, directed just as unmistakably at Veronique. Oscar quickly chalked it up to uncharacteristic labradorian jealousy, and concentrated on gushing flattery:

"Your body is shamelessly arched, as if to incite me to passion," he said.

"I remember," said Veronique. "It worked."

"When are you coming back?"

"That's really why I called. Not for a whole month at least. And then I will have only one or two weeks before . . . you know."

"Yes. Before he returns."

They avoided mentioning Hansie's name and giggled about what they might be able to accomplish in one whole week, especially in cool weather. Oscar revved the sports car's engine and told Veronique he was driving recklessly along the corniche.

"I wish I could be with you," she said. "I haven't been having a good time. Very hot places and having to stop constantly to dress for parties. And . . . he has been ill. He smokes too much for a man his age. And he works and works. I am left alone in houses or hotels with nothing to do and I don't speak any of these languages and the food is never like home even though we brought two French cooks with us."

Poor Veronique, thought Oscar—still imprisoned in the citadel. He did not dare think the uncharitable thought that old Hansie might expire from overwork, leaving Veronique free to find a more suitable companion.

"I'm sitting by our swimming pool."

"You're entirely naked, aren't you."

"That's true."

"Cool drink nearby?"

"Balanced on my chest."

"Ouch. Don't let the servants see you. What does the air smell like?"

"Burning rubber."

Oscar's interrogation continued, via satellite. He made her laugh so that she spilled some of her drink onto her chest. When she said she had to go Oscar heard himself confess rather pitifully that he would count the minutes until he saw her again, and that he was surprised he had not driven off the road when she described the more intimate details of the way her body shimmered in the Southern Hemisphere sunshine. He switched off the car telephone and sighed profoundly. He kissed the photograph and placed it on the dash. He clapped his hands, then gripped the steering wheel and made racing-driver noises. He was so excited—and yet so frustrated—by the news that Veronique would be in his arms again in just a few weeks, that he put the car in gear and roared out of his driveway and up the hill. Up and up he drove, past the convent, past Neville's wife's villa, past Herr Dohrmann's mansion; along the high ridge he drove, gliding and swooping on a sublime cushion of suspension, between bouts of giddy laughter advising himself to slow down.

He wanted to use his telephone. He wondered whom he should call: the windy Sri Lankan? the Anchorage prostitute? the New Guinean postal clerk? the Hanoi war veteran? He had just decided to ring up the little boy in Vancouver who thought Oscar was Santa Claus, when the telephone rang of its own accord.

"Oscar Lemoine," he said cheerfully, one hand on the wheel, an elbow on the windowsill. "What can I do for you?"

"Finally," said a woman's voice. "I've been trying for hours."

"To whom am I speaking?" Oscar inquired.

"I'm just . . . I'm just happy to have reached you," said the American voice. "I hope I'm not disturbing you at work."

Oscar was moving at nearly seventy miles an hour, uphill. "Just finishing for the day," he said "Who is this?"

"Bunny Fenton. Remember?"

"Oh, Miss Fenton," said Oscar. He slowed down and pulled the car over to the side of the road on the seaward side of the corniche.

"I've seen the Christmas cover," said Bunny Fenton. "That is, I saw it when it came out, but someone showed me the—"

"The cactus code?"

"That's right. And I asked around, I heard they fired you. At least that's what your brother said."

"George?"

"That's how I found out. He gave me this number. I'm sorry, I'm not making a lot of sense. I haven't slept in three days. Out on the coast and back four times since. . . ."

"That's okay, Miss Fenton. Take your time. My brother said they'd fired me?"

"Yes. Look, I didn't mean for you to lose your job."

"It—"

"That's not at all what I had in mind."

"I—"

"I can help, if you'd like, to get you back. I feel terrible."

"You—"

"Oh, God, my cat just spat up on my shoes, but listen, Oscar, may I call you Oscar? I just have to tell you something and I'm in a bit of a rush sort of half in my clothes if you see what I mean?"

"I—"

"I just have to tell you. I felt—I *feel* so terrible. You remember our little talk, what I said, what I told you?"

"Of—"

"Well, it wasn't right."

Now Oscar chose not to attempt his side of the conversation. He reclined his comfortable leather driver's seat and listened to the receiver, imagining Bunny Fenton miles up in her Manhattan home, squeezing into her clothes. . . . "Wait a minute," he said. "What wasn't right?"

"What I told you. I was angry. I wanted to hurt you, make you feel awful. Did you feel awful?"

"Still do," said Oscar, not even close to understanding what Bunny Fenton was getting at.

"I was so angry, I was having a bad time—in private ways. I just lashed out, do you see?"

"You lashed out."

"Right. I made up something, something horrible, just to get back at you. I was acting."

"Ah."

"And because of me they fired you."

"That is not correct, no," said Oscar. "I resigned."

"Well even so, if you quit, if you really did quit, you quit because you were ashamed?"

"Right."

"So now I'm telling you you really shouldn't have been."

Oscar collected himself and delivered: "Of course I should

have been, Bunny—May I call you Bunny? The point is, and I hope you will agree, that what you told me *might as well* have been true, whether it is really true or not. I quit because I *could* have done something inexcusable."

The wonderful thing about this difficult, dreary telephone conversation was that Oscar stared out of his open sports car window through a stand of evergreens at the Mediterranean. In New York he would have drowned in his own inarticulateness. Here he found words, at least in his own opinion, of weight and effectiveness.

"There's one thing I really have to say to you, Bunny," said Oscar, sniffing the pine-scented air. "And that is, I am so happy to hear that you are in good health. I was worried about you and very sorry to hear of your condition. The disease runs in my family." This was not strictly true.

"Oh, no," said Bunny. She had lost her voice. There was a long pause until she said, "My mascara . . ."

"Relax, Bunny."

Bunny Fenton excused herself further and said she would like to talk but she had to go to a fundraising extravaganza in Atlantic City and she might miss her helicopter if she didn't leave immediately. She told Oscar rather more than he wished to know about how wealthy people avoided frostbite on winter nights of revelry.

"Off you go," said Oscar, "and thank you so much for calling."

VIII

LIVING IN EXCITED ANTICIPATION OF VERONIQUE'S RETURN, OSCAR occupied himself with lengthy telephone calls around the globe, with stocking up on food and drink, with finishing and hiding his collection of posthumously forged Canine Expressionism. Nothing distracted him but the occasional unnerving explosion across the way at Anton's house.

Veronique's return did not disappoint. She arrived on foot, having sneaked out of Hansie's mansion so as not to arouse the suspicions of the German's loyal staff, on a night warmed by a breeze sweeping off the Massif Central. All was as if she had never left, except that a pent-up passion on both their parts lent a certain physical danger to their reunion. With the town still mainly shut, and the threat of Neville Hacking-Cough lurking behind every wind-bent palm, they stayed indoors by day and drove to isolated villages by night. Oscar related an exaggerated tale of mix-ups and turmoil in New York—the death threats, the false accusation of rape, the adverse publicity over the Fenton Fiasco, his brother's drunken financial and marital dealings, Oscar's departure from the dismal *Lowdown*, the city's general squalor and ruin—and said that he would be lying low in Val d'Argent for the foreseeable future. He joked, or half-joked, that when they ran away together he would have no responsibilities other than seeing to it that Veronique was satisfied in mind and body.

Not until their fourth day together did Oscar sense that

Veronique lived in fear of her husband's premature return to Val d'Argent. She said he could be unpredictable in this way, implying that Neville's story had not been entirely fabricated and that the German might be on the lookout for misbehavior. Veronique's apprehension began to take concrete form, in that when they clung to each other in bed they did so behind locked doors, curtains drawn, escape routes planned. Oscar soon learned what it meant to grunt and sweat under a leery wife.

This was by no means unpleasant—except that Oscar's Naziphobia had been rekindled—and without much difficulty he kept his senses fixed in the present. He assumed Veronique harbored something of a death wish, spending the night as she sometimes did, and that she considered their eventual discovery by Herr Dohrmann to be inevitable. For his part, Oscar was happy to play the game by her rules, which meant no discussion of the matter and by far the most pleasurable nights he had ever spent with a woman. The weather was perfect for lounging in bed and keeping the sweat off one's brow, and overexertion was not an issue for two such young and physically fit human specimens. Oscar therefore gave little thought to the future; only subconsciously did he brace himself for Herr Dohrmann's imminent arrival. Following Veronique's lead, he did not mention the threat aloud, and likewise did not quibble when she seemed to drop her guard and allow their alliance once again to go on show in public.

A particularly severe lapse in security occurred on her fifth night back in Val d'Argent. Sitting up in bed, she claimed to crave oysters. Oscar, who always craved oysters, volunteered to drive down to the Floride and buy a few dozen to be eaten between the sheets. Veronique insisted that they eat oysters correctly, with properly chilled wine, and that this could only be done seated at a table near the harbor. Oscar had to concur. They dressed warmly and walked through unseasonably balmy air all the way to town—unlinking their arms when they reached the seafront's streetlights—and entered the Floride as chastely as possible.

Tight-lipped André presided over their meal; salty oysters slid down satisfactorily. During the past few days Veronique had steadily relaxed from the rigors of world travel. Now she was a picture of composure as she gulped down the milky creatures and sipped her wine between lips Oscar had come to think of as her most provocatively beautiful feature. He would readily have laid claim to living under the influence of the greatest lust ever known by man, if such a state could be measured. Only with huge effort was Oscar able to make conversation of any rational sort, as his speech usually spluttered out in mid-sentence whenever Veronique smiled. It was obvious even to the usually oblivious Oscar that Veronique was fully aware of the power she held over him, but for the moment he was unconcerned by this imbalance.

He became concerned only minutes later, when André was summoned for the bill and vague gestures and wise winks were made indicating that all was taken care of. Everything suddenly added up for Oscar, and he was appalled. The car, the meals, the free telephone—even Hansie's words of approval on the lawn of his mansion. It struck Oscar with nauseating force that, not for the first time, he had been taken in by more sophisticated operators. There was a word for what Oscar was, and as he and Veronique left the Floride, arm in arm, he tried to think of the word. Veronique would know the word. Neville would know the word. There were plenty of words for women in Oscar's situation as he perceived it—ugly, demeaning words. The ingredient of sex-for-payment-in-kind pointed Oscar in the direction of words having to do with whoredom, until at last, as he and Veronique reached a bench in the park bordering the marina, a phrase of Neville's struck him. "I am a toy boy," he said in a soft voice.

"What did you say?" Veronique rubbed up against him on the bench.

Oscar quickly composed himself. "*Hoi polloi*," he said. "The *hoi polloi* will be littering the beaches soon."

"Never mind," said Veronique. "We have our own beach, no?"

"Hmm."

Horrified as he was by the stark revelation of his living on the seamy end of sexual inequality, Oscar threw himself into the business of necking with the sweet-smelling woman he assumed had taken advantage of him. He closed his eyes and tried to concentrate, but was upset enough to open his eyes in an attempt to gain perspective on his situation.

Moments later, through the darkness, Oscar spotted the white head of a man flitting through the shadows from palm tree to palm tree. The figure neared, stopping at each tree and peeking around the trunk, until concealed behind the nearest palm. In a rush of panic Oscar thought Hansie Dohrmann had returned to catch him in the act and to slice him into strips with his dueling sword. His panic was only momentary because he quickly realized that Hansie didn't flit—Neville flitted.

Oscar separated his mouth from Veronique's, and spoke. "You can come out now," he said.

Neville sheepishly emerged from behind the palm tree, brushed his white hair back from his forehead, and approached. His insouciant gait suggested that he had merely been out for a stroll and Oscar's voice had interrupted private contemplation of the seaside. He came over to the bench and sat down next to Veronique. He put an arm around her shoulders and kissed her cheek in greeting, but did not look at Oscar. Now both men had an arm around Veronique.

"Will they never learn, young people?" Neville asked the palms overhead.

"I honestly do not know who is behaving worse," said

Veronique. "Those of us sitting peacefully by the water in the evening, or those of us sneaking around on tiptoe, spying."

"A lonely old life needs spice, my dear. What would I do without the entertainment provided by energetic youth? Still, a bit early in the season to be starting up this way, no?"

"Don't you ever sleep?" asked Oscar.

"Oh, hello to you too, Oscar. Been keeping to yourself all this time, have you? My wife said to say good-bye to you, before she left. You certainly seem to charm the women, dear boy. She said 'Say good-bye to that lovely young man and his splendid animal.' Where is our celebrated Elizabeth, anyway? Keeping a discreet distance, I suppose?"

Veronique turned to see what Oscar's reaction would be, and laid a comforting hand on his arm.

"I never told you," Oscar began, with a sad tone of voice that suggested he would tell the truth. "Poor Elizabeth had an awful time in New York. I can only describe it as a typical artist's nervous breakdown."

"I'm so sorry to hear that."

"Yes. She was close to the edge. Even your wife commented on her unhealthy appearance. We went home and Elizabeth began to paint. She painted compulsively, Neville. Self-destructively. I feared the worst. She wouldn't eat, she never slept, she barked at my door when she needed more paint. I could scarcely keep the paint and canvas coming fast enough.

"How awful."

"She collapsed about a month ago. I found her lying in a pool of black acrylic. She had been trying to sign what must have been her twentieth painting in two or three weeks."

"My God," said Neville. "Not, surely . . ."

Oscar raised a hand. "No, no. Exhaustion. Nervous wreck. Creative overload. The doctors were able to reach her in time."

"Thank goodness."

"Yes. A very close thing, Neville."

"And where is she now?"

"She needed a long rest. Peace and quiet. She's not a young dog, you know. I tried my best to take care of her, but as she grew strong enough to walk again she insisted on going up to the convent. She scratched at the door and mewled like a baby—sometimes five times a day."

"At the *convent*?"

"Yes. One day the nuns opened the door and Elizabeth slipped inside. They had a terrible time dragging her out again. This went on and on until I was able to convince the nuns to let her stay. I have visited her every day since then, and she seems happy enough. Well, a bit deranged looking still, very shy and uncomfortable around anyone but the nuns. The nuns love Elizabeth and they joke that she wants to take orders. Little do they know this is probably the case."

"I didn't know she was Catholic," said Neville, who did not seem to be kidding.

"Of course," replied Oscar. "All the Lemoines are."

"Yes, yes, I see," said Neville, now sitting forward on the bench, concerned and credulous. "I do hope she will snap out of it."

"It's her life," said Oscar. "And the new paintings are superb."

"Quite."

"Now listen," said Oscar, who had gained confidence after his long speech, "I want to say I hope Veronique and I can trust you not to exaggerate our little reunion here. I can see how you might be tempted to jump to conclusions, but you can plainly see that this is perfectly open and innocent."

"Me? *Exaggerate?*" Neville put a defensive hand to his chest. "Ma-high *dear* chap . . ." Neville histrionically denied any intention to rat on the couple, and expressed dismay that Oscar should think for a moment that betrayal of any sort figured in the Englishman's social repertoire. "Look," he said, "I'm off to the Floride to be a tragic and lonely old fool. Do join me later for a drink when you are finished . . . *reuniting*. Yes?"

IX

HERR DOHRMANN'S RETURN TO VAL D'ARGENT WAS UNACCOMPANIED BY the storm troopers and attack dogs of Oscar's nightmares. He knew the German had come back to town only because the normally reliable Veronique failed to keep a late-night rendez-vous. In an attempt to distract himself from this unpleasant-ness, and to rekindle the work ethic that Val d'Argent life often endangered, Oscar threw himself into the business of planning Elizabeth's Paris show. Telling Neville the story of Elizabeth's retirement behind the walls of the convent had been a premeditated bid for publicity, for if anyone could be relied upon to spread the rumor of the canine artist's decision to take holy orders, it was Neville Hacking-Cough. As Oscar packed up his dog's posthumous works, he found himself beginning to believe his own story. It was comforting to think of Elizabeth high on the hillside overlooking the sea, strolling and sniffing the grounds in the company of gentle females like herself. And of course she would look adorable in her little habit.

With his usual efficiency, Monsieur Berlinger soon had all the Parisian arrangements in place for an early April show. Expenses were paid out of the rich takings of Elizabeth's previous auction, but publicity costs were kept at a minimum due to the intervening months' favorable word of mouth. Most of Val d'Argent high society lived in Paris anyway, and would not dream of missing the second Bête Noire showing, especially after news of the artist's nervous breakdown reached their ears.

Monsieur Berlinger enlisted the help of his son, Pascal, and left the shop in the care of his wife. Pascal drove the van with the precious cargo of Canine Expressionism stacked carefully inside, while the fully licensed Monsieur Berlinger piloted Oscar's sports car; this arrangement left Oscar free to man the telephone. They departed for Paris at dawn on a foggy Monday morning. Awakened by his neighbor's activity, Anton came by to watch the loading of the van, to wave good-bye, and to shut the gate behind them.

It thrilled Monsieur Berlinger so much to be at the controls of Oscar's car that he insisted on driving back roads at least half-way to Paris. This suited Oscar, who reclined his seat and put his feet out the window and casually dialed ahead to confirm hotel reservations and iron out details of their artistic mission. Pascal Berlinger had his hands full keeping the van on the winding roads behind the nimble sports car.

It amused Monsieur Berlinger that each time Oscar hung up the telephone it rang again, and that callers checked in from as far away as Auckland. One call came from Brian Fable.

"The man they called Elusive," Fable said. "I got this number from old George. He said to tell you he beat his drunk-driving rap. I was sure he would. I always have."

"Hello, Brian." The hair on Oscar's ankles blew in the warm wind. Steep hillside vineyards swept past the window. "That's very good news."

"Not really why I'm calling," said Fable. "I'm going to make this fast. I'm on my way into the city, after the most amazing weekend on Long Island. Many, many things have come into focus. Are you with me?"

"You bet."

"Oscar, I need you. I can't say it any plainer than that."

Oscar covered the mouthpiece and told Monsieur Berlinger,

in French, what the call concerned. "My old boss," he said. "He says he needs me." Monsieur Berlinger pulled a marvelous French face that said "*Imbecile*."

"Are you still there?" Fable asked over the telephone.

"Sure."

Berlinger shifted into high gear. They swooped down a gorge bordering a river in the shadow of a steep hillside planted with vines bristling with the potential of early spring.

"Here's the thing. I don't have long, I'm getting close to the toll booths. God, the traffic. And it's seven in the morning."

Oscar tried to imagine where Brian Fable was, inching along the Long Island Expressway—the LIE.

"I'm all ears," said Oscar, nodding yes to Monsieur Berlinger, who seemed to think he could drive a high-performance car and pour coffee from a thermos at the same time.

"I need a yes or a no, Oscar," said Fable, thousands of miles away. "The line's breaking up. Where are you?"

"In a beautiful valley. It will be better in a minute. What's the question?"

Oscar took the cup of coffee offered by Monsieur Berlinger and smiled appreciatively. They reached a rise and the telephone line became clearer.

"Right, that's better. The question is, will you pop two more covers in the mail? Just to tide us over?"

"Nope."

"What?"

"No time, even if I wanted to. Next question."

"Actually there is another question. This is the big one."

("Oh la la," said Monsieur Berlinger, who had discovered yet another gear on a long straight.)

"Ask me nicely," Oscar said into the telephone.

"All right, here it is. I have to rush because I'm three cars from the tolls and I'll lose you in the tunnel. Oscar, will you please do me a year's covers for the Paris *Lowdown*? The company bought it. What I mean is, *I* bought it. It's going to be a winner but they need a launch, and . . ."

"Yes?"

"Sorry, I'm paying my toll. And I've heard all kinds of good things about—you know, about your damned *dog*. Why didn't you tell me she painted, that she got *famous*, for God's sake?"

"You never asked."

"Well, I thought—I feel ridiculous saying this. I thought . . . *Elizabeth* could do a few covers for us, or for the French magazine."

Oscar covered the mouthpiece again to relate this request to Monsieur Berlinger, who tooted the horn and accelerated by way of response.

"You can't afford her, Brian," Oscar said.

"Well, *you* then," said Fable. "I really need a yes or a no. I'm almost in the tunnel. You could do French movie stars or something."

"They're naked enough as it is." Oscar recrossed his legs on the windowsill.

"Are you there, Oscar? My old friend?"

"Aren't you going to ask about Elizabeth?"

"What? Oh, come on, I don't . . . All right, all right, how's the dog?"

"Couldn't be better, thank you. Resting after a grueling spate of work."

"Great, I'm so glad to hear it. Now say yes, Oscar. Say you'll help. I'm going to lose you in a second. I really, really need you to say yes. Say yes, will you, Osc . . ."

Brian Fable faded into the Midtown Tunnel. Oscar hung up the telephone and told Monsieur Berlinger what Fable had asked. Monsieur Berlinger repeated his derisive grimace and checked the rearview mirror for his son.

"Did I tell you," he said, wisely changing the subject, "that Cristobal Koch has agreed to attend the Paris show?"

"Wonderful."

"I took the liberty of saying you would reciprocate in the near future."

"Of course," said Oscar. "I am the man they called Magnanimous."

X

OWING TO AN ENFORCED LAYOVER IN A TOWN A HUNDRED KILOMETERS from Paris—enforced due to overindulgence in food and local wine—the Canine Expressionism convoy did not reach Paris until the following morning at dawn, the day before the scheduled exhibition. The splendid city came to life by degrees as Monsieur Berlinger took the scenic route from the Peripherique to the gallery he had leased for the occasion. This was a grand room on the second floor of a building on the Left Bank, around the corner from the Assemblée Nationale, overlooking the Pont and Place de la Concorde. Pascal guarded the van and its cargo while Oscar and Monsieur Berlinger fetched the keys to the building from the glamorous owner of what would be known, at least temporarily, as the Gallerie de l'Art du Chien. Elizabeth was a pioneer of the genre, but who knew how many young dogs, inspired by her example, would exhibit their works there in the future.

All through the day they labored, Oscar and the Berlingers, paying particular attention to placing the paintings in some semblance of order along the walls. Oscar had left one posthumously paw-printed painting blank, assuming that the *cognoscenti* would understand it as a statement of the utter frustration that precipitated Elizabeth's nervous breakdown. Oscar invented titles on the spot, many of them pertaining to New York City, all of them reeking of blackest despair.

When all was in place, even to the perfectionist Monsieur Berlinger's satisfaction, the three men repaired to a restaurant Oscar knew where Pascal could win a bottle of wine by entertaining the patrons with his guitar. As promised, Veronique had used her influence to book Pascal into Le Village in the early summer, and he needed to practice in front of a hostile audience. Pascal won the talent contest with no difficulty, defeating a motley collection of ill-at-ease singers and poets.

Relaxed—not to say anesthetized—by hearty food and drink, Oscar repeatedly toasted his friends and thanked them on his own and Elizabeth's behalf for their indispensable aid. Tears were shed by the two older men as an embarrassed Pascal called for more drink. Eager to get a few worries off his chest on the eve of such an important event, Oscar confessed to Monsieur Berlinger that he feared his affair with Veronique had been betrayed by Neville Hacking-Cough. He said he worried that violence might break out in the Gallerie de l'Art du Chien. Monsieur Berlinger was not short on advice. He suggested that Oscar smile broadly at all times and deny any accusations to the death, no matter how truthful.

"Let's hope Herr Dohrmann is not *too* angry," said Monsieur Berlinger. "I want him to buy the empty one for a record price. Pascal, sing our friend a happy song to cheer him up."

Pascal sang, and Oscar felt slightly better. He felt resigned to confrontation with Herr Dohrmann. Despite his Nazi nightmares, what worried him more than the possibility of being put to death by Herr Dohrmann was the thought that Veronique might be a collaborator. Even if he never saw her again after the exhibition, he needed proof that their romance had been to some degree mutual. Oscar did not like being a sex object.

They retired to their hotel on foot, singing. Oscar slept

fitfully, with frequent trips to the sink for water. The next morning he recuperated from his excesses alone. He trudged from café to café in a state of some disorientation. He bought clothes he hoped might be mistaken for those associated with modern artists, then returned them because he preferred not to look foolish. Instead he borrowed a sharp light-tweed jacket from fashion-conscious Pascal, and in Elizabeth's memory he wore one of her more subdued bow ties.

Monsieur Berlinger went ahead early to the Gallerie de l'Art du Chien in order to greet the guests, while Oscar and Pascal turned up an hour later. As Pascal drove Oscar in the Berlingers' van, Oscar looked in the rearview mirror and saw that something very good had happened to his hair, and that he might never have looked more handsome. Pascal kidded Oscar for his newfound vanity, but pointed out that in this business appearance was all, and that a few purse strings might be loosened as a result of Oscar's cutting such a fine figure. He also said it was the jacket that made the difference.

With his usual flair, Monsieur Berlinger had arranged for a waiter from a nearby café to open the doors of cars when they pulled up to the Gallerie de l'Art du Chien. The waiter took to this task so zealously that he wrenched open doors of cars merely pausing in traffic, but it was best to be thorough. He saluted Oscar and Pascal and said they already had a full house. Pascal drove back around the block to find a parking place, while Oscar entered the building alone. On the landing, Oscar cleared his throat, slapped his cheeks, counted to twenty, then marched into the room.

Monsieur Berlinger had added a few touches to the decor that morning: Oscar's nude caricature of Elizabeth, which he had painted for the previous exhibition, hung prominently over the fireplace; various articles of Catholic iconography surrounded the work; get-well cards, which Oscar could not be sure were phony, had been placed conspicuously on the mantel; a special black sash had been draped over one corner of Elizabeth's supposed last work, which was called *Paw*. Before he could react to these gaudy additions, Oscar was swept along by a tide of handshakers and well-wishers. Each time he answered a question concerning Elizabeth's health he suffered a mild twinge of guilt, but nothing to rival the sadness he felt that she was not here to revel in the adulation.

When he had a free moment, Oscar scanned the paintings on the walls and saw that they were good. Elizabeth could not have done too much better herself. He positioned himself on the far side of the room by the open windows that gave on to a narrow balcony, and awaited Veronique's arrival. He was delighted to see that several Americans had attended, serious American men wearing tortoiseshell glasses, walking with difficulty under the weight of their wallets—Fable's friends, most likely.

The arrival of Cristobal Koch, no doubt orchestrated by his own camp of experts, was flawlessly egomaniacal. Three steps behind his protégés, Cristobal stumbled into the room with the look of a man who had mistakenly entered a ladies' sauna. He made a great show of collecting himself—looking bemusedly at his watch, searching the faces of his protégés for a clue to where he was—then broke into a grin of greeting to all his fans and friends gathered before him, as if the whole assembly were one gigantic coincidence.

With consummate nonchalance, Cristobal plucked a glass of champagne from a tray borne by Pascal Berlinger—whose father cut costs wherever he could—and made his way through admiring fans and pouting critics to where Oscar stood.

"We must talk," he said, after limply shaking Oscar's hand. "Let me have a word with you on the balcony."

They stepped through the French doors and stood along the wrought-iron railing overlooking a peaceful Seine and the orange-yellow foglights of cars growling along beneath the balcony. In the fading light Cristobal—in the same leather outfit and granny glasses he had worn at their previous meeting—looked pale and harried. For some reason he spoke in French. Perhaps he hoped to put Oscar at a disadvantage, in which case he had certainly miscalculated.

"We ought to be friends," he said, simply enough.

"I don't see why that isn't possible," Oscar replied. He had the distinct impression that their conversation was a formality, that Cristobal wished merely to appear intimate with Elizabeth's amanuensis, if that is what he thought Oscar was. The ploy proved effective, as most heads inside the Gallerie de l'Art du Chien had turned toward the pair of artists outside.

"You really have something here," said the famous body-fluids painter. "I'm very impressed."

"Elizabeth will be happy to hear you say so."

"All right, all right, I'll speak your language then," said Cristobal, who meant not English, but the language of Canine Expressionism. "Don't you . . . doesn't your . . . doesn't *Elizabeth* ever run out of ideas?"

"She may well have. I can't say. It is so difficult to gauge her mood."

"I know how you . . . how *she* feels." It seemed to hurt Cristobal to talk about a dog and himself in the same sentence. He hung his head. "I'm at a dead end myself. Everybody knows it." He looked back through the windows at the crowd. "When I see a young guy like you come along, I wonder if there is a future for me."

Oscar was touched and ashamed. He suspected that someone like Cristobal Koch would never admit such self-doubt to anyone he did not consider an equal. "Look, Mister Koch," Oscar said, "please don't say that, don't think that way. Try to relax. Paint whatever you want and let the—" Oscar was about to say "fools," "—let the patrons decide. You have so many supporters."

"What has art come to?" Cristobal Koch wanted to know. He wrung his hands in the direction of Montmartre.

"For the moment," said Oscar, who thought he should end this conversation and return to the business of selling his forgeries, "art has come to me."

"Too right, my friend," said the disconsolate Koch, who behind his granny glasses looked like a very nice man. "I can count on you for Cannes in August?"

"Of course," said Oscar, bowing.

"And your . . . and *Elizabeth?*"

"I make no promises."

The great Cristobal Koch straightened his shoulders and laughed incongruously to ease his transition back into the crowded room. Oscar was about to follow him inside when he felt the shock wave that always accompanied Veronique's public entrances. Only at that moment did Oscar realize he had not really expected her to appear.

Behaving like a single-cell organism, the crowd parted down the center of the room. At Veronique's side was Herr Dohrmann, who looked older and more stooped than Oscar remembered. He winced when he saw the number of people assembled in the Gallerie de l'Art du Chien. Veronique wasted no time enchanting the art lovers with a smile that seemed intended for each individual in the room. Through the balcony window Oscar saw Monsieur Berlinger's face light up at the arrival of so much purchasing power; the Frenchman rushed over to kiss Veronique's hand and make Herr Dohrmann feel welcome. Oscar decided to remain out on the balcony for the time being, suffering an emotional setback at the sight of Veronique in her marital mode. Monsieur Berlinger hustled his son to the fore to provide Herr Dohrmann with a drink and a match for his cigarette; Oscar thought all might still go well until the German made eye contact and showed unmistakable signs of wanting a word with Oscar on the balcony. Oscar cringed, but Herr

Dohrmann would not be deterred. The last thing Oscar saw before Hansie's frame filled the French doors was Neville Hacking-Cough, who had arrived with a number of youthful fun-seekers in tow, and who made his arrival known by shouting, "My *Christ*, but they are fan-*tas*-tic!" He meant Elizabeth's posthumous paintings.

Herr Dohrmann lumbered onto the balcony next to cowering Oscar, and casually flicked the ash from his cigarette over the railing.

"Hallo, Os-car," said the German, in a way that Oscar found threatening—but then his perceptions were biased by Nazi nightmares.

"I'm so glad you could make it, sir," said Oscar.

"Veronique teases me, you know," said Herr Dohrmann. "She says I am in an arts phase. She does not understand how I appreciate these creations. I'm so sorry to hear about the artist, by the way." Oscar wondered if Veronique had told him the truth.

Herr Dohrmann breathed deeply, sucking a combination of car exhaust and cigarette smoke into his lungs. Oscar had almost decided that the German knew nothing, that Neville had not betrayed him, that he might somehow sneak through this evening without unpleasantness, when Herr Dohrmann fixed Oscar with the most horrifying look, his good eye glinting in the searchlights of a Bateau Mouche, and said, "Neville told me everything. I am shocked."

Oscar bit his lip and averted his gaze, only to see Neville on the other side of the window waving hello like an ecstatic bridesmaid. Oscar wondered if it were too late for him to launch into the homosexual imitation of a lifetime.

"What a terrible thing," said Herr Dohrmann, and Oscar looked back at him. Considering what he had learned, Oscar thought, the German seemed to be taking it all philosophically. "A man's home," Hansie said, "is a sacred thing. Do you agree?"

"I agree," said Oscar. He could tell that Hansie wanted to play out this domestic crisis on the highest plane.

"When something like this happens to a man's home, why . . ." Herr Dohrmann flicked his ash again and waited for a buzzing motorcycle to pass, ". . . he feels that his manhood has been *demeaned*." Herr Dohrmann squinted as he spoke this word, so much so that his scar turned white.

"I think I understand," said Oscar. A hand bearing champagne poked out from inside the room, and Oscar grasped the glass; the hand disappeared. Oscar tried to look Herr Dohrmann in the eye.

"When I heard," said the German, "I thought to myself, 'What will I do?' It is so devastating."

"Yes, sir, I imagine it is." Oscar searched Herr Dohrmann's face for signs of violent intentions. "I just want to say . . ." Oscar didn't know what he wanted to say. He supposed he wanted to apologize. Instead he turned and looked back inside the gallery. He saw Neville, taller than the people around him, tossing his head and laughing. Oscar felt no anger, only resignation. He certainly felt sorry for old Hansie, and wished he knew how to say so.

"And what will you do, young man?" asked Herr Dohrmann.

Oscar was about to plead with the German for forgiveness, to throw himself on his mercy, when he caught a good look at the man's expression. He decided that this was not the face of an enraged cuckold. This was not the face of a man who wanted to feed Oscar to his Dobermans, as Veronique had said he would; it was not the face of a man who had killed before and would kill again if wronged, as Neville had warned. If Oscar read the face correctly, and he made a tremendous effort to do so, Herr Dohrmann's was the face of genuine concern. Oscar chose not to speak, not to beg Hansie's pardon, until he had all the facts before him.

"*This your car then?*" came Neville's voice. Oscar and Herr

Dohrmann looked down to see Neville Hacking-Cough, on all fours, creeping onto the balcony. "I'm standing in for the artist," said Neville. "Or crawling in, whatever." Neville barked a couple of times, then stood up. "Hallo, Oscar," he said, brushing at the knees of his trousers. "So sorry to hear the news."

"News?"

"You haven't heard? I was just telling Hansie here—we flew in together this evening. Doesn't Paris look *mar*-velous?"

"What news?"

"Brace yourself, dear boy. You are homeless."

"Excuse me?"

"The most dreadful fire. Only just last night, I suppose it was. I saw the smoke from my bedroom window and alerted the authorities. Your house, Oscar, is a pile of cinders."

Anton, Oscar thought.

"I'm so sorry," said Neville. "I thought surely you had been told. A good thing the artist was safe behind the convent walls wot? Why are you laughing? I tell you it was a *holocaust*—sorry, Hansie."

Oscar regained his composure by exhaling loudly through his nostrils. "It's just that I know who started the fire," he said. He was thankful that he had an excuse for laughing. "I have a young neighbor who won't rest until the entire south of France is reduced to ashes."

Oscar thanked Herr Dohrmann retroactively for his concern.

"There is always my house," said the German. "That is what I was trying to tell you. It is awfully big for two."

Oscar gulped and said he couldn't possibly. For the second time, Neville sprang to the rescue.

"He will stay with me," announced the Englishman. "*Much* more suitable. I'm so terribly lonely, an old man in a great big . . ." A young woman's arm reached out through the French doors, grasped Neville by the elbow, and started to pull .

him inside. "Cheerio!" said Neville, and practically fell back into the Gallerie de l'Art du Chien.

"Do you know, Oscar," said Herr Dohrmann, "that I have disapproved of that man for more than fifty years? Still, he is amusing enough, I suppose. I do not recommend staying with him, though. You are young, I know, but no one is *that* young."

Oscar could now see that Hansie was in high spirits. His ancient eyes crinkled at the corners and his good eye shone. Oscar also saw Monsieur Berlinger, inside the brightly lighted room, waving frantically for Oscar to send the wealthy German back inside.

"Someone is making an announcement," said Oscar. "I suppose the auction is about to begin."

Herr Dohrmann gave Oscar a wise look.

"Very well," he said. "I had a brief glance at the pictures. You wouldn't tell your dog, would you, if I said they don't quite stand up to the last batch?"

"No, sir," said Oscar. "I wouldn't."

"Still, I have my eye on that one at the end. The blank one. By far the best, don't you think?"

"Indubitably."

The German chuckled and punched Oscar playfully on the arm. "I will fetch Veronique for you," he said. "I know she has a little crush on you." Herr Dohrmann gave Oscar a last, significant look. Oscar used all his caricaturist's powers to memorize it for future analysis.

Herr Dohrmann stepped back inside, leaving Oscar alone on the dark balcony. Soon Veronique appeared in the doorway, backlit and beautiful.

"Darling," she said. "You look as if you've had a bad fright."

"Come here," Oscar said. "No, I think it was just fine."

Veronique joined him in the shadows by the railing. She kissed him, then leaned against his shoulder as Oscar put an arm around her waist.

"I really thought he knew," said Oscar. "I was about to confess to everything when Neville came out and told me about my house burning down. Would he have killed me?"

"I'm afraid it is more complicated than that, Oscar. Hansie knows only what he wants to know. Tonight he knows he wants to buy Elizabeth's last painting."

"You told him?"

"Oscar. For heaven's sake, he's my husband. Yes, I told him. Inside information, so that he knows just how valuable it really is."

Oscar and Veronique turned their backs on the Parisian skyline and looked through the panes of glass at Elizabeth's exhibition. At the back of the room, Pascal Berlinger loaded his tray with fresh glasses of champagne. In the center of the room, Neville Hacking-Cough raised his hands to hush the crowd. With his back to the first painting in a long line of forged Canine Expressionism, Monsieur Berlinger mopped his brow with a handkerchief and cleared his throat. To one side, with his blind eye toward his young wife, Hansie Dohrmann inspected Elizabeth's last paw print.

Oscar held Veronique tightly to his side, and closed his eyes. He felt Veronique's lips on his cheek. He heard the crowd go quiet. He heard Monsieur Berlinger's welcoming toast. He heard Neville shout "To Elizabeth!" He thought of Elizabeth, and of the people who had come to celebrate her art. Oscar had to smile.